Dodge Rose

Jack Cox

Dodge Rose

DALKEY ARCHIVE PRESS

The cover images, of an envelope belonging to Dr. M. Napthali, are reproduced from Isadore Brodsky, *Sydney's Little World of Woolloomooloo* (Old Sydney Free Press, 1966).

LIBRARY OF CONGRESS CATALOGING-IN-PUBLICATION DATA IS AVAILABLE UPON REQUEST.

Partially funded by the Illinois Arts Council, a state agency
This project has been assisted by the Australian Government through the Australia Council, its arts funding and advisory body.

Dalkey Archive Press
Victoria, TX / McLean / Dublin / London
www.dalkeyarchive.com

Dalkey Archive Press books are, in part, made possible through the support of the University of Houston-Victoria and its program in creative writing, publishing, and translation.

Typesetting: Mikhail Iliatov

Printed on permanent/durable acid-free paper.

Dodge Rose

Revenge is a wild kind of justice

Then where from here. When the train rolled over a canopied bridge the eyes of the boy in the opposite seat opened and closed to the broken sun but he dozed on. His head was rocked against a woollen sleeve. Eliza had stretched her legs out in the space beneath his feet and now she crossed them and pressed her thumbs to the bundle in her lap. The shoes above hers swung back and forth like pendulums staccato lights between the shadows that beat through the carriage from the bridge but for all his moving parts the boy remained oblivious and his brief eyes gave back nothing but the wrong end of his reveries. Eliza yawned and turned towards the window. Before wide green plots the spokes of the canopy blew past, then they were gone.

She looked down at the pair of ripped envelopes beneath her hands. In one was a letter from the family solicitor that said her aunt Dodge was dead. Eliza was coming to deal with the estate because her mother couldn't. I wrote the other letter, to cut a long story short. After a week in the post it arrived a day later than the solicitor's, and so the envelope itself with its return address was a surprise because she was expecting to travel to an empty flat. She unfolded the sheet of paper faded to azure once on the train. She had never met her aunt and her mother had not told her much about her, so she was used to considering her relations tolerably less than they may have been. Dear Max she wrote back, who are you and can I stay at the flat. The sleeper shuddered. It was a clear winter morning and the air that hissed through the window began to taste faintly of salt.

Eventually the open country had given way to the suburbs and now a sharp bend in the tracks threw up the glass towers of the harbourside, and shifted them, and spun them away again. Eliza had been raised on a sheep farm near Yass and gone to a local school and rarely travelled this far east. Nothing in the window was familiar to her, neither in form nor the speed at which it altered, and when she recognised an old biscuit logo from the loose change tin in her living room it was swung past on a wall left exposed by a demolition in the neighbouring lot, enormous, faded almost to the brick. She packed the letters away and folded her arms against her chest as the banks of facing windows crowded in and the train wound up the rusted arteries to Central Station.

The boy was still sleeping when she shouldered her luggage and walked out to the platform. As she passed along the vaulted causeway she checked the bronze timepiece hanging from the rafters and found it was earlier than she had expected. She glanced back at the standing train. At dawn she had put on a clean pair of jeans, kissed her mother goodbye then stood a moment in the doorway and the older woman bedridden, breathing through a plastic mask had raised her arm in a wave that stood still as the red gums out the window, and now Eliza thought of that arm falling, in the full sun, as if she had turned up here in the interval. As if all the old years had blown away at once.

Assonance, the patchupperer, I have you at least. Before letting her go her mother had given directions to the flat that Eliza had decided to commit to memory. She took an escalator to Eddy Avenue and walked through Belmore Park scattering sticks and debris with the uninhibited stride of a born rentier. The light tumbling clear through the bare plane trees caught the down on her cheeks and her curls, assembled in a red elastic, shone as softly as an old waxed intaglio. Russian clouds hung still in the treetops. We were twenty one and halfway into 1982. One day sheep were going to make Eliza rich, but by then she was going on three years out of school and felt the need to make money and the letters turning invisibly in the shallows of her knapsack weighed almost nothing at all.

A line of nuns caught her up on Castlereagh Street and she walked behind them as far as the district court. Above its opaque windows the blue and yellow tiles of the old arcade still spelled out mourning, lace, gloves. Already the vague map in her head had begun to unravel. Ahead of her the nuns went over to Hyde Park and she should have followed them but turned too late and finished up walking down Macquarie

Street towards the water. She almost ran into a milkman pushing a trolley of empty bottles out of the Mint but when she opened her mouth to ask for directions the words failed her and he swerved past and went clinking over the road to Martin Place. Eliza burned and ground her boots into the pavement. She had never been lost before. Where was north. The sun reverberating off the towers on the far side of the street hit her like a white noise it was impossible to cancel out even when she closed her eyes and the panoptic burr of the traffic made her reel again. She tried to think where she might have gone wrong and couldn't, so in shame she kept on the way she had been going until she spotted the baize harbour winking at the end of the street and knew for sure she had come too far.

She spun on her heel and kicked something.

Respect said a man standing in the shade beside her. He wore his ponytail hooked through the clasp of a sweat streaked baseball cap and carried a bundle of newspapers under one arm. With the other he was pointing at the big iron gate still ruckling from the blow. Eliza frowned. I need to get to Kings Cross.

You have to go the other way.

She nodded. I'm not from around here.

The man was taller than Eliza and held himself so rigid that to look at her his eyeballs rolled down in his face like a pair of lead sinkers. The quickest way is through the gardens he said. I'm going through to Bourke Street, I can give you directions from there. She thanked him and followed him through the gateway. He did not ask her what her business was in Sydney, his long legs quietly swallowing up the ground before her. She wanted to know what place they were in. He told her they were in the Palace Gardens. Where was the palace.

Here he said. It ran more than two hundred metres this way and that way. He began to tell her about it because Eliza had returned him, helplessly, a blank look. A glass and wood and corrugated iron monument to trade and industry and shop and housekeeping. A dome rose in the middle as high as five stories. The architect had worked for the English greenhouse expert whatshisname, Paxton, who drew from the example of a giant water lily the load bearing beams of the Crystal Palace in London. The building here burned down one night and the land reverted to the gardens. There is a sunken pavement where the dome used to be and a bronze cupid in the centre whose eyes are covered in fruit bat crap, his face turned up in glee or wonder to where that ceiling imploded and fell five stories in a bloom of galactic cinders. A plaque beneath his feet says love lead them. Always wondered what the hell that means.

As they walked the man had folded the newspapers behind his back and Eliza, seeing how brittle they were and hatched with creases, scanned between his fingers for a date. They came to a flight of steps and stayed there. That must have been a long time ago.

One hundred years.

O said Eliza. The hours spent on the train had wrung her out. A line of tourists walked between them and down into the lower gardens, their voices echoing back on the steps. Eliza brushed against a statue of winter holding a dead sparrow in his hand, little left to divine. Not once I'm through with my lapidations, if I have anything to do with it. The plinth for spring stood empty. How did the palace burn down.

Some say arson. After the exhibition was removed it became quite a volatile species of miscellanea. Lots of apparently innocuous objects were kept on display in the wings and places, including the complete collection of the Linnaean Society library, but the basement was turned into a store for government records. Land deeds, the census. The 1888 census went up in smoke, so they say it was arson. To get rid of the stain you know. You go up and back and the family is begun in bondage. Could be a speculator on Macquarie Street just wanted to clear the view. He shielded his eyes and looked out across the harbour. Boats were scattered around like rice. A million dollars muttered the man in the baseball cap, and rolled his papers into an iron scroll. Eliza stretched until her shoulders cracked. That is a lot, she said, of useless water.

From the farther side of the gardens he pointed her up William Street to the Cross, and so she went along that concrete geodetic and alone wove under the pale neon rain of the strip clubs towards the address I'd cobbled together a week before over Dodge's ancient, fractured stationery. It was after midday and people had thrown their jackets over their shoulders and come onto the street with empty stomachs, cockeyed with the chords of forgotten ways, relics of a senile stage, bed to the river of the living. The street, it got away from me. Those were the days. Who were they all these people. Eliza might have ended up lost again but she had been watching a sailor flit like desire through the crowd ahead of her when he turned a corner and where he disappeared she read the name of Greenknowe Avenue in bright letters.

The latticework of pipes running up one side of the building was, when she saw it, burgeoning with rust, the brass panels of the street door as encrusted and clouded as a high water mark. Since a stopper had been lodged between them Eliza pushed through to the lobby without buzzing the flat. Her foot caught the stopper and the daylight snapped shut behind her. She blinked uselessly. In a gloom where the glass torches of four electric angels had raised as many overlapping moons along the wallpaper she could make out the silhouette of a staircase, a narrow pot plant and nothing else. Her fingers groped along the wall until the pressure of a scratched plastic button brought the lift down and she took it to the top floor.

She came straight in. I don't remember how the lynx or I got here. Along with the front door I had thrown all the curtains open and unlatched the windows and the polish on the dresser and the chairs our side of the dining table shone like gold dust in the first bleed of colour to the afternoon. She surprised me standing in the kitchen doorway, the toes of my kid leather shoes given false life and sclerosis in the

long run by the washing up water, a fistful of plaid tea towel
at my hip. She looked like Dodge. I once thought I looked
a bit like Dodge but since then have had less tenuous no-
tions.

You must be Max. She swung her bag off her shoulder
and seemed as if she meant to drop it where she stood but
hesitated.

Hello Eliza I said. Make yourself at home.

So the knapsack fell and because neither of us approached to shake hands we grinned and glanced around us
and Eliza wiped her nose with the back of her hand and
said yes she would like a cup of tea thanks and flopped
down on the nearest armchair. She said I bet you don't have
a T.V.

I know it's old fashioned I said and tried to imagine
the place through the eyes of someone who had grown up
elsewhere. Eliza had landed before one of the bay windows that opened over the Avenue. A suggestive view of
the interior. The contents of the living room had been
there a long time. The yellow and pink furniture was
clean but threadbare and there were patches in the faded carpets where the strings of the warp showed through
like a bad signal. Some of the furniture that used to be
pink had become yellow. Between a pair of sliding doors
ahead of her she could make out a line of the rubbed clutter in the dining room and to her right a corridor whose
far end glowed with what might have been the coloured
rhombs of a leadlight portal. The living room had begun to
blaze.

She said it's like some kind of museum. I said they ro-
tate the exhibits there. Should do for the he said she said.

She nodded and we stayed as we were for a moment
looking at each other. I hadn't heard of Eliza either before
Dodge's funeral. I had assumed, living in a place like this,
that the family was dead. Dodge had spoken about them
but always in the past tense and her sister had seemed to
flicker so dimly through the rooms of her memory that it
was somewhat skipping a beat to be facing the issue without

a chance first to get accustomed to the idea of that error from her childhood endowed enough to make her own mistakes. Apparently. Some hooch. I had never heard about a farm either but that was not surprising since it belonged to her mother's side and that far out in the family Dodge only had stories about the Dutch bankers who made her father.

I left Eliza in the living room and went back to the kitchen. The armchair groaned behind me as I bent beneath the drying rack to let the plug out in the sink. She must have been curious, bewildered even. She was obviously not going to explain anything but all the same it was nice to have a change of company. It was not the same. The dishwater gurgled off in a nacreous slew of grease and detergent as I dried my hands and lit the burner beneath the kettle with a damp safety match, then I carried two cups on their saucers into the living room.

Some things you can do without thinking.

Eliza smiled again, her broad back to the bookcase that stood between the kitchen door and the sofa. We had too much in common to be embarrassed but it was hard to begin with nothing to go on. She had been looking at a photograph that sat locked among the knick knacks in the bookcase. The photo was small enough for a passport but gave back the full length of a girl buried to the neck in a fur coat, her glossy brogues spliced awkwardly through a moraine of rubble and bright frost while one hand gripped at the edge of a kind of vertical ice sheet, perhaps a squirt from a frozen waterfall or the shard of a glacier that had come to pieces. Her felt hat had been turned up at the brim so her face would come out in the developing fluid. Her eyes shrunk by the sun. A blur of arrested speech.

The kettle whistled. Eliza blinked and followed me into the kitchen saying I got lost on the way here. I came through the Botanic Gardens with a guy who told me they once built a glass palace in it full of giant furniture. He said it was the first building to be raised under electric light.

And the first crops grew there I said. Seeds and plants in the ship, instant botany.

Eliza clapped her hand to her mouth. I have to make a phone call she said. Do you have a phone.

There was a candlestick in the dining room I showed her how to use. When she came back she had taken off her jacket and let her hair out. She stretched the red elastic between her fingers. Mum says Bernard called. We can go and see him tomorrow at ten. Her voice faltered. Something obvious appeared to be beginning to dawn on her and she frowned until the elastic had slowed to a stop and her thought come home. She turned back to the bookcase and her finger slid as if longingly over the glass, tracing the xylonite frame. Is this my aunt.

She used to say so.

Eliza wrinkled her nose. Puny us. Looks like a mouse stuck to an ice cube. She squinted in at the dark little mirror, repeating odd points of the room behind her in a glance the chairs their torqued legs and the broken arabesques in the carpets, the coffee table and the writing table beside the window, the acorn lamp suspended from the ceiling on a brass chain. In the base of the lamp a pile of dead moths made a star shaped smudge in the frosted glass. No offence. She frowned. I didn't know her. Outside some kids had begun to play in the street and the impact of their basketball ricocheted up the walls like aftertouch. Eliza squatted to open her bag.

Could she smoke. I gave her a saucer to ash in. She rummaged through her clean clothes and I poured the tea. The steam looped around my wrists. She picked a strand of hair from the corner of her mouth with her free hand then she lit her cigarette and said you didn't say a lot in your letter. I have no idea why Mum and Dodge stopped talking but it must have been before me because I never heard about her.

Did your mother know about me.

Don't think so. I read her the letter but you know she isn't well and the drugs keep her quiet. I guess if you don't remember there isn't a lot to tell. What did Dodge tell you.

The usual garbage at first, until I couldn't be bothered asking anymore.

My mother told me I came from Heaven.

Told me I came from Hollywood.

Eliza snickered. Why.

The building was full of entertainers when Dodge was growing up. Some of them used to play the piano and have parties in the flat. A magician pulled a chocolate coin from behind her ear. Left an impression. She used to talk a lot about them. It could have been something she remembered hearing. New girl. Babe from Hollywood.

Have you met Bernard asked Eliza. A glow between her fingers and a jet of smoke. They have the same lawyer.

I said I met him at the funeral. There was a bit of money left over in the house so I put an ad in the paper but the only person who came was Bernard. I think he was drunk. Wildly groping man lurching out from between the pews. Max*ine*. You *were* a surprise. Here we go. Look around you. Flebile principium melior fortuna. Jackey Jackey. He told me about you. He said your mother had given you power of attorney so I wrote you that day. I didn't have a phone number for you and he didn't have it on him.

Eliza smoothed a crease in her jeans. Mum told me he would handle things well. He's worked for the Roses forever. From the deepening sky a split second of lightning lit the window. She turned and looked over the acacias still shaking their green leaves, then got to her knees and stubbed her cigarette in the saucer.

The new day fell in sheets of rain. We had
breakfast facing one another along the cracked window of
a diner in Kellet Street, the collar of her stonewash jacket
folded up to her ears, an abortive gulf of coffee, almost, almost inedible toast and a cigarette between us. Fifteen
members of the Canadian Black Leopards Karate Club had
recently demolished a house with bare hands and feet on
the radio and the planes were still crashing and there were
wars. Eliza had not slept well. Dodge's feather bed had giv-
en her a bad sinking feeling. She drew circles in a pile of
spilt sugar and stared out the window at the wet traffic.
Never thought the city would be so dirty she said.

We ran under awnings and then down the hill from Potts
Point in the rain and the shattered pollen to the solicitor's
office at the corner of Bland and Bourke Streets in Woolloomooloo. Once we had taken a resplendent flight of linoleum
stairs, Eliza struck the open door, at which lesser adventure
two small disks of glass flashed out from then disappeared
among the piles of cartulary greying in the morning light.
Excuse us. He waved us through with his spare hand, nodding into the phone while signalling it for the benefit of
the other side in a run of significant noises, then dropped
the receiver so the bell clanged, pressed both hands
to the desk and lifted himself above his files to face us.

The Rose girls. You should have warned. Good morning
come in. He looked from one to the other, a bemused smile
abandoned on his mouth as he stepped forward with his
hand outstretched. You must be Eliza. How is your mother.
I am sorry about Dodge. We go back an age but the last time
I saw her was. I went to the funeral. It was a closed casket.
If it had been an open casket I might have started reminisc-
ing but I'm too old for a closed casket. St. James' really is
a lovely church. Very austere. All that marble. Cleansing.
Makes you feel clearheaded. He gestured vaguely for us to

sit then went back behind his desk. Eliza perched on the arm of a chair piled with empty springback binders.

The room was very small and full of both opened and unopened boxes and there were piles of paper on the floor as well as on the desk. The shade had been pulled down over the window and through it the sun made soft shadows of the backward letters that spelt out the firm for the street. Bernard took off his glasses, pulled a handkerchief from his breast pocket and began to clean them. He was large, in the chest and the face and the elbows of his cheekbones shone blasted pink. Two thin sheaves of white hair swept up from his temples to his bare skull and wrapped it. Still blind, he cleared his throat and nodded in our direction.

It really is unfortunate he said. You must borrow an umbrella when you go. Maxine I met last week. Very interesting, very glad to meet her. As soon as I read the ad in the paper I went straight for the Rose file but the fact is I haven't found it yet. Of course it ought to be in the safe but it isn't. He pointed at the piles on his desk. I've been looking ever since. Not normally such a mess in here. I didn't mention it earlier because I hoped I might get lucky before you arrived but it seems to have disappeared. Mea culpa! We had an accident a few years back. Some documents were lost but they've all been accounted for. Your family's file, I frankly just don't know where I put it.

Eliza opened her mouth then shut it again. She stuck her thumb between her teeth and took it out. And Dodge's will.

In the file. There were no copies. He pushed his glasses back up the bridge of his nose and raised his eyebrows. You could get confused even with these on.

Eliza frowned. What do we do now then.

He tipped his head to one side. An automobile made a slish in the street. Well in essence since Dodge had so few relatives it ought to be quite straightforward. First you apply for letters of administration. You need them to handle an estate without a will. Then the property goes down the line. Only we don't know. We don't have any papers for

Maxine. Not a birth certificate, nothing.

Eliza looked at me. Is that true.

I almost shrugged. I've looked. I can't find one.

Bernard placed one hand over the other on the desk. You say Dodge was not your mother.

I don't think I said. I said I think she would have told me. It's a problem for the inheritance isn't it. If I was adopted there would be a record somewhere wouldn't there.

You might begin he said by asking at the Department of Community Services. Otherwise there may be a record at the Supreme Court or at the Registry of Births Deaths and Marriages. But it's not guaranteed. If it was a private outfit, say if you were adopted from out of a religious institution, they might have the only record left but you'd have to know where to look. You could. Well. You could try the state archives. This kind of information has a tendency to disappear sometimes. It can take years. He coughed. Of course with the whole family file missing we can't check up on it but I don't believe *I* was ever given anything relating to adoption. I'm sure I would have remembered Dodge Rose adopting! Like a little girl when she was old enough to. I used to take her out on the weekends sometimes. She tied knots in her handkerchief to remind her of her errands but it never worked and she'd never undo the knots as long as she couldn't think what they were for. Afraid of losing. Some childish superstition. Fine young woman to be going around with her handkerchief tied up like a lobster net.

What if we can't find a record.

Then you may not even be entitled to the place you're living in. You see as administrator Eliza is bound to distribute the property according to the rules of intestacy.

Eliza had begun to slouch and press one foot mechanically against the other.

What are they.

If you couldn't prove that you were adopted Dodge's sister would be in line to receive everything. The definition of child in a case like this is restricted. If you wanted to seek maintenance you would have to do it under the provisions of State maintenance legislation rather than the Family Law Act. It would be a difficult situation. Perhaps, capitulation. But you know. Well. Hang on. Bernard half rose and began to turn over some manila folders on the desk when his elbow knocked an alphabetical filing box causing it to tip and spew its contents across the floor. The slightest suspicion of a faintly acrid perfume hit the remaining sense. He glanced aside, his hands hovering a moment over the spill, then as if the information he was looking for had been knocked out with them he waved the scattered index cards into the undependable future and made a fist that fell in the space just cleared on the pinewood desk.

Family provision. There was an act passed this year that might help you. It makes it possible to get a provision from the estate even if you're not a blood relative and so I guess also in a case such as yours where you don't have adoption papers yet but might have. He sighed. It might be your best way forward. Of course the rest of the family has a bearing on all this. You seem sympathetic to the situation you had better talk to your mother. I'm sure she is. I'll confirm the details of the act and we can meet again at the end of the week. As for your immediate business with the court, determining next of kin under the rules of intestacy requires you to document the family tree, just the relephant part, so collect the birth certificates that link Dodge and her sister and yourself, start valuing the estate and find out if the poor woman had any outstanding debts. He swung back on his chair and tipped up his hands as good as in benediction. Judgement and sentence according to law and *equity* you know. Fair's fair.

On the street as I opened Bernard's umbrella above us Eliza looped her arm in mine and said I used to wish I had been adopted.

When I got back from the local Department of Community Services office the phone was ringing out the cankered traces of its own preterite neglect, its fast ablating corrugations as it were wavering over the derelict living room like the fading echo of an apocalypse that had not come to everybody after all.

I ran for it but when I answered the voice on the other side rushed through in a thin stream of vowels and consonants, so I jammed the receiver against my ear and froze. I tried to talk back to stop it but before I knew what I was doing I'd dropped the phone and retreated into the living room. Above me the water in the pipes jumped and a moment later Eliza was at the end of the corridor wiping her hands on her jeans. What's the matter she asked.

It's Dodge I stammered. On the phone.

Eliza raised her eyebrows but held her tongue and went into the dining room. We aren't puppets, what did she say. What was she trying to say. After a minute she was standing between the sliding doors with her hands on her hips. It was my mother. I called her when you were out to tell her about the will. You know what she said. She said we two should divide everything between us.

I had taken a seat by the window and drifted off a bit but now I glanced back at Eliza and in her eyes. Something in one. How could you understand what she was saying. I could barely make out her voice.

Eliza shrugged. I've had to make out what Mum's been saying for years now. What does it matter.

Make up do you mean. Not out.

She waited for me to say something more. She put her hands on her hips again, over two sets of damp fingerprints.

I've just been to DOCS.

What did *they* say.

They couldn't get a hold of anything on the spot. They

have files up from the mid fifties and some from adoption agencies that have closed. If there's nothing there they could help me look. I think it would cost some money and in any case they said it could take years. It's not very practical, for the circumstances. Eliza crossed her arms and looked me up and down. In my reply to her letter I told her I had been living with her aunt at least since I was six years old, before which I don't have any memories. I remember. The first thing I remember is that I was bringing Dodge lunch on a round pewter tray and she was defecating all over our shoes. She had been saying thank you but now she was wailing and her nails were in my shoulder and I was staring into the whites of her eyes and trying to hold the tray steady so she wouldn't topple it into the shit.

I don't know how long I had been in the flat when that happened but later I took a clean pair of socks from my suitcase so it can't have been long at all. Dodge ran a bath. She trod shit through the house but what could we do, so did I. I put our shoes on the balcony outside her bedroom and I scrubbed the carpet with half a bar of Sunlight soap then put some in a bucket of water and on the balcony I dunked our shoes and hung them from the balustrade by the laces. In the evening when I went in to wash I found the rest of her clothes in a bundle under the sink. Dodge had shut herself in her room so I rinsed them in the tub and threw them over the curtain rail.

We never spoke about that afternoon though it turned out she shat herself more frequently than any other woman in my experience.

In your experience.

I'm sure I would have remembered one.

Dodge was incontinent.

I think it was her porcelain bladder. It pressed in on her. Towards the end she rarely even left the flat, and if she ever had to she was so relieved to get back she usually sank into the sofa and stayed there until I came home from school and took away whatever it was she'd bought rum, tobacco, some flowers, a bolt of fabric. A hatchet. No only on Fridays. She

didn't go out other days. Once she did but I wouldn't clear
up the shopping dumped by the sofa on my entrall. Fuk
this shit I said I hav rites. One evening I found her sitting
at her desk by the window, her fingers gripping her pencil
to a shopping list. She wore her hat and her gloves already.
Her hounds tooth coat had slipped down from the arm of
the sofa and her bladder had gone. I opened my mouth but
stopped there. Above her hand, clamped shut forever, her
pearls winked with the motes turning briefly in the levelling sun. All those years she had been like a mother to me.

When I was older I didn't ask her where I came from
anymore but then she had a nauseating habit of telling stories. She would dredge up all the people who ever came or
went from the flat and the more often she told a story the
more they slid around. By the time exhaustion took over
and even the words began to loosen from her sentences the
only thing that was staying where it started was the furniture. Even the photo albums were too many. It became
harder to tell apart those that had been inherited. You could
find a pair of neatly creased serge trousers in every one but
together they covered at least a hundred years and some
had been taken on the Riviera and some came from cities
we had never known. Dodge was a collector. Photo albums
were cheap and her favourites.

I used to leaf through them myself during the brief periods
she called for silence. One afternoon in the school holidays
I lay beneath a window in the living room with an album

whose scribble of blue ink spelled Summer 2. Under it flew
an embossed bow as slim as infinity. Dodge was out. I was
turning the pages slowly in the glassed heat when I saw
something I had seen before, come unstuck from the grey
cardboard mount and slipped down to the spine of the album. Not the photo but that blur of hooped skirts in the
sand, a loosened fist by a clutter of soiled plates and tumblers and those spots in the ocean. I had been here. Where
the sand is hot but you have to take off your socks and walk
on it. And, oh the wind in your face, the salt wind that mas-
sive breath that smacks you up as the grains rise between
your toes like yeast. Warm glass powder that stars your feet
on the way to the water. Obliterated conches. Voices glance
over the surface from the boys in the deep. They used to
look awkward dandled by the unbroken waves but now they
can dive and when they turn their shoulders to the water
their blades wink in the sun. And the sand burns your feet.
You are in the water and it's good to float in the fold between
the sky and the sea. The sea! Whose hand was that. You are
lifted in the belly of a wave, held by an upward weight then
hurled through stinging stuff up all the holes in your face
over feet over face in the white water. It carries you into the
sand. You struggle up to your knees and vomit. I felt sick in
the flat. The carpet seemed to be slipping me out so I sat
up against the mullions. When I closed my eyes I could see
the whole dead day again. It happened more than once.

Eliza looked at her watch. What have you been living on
this past week.

On the cash left over in the house. Dodge went to the
bank every month and she kept what she withdrew in that
tin box over there. With the coroner's fee and the funeral
costs it's almost empty now. I was waiting for you to arrive
before we went to the bank. Eliza looked me up and down
again and bit her lip.

Are they Dodge's clothes.

At this I could not avoid tucking the faded skirt of a gab-
ardine pinafore between my knees. It had been royal blue
once apparently. Dodge had kept everything bought for her

since she was a girl so if I ripped my stockings climbing
over the sandstone crenulations of the school steps she just
opened a drawer in her dresser rolled away the mothballs
and shook out a new pair, like the last glimpse of a dis-
turbed octopus beige turning coral pink. There were even
shoes wrapped in oilcloth tucked away on the mother of
pearl paper with the gloves and scarfs. You had to be careful of those mothballs though, a new stocking might con-
tain a painful grain. Indeed the versicles were there from
the beginning, between her howling and my own, I will always have that to fall back on when I run out of connect-
ing words. I also inherited hats, and bloomers with slugs of
thread where the silk had rotted off. We were economical.

Where did Dodge get her money. Do you know.

I shook my head. Some kind of pension I guess. She
never worked. But like I said we didn't spend much. That
is. I raised my hand as if I might have pointed at something in the room but it fell in a limp arc at my side. There
wasn't much need. She only ever went to the hospital once
as far as I remember despite the things that were wrong
with her. There was no expensive treatment. The money
she put in the tin box was never any more or less than it was
at the beginning. I had no real pocket money, I thought it
worth underlining. I didn't mind dressing like this. I liked
the clothes.

Over the pinafore provided it isn't only more natural lard to cover up what has long since beaten a retreat, I
had on a rib knitted cardigan if you can believe it, orphi-
non, with one, elliptic celadon wafer button; celadon yes,
it fell between my margins of error, for the other I go by
the gardener's method, if it's possible to use such an expression without foundations, plunging the first stake into
my own hearth. Should have been born in Carrefour. Eliza
eyed them in all seriousness and said they look good. I wondered if I dressed like her mother. She said no her mother
didn't wear anything anymore. Slept like a baby. Of course
Eliza still dressed like a cowgirl, a plaid shirt rolled above
her elbows, football socks.

What exactly was wrong with her.

At first it was just incontinence. Then the bladder cancer. It can be difficult to treat once you find it because by then it's usually advanced. Sometimes there are no symptoms, and anyway Dodge was so acrazed she might not have noticed if there had been. Maybe she did notice and she was just scrimping.

Something almost like a smile had been curling up in Eliza's face for some time and it broke then in a ripple of hilarious twitches. So you think she lived on a pension.

What else.

Heritance you never heard of.

I shook my head.

When the older Roses died they left everything to their daughters. I guess Mum settled with Dodge before she left for the farm and maybe she took more because Dodge stayed behind in the flat but it can't have been a lot more when everything was weighed in the balance and she's bought land and a fifty thousand head of sheep with her bit and has got them through the drought so far without using it up.

How much.

I don't know. That's two million dollars' worth of sheep though.

I trust I am remembering that number correctly. As it was, until our time together I had handled only a very small amount of cash (some inescapable expenses carried in coins in the pocket of my school dress but everything else Dodge saw to herself, writing cheques wherever she could with an ostensive if incomprehensible scruple apparent in absolutely nothing else) and so it must have been from lack of contact that this information was absorbed by me as with the the infamously immediate and arresting force of pure theory. Her words came and went as a revelation, everything in the wake of that great property expanding into so many impalpable and inadequate dividers, being at first just a vague tergiversation and then as if the same abstract shades that had clabbered every particle in the flat turned for a moment

as full and fleeting as a rush of oxygen into a spumous surplus, leaving me floating in their airy mould, surprised. I
had never made plans, being by nurture far from pleonectic.
I made some.

There was no pension said Eliza. I can't see why there
should have been. She was probably living on interest.

We'd better go to the bank.

They'll probably want to see my letters before they let
us have anything. Better wait until we see Bernard again.
I'll write off for Mum's and my birth certificates and we'll
need to find Dodge's. It's really too bad you don't have one.
Do you know did she have any debts.

I shrugged.

How do we find out.

I guess we just wait to see if someone calls them in. Before we left him Bernard had shown us the template for a
notice that had to be published two weeks ahead of apply-
ing at the court for letters of administration and we had followed it on the spot and delivered our version to the front
office of *The Sydney Morning Herald* on the way home, so
by now it was not simply from under the stone cold teapot
and sticky breakfast plates deserted over the coffee table
in the flat on Greenknowe Avenue but from any number
of the volar errant facets of the daily press that the words
after fourteen days from the publication of this notice and
application for administration of the estate of ROSE DODGE
late of Sydney, *spinster*, will be made by Elizabeth O'Rourk
the niece. Creditors are required to send particulars of their
claims upon her estate to Looper and Russett solicitors,
1/2 Bland Street, Woolomooloo might have been seen by
anyone. As grammatical error or a hole was inherent to the
template and because we didn't know any better we didn't
think our own defect would cause any trouble. We figured
anyone who had an interest would understand whichever
way it happened to come out.

Dodge didn't have a filing cabinet or something.

No. There's nothing left. She didn't keep any. Papers.
There are none. At least I don't think so. Where would you

keep them around here.

Eliza was trying the drawer of the writing table by the window. It opened with a hollow cough. She flinched. It's empty.

They all are.

Oof. Looks like the kind of place that'd be full of stuff to read. What about in there. She pointed at the glimmer between the sliding doors.

Things for eating.

What did you do all that time without a T.V.

Dodge talked. We had a radio once but it broke.

The birth certificates came express courier, the envelope otherwise empty but signed by the neighbour Eliza had left in charge of the property and her mother's vital needs. At the end of the week we went back down the hill and found Bernard hunched over his desk again which was clear now except for a blotter and a glass of something orange and softly hissing. He remained seated as we came in, smiling to avoid wincing and nodding, taking back from Eliza his umbrella, dry, wound up, and buckled in. Don't be fooled he said lifting the umbrella slightly. It looks much better but I still haven't found your file. Obviously he was referring to the old disorder though apart from the surface of the desk and some space that had been dug out in the corner of the room to the left of the doorway there was now a pile of manila folders and loose purplish paper leaning against the benighted window where there hadn't been before and where there had been a chair there was another stack of boxes. I'll say the rest of the room looked exactly the same.

We gave him the certificates and told him it might take a while to turn up adoption papers. We all agreed it would be impractical to hold off dividing the estate. In any case he said inhaling deeply I was right, the Family Provision Act makes it perfectly possible for Maxine to be provided for without them. Dodge finally transcended her bad timing. Recte facit, if you'll pardon my rudeness. You see the old Family Maintenance Act only worked on behalf of blood relatives. Now in the absence of a legacy the court is allowed to consider the contribution of any eligible person to the welfare of the deceased, including contribution as a home-maker, the character and conduct of the person before and after death, her circumstances. Having been a dependant also makes you eligible to be provided for. What does your mother think.

She agrees.

Bernard paused. He had picked up the glass from the desk but put it back now without drinking. Good. Recruit to dilute. Well that's good but a decision made under the Family Maintenance Act is a discretionary one. That is, it's up to a judge to decide whether there are grounds for an order in Maxine's favour, even if you've come to an agreement amongst yourselves. You may decide on your own how much Maxine should have and you two could in fact apply to be joint administrators of the estate but that would take another twenty eight days to come into effect and even then the judge has to agree to the amount that you both agree the defendant, in this case Eliza, owes the plaintiff, Maxine. None of this is difficult or riskful but it does mean you have to go to court.

We're in a bit of a hurry said Eliza.

Isn't everybody. He moved his hand from the glass and lifted the notepad with two blurred fingers as if he might have flung it off the desk but only dropped it there as an actor throws down evidence. More the same. He said that, I didn't say that. Anyway going to court is expensive. My advice is that you can avoid it by offering Maxine a certain amount of money as a settlement. The formal agreement then is that on acceptance of the settlement proceedings are dismissed. You could agree on a provision and hand it over right away, then you'd be square. It depends how much capital there is and how much you think Maxine should have. Of course if there wasn't enough you could liquidate some of Dodge's assets. Save time and court costs.

How do we access Dodge's money.

You need your letters of administration. I'll sign an affidavit for the lost will and you take them with your certificates and a summary of the value of Dodge's estate and liabilities to the Supreme Court. Get a real estate agent over to tell you how much the flat is worth, and how much it'll cost to sell. Plus there are her possessions. You should have a professional value the contents of the flat and the cost of sale. Afraid with property and gold plummeting together, well, whaddo I know. Anyway you need to give all that into the court. I'll help you write the forms now and give you a list of everything else you need.

We can at least look at her bank account can't we said Eliza.

Bernard nodded swallowing. Uh of course. You need to, and you'll have to include the balance in the value of her estate. With power of attorney you're entitled to see how much is in there. Just go to the bank and show them her death certificate.

Certainly. Eliza turned to me. Do you have that.

I did.

Later as we were taking a long way home down Bourke Street Eliza said you don't seem very curious about the adoption or whatever it was.

I said I didn't know what there was to be curious about. I didn't know what there was. Besides, the less we know about it the better it is for you.

Why.

Because if I was adopted I'd inherit everything.

Apparently Eliza hadn't thought of this. She stopped walking and cupped her hand on her belly. Did you expect to get it all. You must resent me.

I demurred. Dodge literally died sooner than I anticipated. She didn't tell me how sick she really was and I never thought about what to do after it was over. I suppose I always assumed it wouldn't concern me by then. But she just hit, you know, one afternoon all of a sudden like death into the Mirrour of Justice, and now here we are, her own metabasis. I'm glad she was rich but frankly I would not want to pick up alone, that would be a bit much.

Eliza looked ambivalent but we went straight home and made lunch with the leftovers in the fridge and half a bot-

tle of flat apple cider then we collected the death certificate
and set off for the bank.

A jet was evacuating its load of soot and
tiny ice crystals through the washed out sky over Martin
Place when she pointed behind her, hush, the breeze scuffing her hair across her lips. She said she had come along this
way, that way to the park, the first day, where that bum told
her about the big glass building. Wafted to me with his pit-
ted fist. Her eyes like a dug up sailor's. Strangely iridescent.
Uh huh, like Bernard, who couldn't throw anything out, the
mauve print rubbing off on his fingers. Spirit paper.

We talked about how to divide the estate. I pointed out
that it was her mother, not Eliza who stood to inherit, so
I would have to be splitting with her. Eliza without going
as far as to say that she could rob her mother said that was
fine, which was to be the last word on delectus personae.
The architectural terra cotta tiles of the bank, shimmering
in the sun as it slanted into the square before us, lent it
the appearance of a giant Königsberg amber box, some tall
Pharos. A row of fluted columns appeared to lift the whole
edifice into the air like a solid pipe dream, like a trick of
perspective. It was wide as the block. We went in by a side
door.

It had only been sifting back for a dropped word that
I remembered Dodge had belonged to the Commonwealth Bank. The tall beaux arts or something building being its most conspicuous office in the city and a
cultural landmark was the one branch I could bring to
mind so I had chosen to take Eliza there. I had never been among the veined green columns of the interior, in fact raised in a growth spurt by hundreds of la-
bourers and craftsmen from Friuli whose employers, the
Melocco brothers, had a showroom in Annandale stamped in
marble with the motto refloresco but who now as I stood inside seemed to have fallen away like the scaffolding of dead
time to reveal this permanent fantasy of brass elevators and

long polished benches, a winter garden of hard currency. The noiseless feet steal swiftly by. We stood around and counted the swastikas in the magnesite floor until a man in a far booth called us over.

He took the certificate and told us to wait, then he walked to the end of the immense room and got into an elevator. Is he going up or down asked Eliza. Up I said. The gold used to be stored below but not anymore.

The clerk came back out through the brass doors with his hands behind his back, plying in our general direction an officious, congested vacuum the time it took him to recover the length of the off white pavement. Above his navy suit a tightly knotted yellow tie seemed to have pushed up both the cleo ring of his closely shaven neck and the roundish head that ducked now between the bars of the booth, turning to one then the other of us. Miss Rose. He was holding the certificate and a new sheet of paper. He said (it was true he had a cold, a repressed sneeze dislodged his steel frames from the apparently Pyrrhonian strand of his brow) we would be quite happy if you wished to withdraw the lot presently and close the account.

Later when we knew that there were four hundred dollars in it this was remembered as an obvious bad sign but at the time Eliza only fluttered her lashes in concert with my insides and said of course we'll open a new one.

He assented indifferently. Then he pushed a printout of the balance of the account across the bench so that Eliza could read it. She must have thought she was seeing the dot in the wrong place or counting fewer zeros than there were in reality. This ambiguity is killing. It was some time before she raised to me eyes blazing with marvel if not a mere hint of starry terror. But between the clerk and myself they must have triangulated with the bottom line: when they had dipped again to scan the columns of ciphers, since one also happened to show the withdrawals for the last month, she simply clanged down her own glassy margent of what I had to presume was suspended judgement. A foul reserve as it turned out, monosyllabic and undeniably less than edifying. From that moment on she treated me in any case with the more or less tacit respect that a swindler does someone whom she suspects to have plundered the ground before her.

I beg your pardon said the man in the yellow tie.

I said we'll close the account. We'll take it in fifty dollar bills please.

We went back home through the gardens, past the muted ecstasy of the bronze cupid, keeping an eye out for the old beggar. Eliza appeared to want to retrace her steps and gather her thoughts to begin again with. But we saw no one we knew and ended up consulting an illustrated plan whose red roads all seemed to twist into rather than lead out of the cardiac blot labelled you are here. We followed the path through the fern forest reading the plaques tacked to their trunks like the names and origins once tied to the necks of infant refugees. Ponytail Elephant Foot Tree. Slender Lady Palm. Chinese Fan Palm. Cheese Tree. She Oak. We quit browsing and went east as soon as the path turned that way but the incline only led us to a glass plated shed baptised as it were Cryptogam House and then past a fernery whose soft cornered sandstone walls had apparently been carried up in 1924 from the Governor's bath house in Farm Cove. Everything was labelled. Somehow among the mulch and rotting branches this mania for provenance seemed a bit unhinged. But maybe I said to Eliza even here in the waste of years and hours a few of the older trees were nurtured by the ashes of the library dedicated to the botanist who first made the analogy between plant and human reproduction. We walked back the way we'd come in the wrong direction but found the right one next to the what the stink pipe no the obelisk with the. XLIV. The remains of Allan Cu. A croft. Who's he when he's at home put Eliza.

Cunningham the colonial woodcarver. His coats of arms in the King Street Courts. Associates in poverty. Worm in the nombril. Rise. Quinine. Dem, dom. Madeira. No. Brucine.

Enough of interiors. We'd better go or I'll start spewing out my off cuts.

Haven't forgotten the French if that's what it was, might
never have got out of there otherwise. That's it, den Adern
deiner Brüder. Ex villatic. That's starting to cover ground.
She followed me through the Domain and down the steps
to Lincoln Corner, where a flock of silent gulls was circling
the abandoned finger wharf. What else. Beneath them a
man grabbed at a flash of silver that buckled in the air before
his knees then slipped, before we had reached the other
side and damned his memory, out of his hands into a hec-
tic bucket. The wind off the water was blowing her skirt
against my legs and sending a handful of paper garbage
scuffing along the pavement before us as if it was a mirror for the birds. The sky was clouding over again and the
first drops of rain were falling before we got home. Inside
the street door I unlocked Dodge's box and picked up the
mail that had been overlooked for days while Eliza called
the lift. We were not talking much by now. She seemed to
be thinking.

A window had been left open in the flat and as I came
back from closing it Eliza took the eight notes out of her
breast pocket unfolded them and laid them on Dodge's
writing desk under a millefiori paperweight the scratched
surface of which blurred and multiplied the fractures between the coloured glass rods as its atmospheric equivalent
is dispersed with the accumulation of its own substance.
I had dropped the mail in the same place, next to it is paperweight, where I usually left it, and turning back had
the sensation that I was seeing the gesture I had just made
made for the first time, right over the letters lying as they
had for thirteen years, and it dawned on me in a perfectly
good manner of speaking that Dodge was dead, that Eliza was not Dodge, I was not Dodge, that we would have to
do what was undone. I was looking into the hard wet patch
of my own reflection. No. Because. Though the drawers
of the desk and the bookcase still hung open because we
had not in fact been able to find Dodge's birth certificate
and had kept looking for it until we couldn't put off leaving
for Bernard any longer without being late, that centripetal

invasion of blank space only seemed to point to a deeper reticence, a fixture as secret as the clamps in a family portrait, even now the patch of damp carpet beneath the window returning as if the shock of her death had exposed the room to an image that no matter how well you cleared the place out would come back like a photograph blooming under the alkalies across a furious sheet of paper.

Well said Eliza quite frankly. What do you think happened to the money.

I have no idea. Maybe she never had any.

She shook her head. She must have. I can't believe Mum took everything.

Maybe she spent it.

On what.

There used to be a lot more in here. Dodge was always going out to auctions and second hand stores when I was younger and taking things with her and bringing back more than she took. Heaps of old stuff really. It all seemed worthless to me but you know you can't tell with old stuff.

Eliza drummed her fingers on the back of the threadbare sofa. What happened to it all.

We got rid of it. It's gone. That was a long time ago now. I can't think what she could have ever got for those trinkets. I want to know can't I say anything straight. Have a real cigarette. Eliza tapped up a slightly squashed Stuyvesant from its packet and began patting the pockets of her jacket for her lighter with a rapid movement that might have been nerves and I realised also as if for the first time that in a shallow way I was falling in love and maybe she was too. Maybe it was just beginning to have a friend. I guess it must have been as lonely on the farm in Yass with no one but her mother and the surrounding sheep as it was to live exclusively for a mistress in the Cross. It was Caprotinia the day of the. Caprio. Went under, no a loir wild fig tree. I love long life. Posh, damn short shrift high school don't remember anything. *Two* figs to the captor of that profound navel from down here over your pretended arsehole. Who the hell gave me this extravagant education.

That night I was woken by the sound of something metallic crashing onto the floorboards of the dining room. At first I held still in order to put nothing between my ears and the other end of the flat as my eyes adjusted to the moonlight that fell in through the open blinds spreading pink amid the wales of my woollen bedspread, shining on the rim of my alarm clock and in the silence that followed between the ticks of its infinite helix I threw the cover off and walked carefully, I won't say I pattered down the corridor to the living room. There was no light on anywhere and still no noise. I did not want to go any further without some kind of weapon but standing in the dark of the corridor at the entrance to the living room I could see through the open doors of the dining room to where a faintly luminous body was bent over something on the floor. It was Eliza. Again. Who else would it be. When she saw me walking towards her she jumped up with the metallic object in her hands and I reached and grabbed it only out of fear that she might drop it again but as she raised her hands in surprise now two pale palms against the shimmering obscurity of the dining room that for years had been no more than a hoarding house for family silver if it wasn't the effect of Fagan himself it was Jack Dawkins or the Artful Dodger coming at me for his share with streaks of ash down the thighs of his nightie and with an equally vacant reflex I swung the lidless urn to one side and out of her reach. She yelped, then recovering she said my name and asked me to turn on the light. I did, and saw that her hands too were covered in ash. What is that she said.

It's an urn I said.

She flopped down on the floor one bare leg either side of the little pile of burnt bones and the copper lid. She seemed as half asleep as I was. Come on I said in the atavistic fuddle of the early morning, no use crying over spilt milk. I was not long recovering my senses though. What I asked was she doing.

She looked at me and waited, her eyes resting opaque and patient on mine until at last her mind seemed to withdraw something that it must have been almost holding out, face down as it were, and it was with the kind of disappointed but levelling calm of a card player who folds before getting in too deep that she said she was looking to see if Dodge had hidden her money anywhere and I didn't bother to ask why she was doing it at one o'clock in the morning. O God how can I wash my hands. I suggested she rub them over the top of the urn first. She did, interlocking her fingers, rubbing the backs, making a fist of each hand and rubbing out the ash from the creases in her knuckles. She went to the bathroom then and I got a dustpan and brush. I had to feel for them in the dark in the cupboard under the sink then I took them back to the dining room and crouched and swept up the ash that had fallen on the floor and turned up the dustpan so that it ran off one corner into the urn. Thanks said Eliza through her collar as she wiped her face in the doorway.

How do you feel now.

She almost said she felt like a cigarette. I thought she was going to start drooling again. Here I said and pulled out a chair from the dining table. Let's talk a bit before you go back to bed.

She sat down and put both elbows on the table and her head between her hands. Did she say what she wanted done with those.

No. Remember she didn't leave any instructions.

That's right.

It's cheaper to cremate than bury.

How could she not have any money. It doesn't make sense. She should have been rich.

Maybe she had an expensive habit, that can add up.

But like you said she must have had a pension or something. Otherwise how else was she keeping you. And anyway it was more than two million, that's just what Mum spent on the sheep. There must have been a real fortune between grandma's and grandpa's families. They were bloomin bankers and squatters. It was ying and yang. Someone's money must be hidden somewhere.

What did you want to do with it.

Get off the farm start a business.

What kind of business.

I don't know, travelling sales. I'd like to travel.

And the flat.

What about it.

If we sold the flat.

But you live here.

There is a law you know that it goes to your mother.

Mum wouldn't kick you out, she doesn't need it. Besides what about the family matinee act or whatever. You can have the flat.

We could sell it I said. We could go halves and then you could get off the farm and I could get out of here.

She drew back slowly. It struck me then that I might have taken her reserve the wrong way, that she may rather have doubted her good fortune from the beginning, suspended as she was between the files and musters, deferring even conjectural investment until she could put her hands on something concrete, afraid to find that there was nothing there but unable to admit that it was possible, as if she had been holding her breath, not daring to let herself go in case there was, impossibly, nothing to take back. But no sooner had the idea rung out than I felt with all this outward stimulation that I recognised another kind of restraint, that Yass, whose misted hills appeared to roll about her pupils as they drifted from me over the dim walls of the dining room held her somehow locked in like I had been that she was still in some sense pinned back to that far from littoral shore as for thirteen years I had been by Dodge and the keys and some other illegible force, some manifestly prurient though untold indenture, perhaps her false but fantastic interest, in the foul and motley wallpapered flat (apart from skoo l, I'll have this coven between the covers in no time), the former's, I mean Eliza's eyes flying open even as I told out to myself for the last time and with the faintest, the very faintest regret the modest changes I had briefly foreseen, which were I would be the first to admit rather a failure of imagination than otherwise, all more or less this side the dictates of my intangible legacy, flying open as I was saying at the sudden recovery of such a pinched square of floor space, like a stump grubber's on still colder ground who, severed the red thread in the navel string, hoes up from the decorated threshold of an expired cult the tessera going to reveal the actual value and dispensability of the whole familiar plot, our anonymous, adverse brother, adrift in the unbounded troughs. And Eliza, I have not forgotten you, pushed up against me, cast forth before your time from the same infant quarter that might in a single blow be subtracted to a real escape route, through whose b darkened rooms da you, of your dried tears like the underglaze, in the French sense, were beginning to sense a way out of the vast and smothering enclosure of your immediate inheritance.

I think I'm starting to get the hang of these peripli of the mind.

As I was unequipped at the time to unload such sonnets on to her, she nodded and smiled and kept nodding equally dumbly until I suggested we go to bed and talk about it in the morning. It was not, she admitted then, referring to my earlier contribution, a shite idea.

We were woken up by the phone. I was back in the dining room to answer it before Eliza arrived with her pyjamas tucked into her jeans mussing her curls and resembling under the foreign velour of the morning light nothing so much as any other punk kid. There goes the beggar king. The morning makes us new.

Hello is this Mrs. O'Rourk.

Still that pulverised voice cascading nonsense out of the receiver. Ont ont.

I passed it to Eliza.

What did she say.

Sounded like something about hell and a house.

Since I knew by then that she didn't have any better idea than I did what her mother was saying I went to see about breakfast. But we had eaten the place bare so when she was off the phone I told Eliza to get dressed and took

fifty dollars from under the paperweight and we went down
to the Piccolo Mondo for a meal then doubled back to the
Woolworths on George Street to buy groceries. The glass
doors slid open on more rows of packaged goods than Eliza
was used to taking in at once. Even the flagship supermarket on George Street was no Roselands but somehow the
way she flew up and down the aisles in acquisitive figure
eights made it seem like enough forever, a millennial store-
house. What shall we. We bought mineral acids, milk,
Cornflakes, Wheatbix, sugar, apple juice, tea, a large bronze
packet of Vittoria coffee, a dozen eggs, sprouts, bread with
a rising sun on it forget the name, ham, Swiss cheese, other
cheese, butter, plain flour, jam rolls, ribbons of bacon,
shaved turkey, a sack of frozen peas, canned fish, water
crackers, peanut butter, popcorn, stuffed olives, garlic,
lamb chops, greenish oranges, the biggest iceberg lettuce
we could get our hands on, sprouts, onions, potatoes, India
rubber, noodles, rice, something resembling spinage, new
and pickled cucumbers, button no, yes that's right button
mushrooms, shallots, shamrock, rosemary, fennel, aspara-
gus, cans of Queensland tomatoes from a pyramid of canned
Queensland tomatoes, carrots from South Australia, hope-
fully stoneless sardines in cans, maybe they all are, the lucky
dumb animals, an elegant variation on cream buns, Black
Forest cuckoo, macadamia nuts, almonds, green and ruby
table grapes, kiwi fruit, dates from the U.S.A., Monte Carlo
biscuits, sour cream, marmalade, mayonnaise, a whole
chicken, canned peaches. Brother. If that doesn't put me
on the syllabus nothing will. I have to foam out my own
confusion on the poisoned pastures. We piled what was in
fact our carnival into a shopping trolley and rolled it up the
street to the flat, then we crammed the trolley into the lift
and took the stairs at a gallop to catch the doors before they
could close. We had breakfast again. I put the money that
was left over back under the paperweight on the writing table and took out the mail.

   You know we're not going to be able to pay for groceries
much longer at this rate.

Eliza said through a mouthful of burnt toast something like it won't matter if we make a quick sell.

A what.

You remember she said licking her fingers. What you said about the flat. If we sell the flat quickly.

You're sure you want to sell it. You sure you aren't. Overr. I mean are you sure that your mother, since she's the only one left. This place is the only link she's got to. Eliza raised her hand against such impressionism and said it won't make a difference to her who owns it.

The mail was three envelopes and I had seen them all before. Still standing by the desk I had torn into the one branded in red ink with an insignia shaped like a cameo brooch whose crucifix or crossroads already reminded me of the shield on Loftus Street, perhaps because, though it lacked the crown and the waratahs, it seemed to be grown over with something. Orta recens. One for the archive. Ms. Rose. I got halfway through before returning to the top and reciting the whole thing. That's a rent notice said Eliza.

It's a rent notice.

She didn't even ask to see it for herself, the truly incredible thing by now being possession, whereas she seemed quite ready to throw up everything including what she had just got her hands on with hearsay. The promise of the night before went the way of the rest of her malapropisms. Eliza extended herself on the sofa and closed her eyes. She mumbled something about where had it come from but then said never mind and clearly, how many weeks are owing.

Six. We don't even have enough to pay the rent.

How did that happen. How did she lose all that money and then the flat and no one know when or how and there be nothing left but old furniture. That is unless the furniture is spoken for. Damn it I guess we have to go and see the lawyer again and find out what kind of a ball up we're really in.

We went to the office but the door was locked and the light off. On the way down the stairs we ran into a man in

a burnished suit with a face like a layer of crumbling plas-
ter cradling a smeared paper bag and an open book in both
arms and Eliza either guessing right away or grabbing at
straws said are you Mr. Looper?

He was. Bernard was at court but if we went there now
we might catch him at his lunch break. So it was back to
Macquarie Street and over to the Supreme Court before
we'd counted on it. The steel ribbed glass panels of the
new tower in Queen's Square rose from street level like
the facets of a quartz crystal or ice, the entrance not its
most conspicuous feature. Inside an employee with a thing
around her neck pointed us from behind a red hooded information desk to the busy wall where the court notices
were tacked together on a notice board in one long patch-
work bulletin. Eliza had written the key points of Bernard's
matter on the back of her hand and I elbowed our way between the varied, ebbing crowd until we had a place before
the notice board from which to look for a matching copy.
Looper had remembered right, their case wasn't coming up
for another hour, so we asked someone how to get to the
cafeteria and were shown the red doored lifts and told to
go up to what would become the Buena Vista Bar and Café
on level fourteen. It's important to have an historical perspective. I believe I'm coming to look back on all this with
something like the rigour it has been asking for.

A hard right from the lift, we found ourselves before an
expanse of haphazardly furnished carpet edged in kind by
the panorama in the glass walls, the almost undivided view
out that corner of the building extending from the thrashed
cement at the once leafy embouchure of the Domain, over
the Cathedral with its imported enhancements sitting rigid
and far from broody in the bright, inarticulate midday sun and
back on to the east west axis of the C.B.D. The built shelf of
Potts Point, stacked to an inch of its limited, mineral life by
the archived middle class to repulse the rising slum below,
itself appeared an eburnation of biscuit. Was bound to return to my rock bottom sooner or later. Wasn't the right
word anyway. There must be something else in here. Win-

ter's less imbricated rectangle of Hyde Park. Our patron de-
fender, watering his dominion. Not the mansard roofs of the
Bon Marché either. These gaps in my memory aren't even
obscene, not scales even if they did fall out of the night, mere
sloughed off vestiges of the hautpaanupwego. Who needs
undertones. Not of earth. No end to these comparisons.
Tell it to them, it, them, she could drown in them. Watch
out. That's no raven. Let me draw you a map. Eliza tugged
at my sleeve and pointed until I recognised an obscure bulk
against the light flooded glass and we made our way to the table where Bernard sat alone with someone else. Not Darling.
Who else was there. Bernard saw us and waved the wedge
of ham sandwich on the way to his mouth. Hello you two
welcome to no man's land.

The other extended a slim translucent palm in our direction. Eliza shook it. Smith. He offered us the remaining
seats. His colleague, he explained, was morbidly referring
to the tactful architecture of the new building, divided as it
was between the Supreme Court, which occupied the lower
thirteen floors, and the Commonwealth Courts, which were
above us. The cafeteria and the library on the next floor
acted as a buffer, or a dead zone as Russett would have it,
just for fodder, for the separation of jurisdictions was considered so important that it needed to be physically delin-
eated. The design was rather subtle. It was surely not obvious to a visitor but there existed barriers that servants of
the law and its residence knew were literally impossible to
cross. One entered the courts from different lift wells, for
instance.

Bernard wanted to know what he could do for us.

Eliza explained about the letter, were we going to have
to pay the rent owing and how had Dodge managed to sell
the family home all on her own and could we get it back.

This isn't like with wills said Bernard. You can't plead in-
sane delusions or any of that. If she sold it—

You were her lawyer weren't you.

Smith took a breath politely but Bernard cut him short.
I was her solicitor as I'm your mother's but if she had help

selling the flat she didn't come to me for it. What do you mean on her own.

Eliza said the flat belonged to the family she didn't think Dodge could sell it without her sister's consent.

You believe they were joint tenants, interrupted Smith.

Not tenants we owned it it was ours, my grandparents bought it.

Property is an elusive concept, said Smith. Due to the doctrine of tenures and estates one can rarely speak unreservedly of ownership even in relation to family homes.

Please what are you talking about.

Whatsoever, with the help of such amusing girls, the tongue picks came the answer. The doctrine of tenures and estates is the foundation of English real property law. It was in a number of ways worse than buttered mackerel for the settlement in New South Wales, but, as Blackstone wrote, if such a country be discovered and planted by English subjects, all the English laws then in being which are applicable to their situation, and the condition of an infant colony, are *immediately* their bithright—

There what.

Bernard said that's called black letter law. Jo has a you know, a photographic. He doesn't miss a thing but he's incapable of improving or abstracting.

Bernard said Smith, is a fat liar. I am selective, and already as indicated oversimplified. In 1833 Justice Burton quoted from Blackstone in the same way during Macdonald v Levy in order to argue that the English usury laws were in place here the moment one person became a lender and the other a borrower, but despite Burton's public intention to remedy the apparently enormous and ruinous change of property which occurred in this colony at that time and his private desire to correct what he called the cupidity of the half-reformed rogues of Botany Bay, the Chief Justice, the first, author of *The Improvement of Wastelands: Viz. Wet, Moory land, land near rivers and running waters; peat land, and propagating Oak and other timber upon neglected and waste land. To which is added a dissertation on great and small farms;*

and the consequences of them to land-owners, and the public,
opposed him on the thoroughly reasonable grounds, principally, and apart from the fact that if, ignoring not only the
general practice in New South Wales at the time, including the court's own ruling on an interest rate for the newly
opened Savings Bank that would have been illegally high
in the mother country, of 8 percent, as being against the
statute of Anne, but also the diverse outcomes of that legal
inheritance in the other possessions of the Crown, Ireland
Jamaica or the American Colonies for instance, since the
first regulation of the interest rate under Henry VIII, if the
court ruled that the law that fixed the interest rate under
Queen Anne at five percent *had* been in place since the beginning, then, in the words of Justice Dowling, the public
credit of the colony must be shaken to its foundation, and
the most irreparable injury produced, it was simply not the
intention to broad cast the whole body of laws in existence
in England upon the colony but rather, as Blackstone himself proposed, those that were applicable. Indeed, in that
case the plaintiff's argument that a part of the Act may hold
and a part not, depending on local custom, so that the statute would then stand as a *blank* as to the rate of interest in
the colony, was upheld by Forbes' drawing attention to the
recognition given in the so called statute of frauds to the
force and effect of local usage in determining the application of any particular statute to the colonies.

To remover certain doubts Jo, avoid all unnecessary dila-
tory or vexatious forms of proceeding.

What I want to say to these young people, he continued
soberly, is that in much the same spirit as met the usury law,
the impracticality of the doctrine of tenures and estates was
in fact recognised and gradually acted upon, which is one
reason we have two kinds of real property law in place simultaneously, the feudal doctrine as embodied in the English
Common Law System of conveyancing, and Torrens Title:
hence why it should be perfectly easy for you to find out
to whom the flat was registered. But Russett did well to recall me to the rules. Allow me momentarily to take a bourne

in lieu of the confins and remove down to basics, immo, are we on the same page, like Félicité peering in upon the vanishing point of la carte du pays perhaps to find out new heaven and earth (here we are), to stuff our common fancy through a back window of that ultimate refuge where one hopes to put one's feet up, scilicet, to wit, to woo that hypothetical complot where property and law, as Bentham apparently discovered, are born together, and die together, for all purposes coto y termino (we needn't let in the hordes of Boa-constrictors just yet, not for the moment to amalgamate princes and merchants, but in a foyer where some king worms live longer than bronze, in their insolvent progeny I mean, the bust will perhaps survive the ardent city after all, as a famous poet once said). I know what you are thinking. Our abstruse training can leave even the most stringent of us with delusions of hypotaxis. But anyone who stands with the people can make himself perfectly understood. If immemorial usage is the proper evidence of custom, the vicious circle of applicability is a mere surface manifestation of that inconsistency that sets every one of us here moving, accessorium sequitur principale, abyssus abyssum invocat, and one is leery even in common law, which in fact generally tends to consider any authority immemorial that has not ceased, of deferring justice to the source, but to be emphatic in an exotic way, if what for instance comes to be defined as personalty, involving as it does a fundamental abstraction wherever the proposition remains so to speak even remotely tenable, that a piece of stuff which is actually in the Indies may belong to me, while the dress I wear may not, binds us as well as those legal incidents with which we say that a court is clothed, it is that dress, as Charron says, is where yours and mine begins, a sort of tunica molesta one way or another, whether it binds you to the stake or lights your way through the Imperial Gardens. I can put it another way. Where in contrast to the limited assertion of finders keepers, for all that this encompasses nine tenths right to anyone's gems once swept glowing from the above-mentioned fireplace to be misplaced in my pocket or some other fictive apprentice's pillow, say the poor man's proskephalion basilikon, we will get to the nut-shell, property classically appears simply as what is enforceable as against the whole world, I will remind you it is a monopoly in which the *thing* in question already regards the others, absolutely Hap Hazard as the case may be, and whereas in the first instance there also obtains some manner of reciprocity, for at the very least one cannot, cf. the imprint in the sand, own anything in isolation, in the second its essence is revealed to be pecunium, whence one returns to the principle, embracing both inert and moveable property, that the interest in rem, more or less rigorously extracted from the interest in personam, does not depend on what we may desire to idealise in terms of inherent value.

The Health Act, 1958, Victoria: property may exist in a lock of hair or in nightsoil.

Your gilded pills. Don't get me started on Victoria. Solo cedit. It's Yarmouth versus France, de meuble en immeuble etc. I do not intend perishing in the abyss of nonsense. Our bell, book and candle is the fundamentum divisionis. I've watched too many movies. But quibbles and the larger part of the almost innumerable channels into which the effectively mythical and undeniably nicht festen Grund of the really universal position of private ownership flows aside, afloat as we are in the modesty of your explicit predicament, I would eventually like to draw your attention as we are swept heretofrom towards the more dispersive spheres of jurisprudence to the desirability of apprehending something of the distinction between real property and personal property, as it is therein one encounters the peculiarity, je baise mes mots, of the situation pertaining to the Colony of New South Wales. Difficile est. Do not think that through the mere process of elucidation I exaggerate those incoherencies adhering in many a mechanical affinity that, automaton-like, continues to function in the absence of more than a soul. They present nonetheless no deficiency of occasions to take fright. When Forbes ruled in 1825 that no grant from

the Crown is good, unless the Great Seal be affixed to it, and
it also be of record, the portent of Dr. Wardell's response for
the *Australian* deserves neither to be dismissively calqued
from the distended lines of the extra-quotidian persona of
journalistic declarators, assuming one knows the Chief Justice's reply, nor merely felt in the lightning-like appercep-
tion of something profoundly amiss, viz. if something is not
done somewhere to ratify all the grants and leases which the
Crown has hitherto made, it strikes us, (assuming the dictum
of the Chief Justice to be law) that there is no legal title to
a foot of land in the colony, but arrested rather in what he
does not say. In 1829, another dry year, the same Forbes was
successfully petitioned by pastoralists for a suspension of
quit rents, when an overwhelming number of actions to
recover debt began to pour into this Court, resulting in the
Bankruptcy Legislation, which removed associated prison
sentences, and generally loosened restrictions on debtors,
such as to allow them, item verbatim, a fresh start (an imperial statute of 1813 had put land in New South Wales in terms
of debt recovery on the same footing as personal chattels, allowing a creditor to take possession of all of a debtor's lands,
whereas in England, where the prejudice was for the con-
servation of title, it was only half), Governor Darling reacted
to the situation in Sydney, where the greater part of land was
held by leases from the Crown or by urban squatters, by pro-
claiming, with the unanimous approval of the Executive
Council, that on application, a grant in fee simple would be
issued, on conditions prescribed, to every person, or his
lawful representative, who, on or before 30th June 1823 (a
period when every rural grantee was required to keep and,
nota bene, clothe a convict for every one hundred acres,
which may stand as an illustration of the asymmetry arising
between the country leasehold in New South Wales and the
large English estate, a formal conflict that culminated in the
British Government Crown Land Sales Act, passed the same
year as the Waste Lands Occupation Act, which was itself
helped in by an alliance of squatters and a London-based
cohort of wool-importing firms, land appearing to the con-

cerned parties in the form of a commodity that, unlike salt,
tended to perish under monopoly), was bona fide in possession of a tenement by lease from the Government, whether
it had expired or not, or who occupied any allotment of land
in town not hitherto alienated by the Crown, and not speci-
fied, in an Order of even date, as 'parcels of land in the town
of Sydney reserved for public purposes.' You will allow me
the mise en abîme. In the absence of lacunae I find there is
only one way to extricate: reach further back and see where
it leads. Dig in, please, there are almost no surprises. One
parcel of land reserved for public purposes took in three and
a quarter acres of the Government Domain, he indicated
generously, leased in 1802 by King (the Governor, not the
alleged Joseph or the supposed deceased Nicolo) to John
Palmer, the Colony's first commissary, in exchange for a
Lumber yard in the heart of the town held by Palmer of a
very limited duration. Now, this change of hands may not
represent such a Sea Mystery At Our Back Door as the ten
thousand acres granted to Forbes himself, of which Darling,
facing the for him rather regular accusation of abuse of pre-
rogative, said, with malicious veracity perhaps, I have
merited reproof by allowing myself to be betrayed into a
belief that this 10,000 Acres given to him by my Predeces-
sor, was intended as an equivalent for some Land, which his
Mother was to transfer to Government at Bermuda, but since
the Domain lease was for five years with a prospective lease
of another sixteen, it was certainly against the instructions
of the Home Government, which in 1801 ordered no land
reserved for government purposes to be leased for more than
five. The imminent expiry of the lease notwithstanding,
Palmer erected two kinds of windmill and a large bake-house
on the land close to the frontage, but by the time the Governor whose name would be given to the street that forms
that frontage decided to use the parcel for an extension of
his official residence, the lease had already been transferred
with improvements, for a substantial consideration, first to
Robert Campbell, then, by him, to Fairlie & Co. of Calcut-
ta. In 1814 Macquarie communicated to the outfit's Sydney

agent his intention to pay for the reprisal, and in 1815 demolished the wooden windmill and the bakery, with,
however, the question of compensation remaining almost in
abeyance until the arrival of Governor Bourke, who had his
own plans to build a new Government House on the top
portion of Palmer's original lease, where the dismantled
stone windmill had since been converted into living quarters for Government-men and a tool house, as was attested
by the Assistant Superintendent of Botanical Gardens, who
was also asked, though he could not say why they had been
destroyed, nor why the men had left the place, to prove that
he had planted trees on the land for Government in 1832,
the matter of reprisal having reached litigation after the
current claimant to the parcel, one Mr. Steele, answered the
Governor's offer of compensation by placing a lock on the
Domain gate. What are robber gangs, except little kingdoms?
That is mind you a real question I intend to answer. Evidently it is the tension between the different forms of property represented by leasehold and freehold, not their under-
lying dynamic, that is novel here. If the feudal jurist already
sticks on to pure monetary relations the labels supplied by
feudal law, the Statute of Tenures, which, after the English
Civil War, did away with the old taxes and obligations once
due to the Crown by tenants in capite, that is, those who
were supposed to hold land directly from the Crown, and
initiated a system whereby all freehold or fee simple estates
were created by the Crown in the form of free and common
socage, causing a distinction to emerge between real and
personal property as relating to the nature of a tenant's rights
to that property, the former generally taking the form of land
not because it describes it but rather the nature of the right
to it, with freehold a form of real property, or chattel real,
and leasehold a form of personal property, or chattel, freehold, being inheritable, coming to be called a freehold of inheritance, thus marking the domestic as well as territorial
basis upon which that circle of interest revolved, land being
difficult to alienate, title depending on an unbroken chain
leading back to good root of title, insofar as it was a step

towards the full right of alienation however, did little to mask
the advance of the notorious patriciate of money, and with
the princes in France, who were similarly allied, the bour-
geois reveals himself as the very paleographic origin of the
aristocrat: as any amateur belles-lettriste will tell you, the
particule is not proof of noblesse but rather the sign of the
franc alleu. One was named after one's holding, and the
branches of a single family were distinguished by varied
desinence. On the other hand, if the calibrations of the freehold are at last vainly intended to still so many teeth in the
corporate clock of the English landed gentry, in the colony
of New South Wales, where land is principally divided
between small urban freeholders and large leaseholds, it is
the former that appear to be vulnerable, the latter purchases
for entrenchment. The courts here increasingly appear to be
out of joint. I wouldn't take one of those, in some ways we
are further from the ocean than you might think. Above all
perhaps, the somewhat redundant interests of government
and large landholder appear to be eliciting a conflicting tendency towards both an exacerbation of the old arbitrary
powers vested in the Crown as the ultimus heres and a new
practice of immediately handling land as goods of exchange.
More than one contradiction undoubtedly exists where the
law pertaining to leasehold, falling as personal property on
the side of what was generally considered to be moveable in
the distinction that prevailed in England by the end of the
seventeenth century, but which was increasingly felt to be
irrelevant here, leasehold having become the chief form of
holding land by the 1840s, can supply a certain Windeyer,
defending his client against an accusation of intrusion on his
own land issued by the Attorney General in New South
Wales in 1847, the coherent and even compelling argument
that to maintain the grant of Crown land with all its statutory reservations and restrictions would be to maintain all the
old principles of feudal slavery which the Statute of Charles
II abolished. The question of reservations in fact, throwing
up as Windeyer argued the distinction between dominion
and ownership, and hence the question of the Crown's

radical title, opened on to what undoubtedly is that highest of contradictions that is constitutional monarchy, where, under fealty, to cite veritas non auctoritas as, between ourselves, goes without saying, it almost appears that the power of the crown is the power of private property. I hardly need to insist that those who took up the omnipresent atom of the latter to examine it, found the slightest agitation sufficed for this incensed and practically neutral power from whom the tenant in capite pretends to hold his lease to appear enthron'd in the marketplace, reemerging upon the field of law as no more ut ita dicam than the negative earth of the capite censi, which may yet be the expression of au bout du fossé with a vengeance, for that other, rational pole of the system, drawn upon as this was to define moveable property rights not only on the continent, where the Roman code was the basis for all law, but also, crucially, by our own forebears, could name such a *but for vacancy* precisely because it never vested private property in the state, taking the basis of private property to be a factum and not a right. Such a very gap in nature is the reason that Blackburn can decide in 1889 to address the question of whether the colony was previously settled or not as one of law as opposed to fact, a decision congruent with a set of prescriptions of which Blackstone, who, with Coke, developed the modern notion of property in land, helping to turn usages into properties which could be rented, sold or willed, noted, Pleased as we are with possession, we seem afraid to look back to the means by which it was acquired, as if fearful of some defect in our title; or at least we rest satisfied with the decision of the laws in our favour. As our great colleague in Kaliningrad used to say, you must not take it too far. Or as R. Torrens' own ink-stained March fly is made to say for us, A banker's fortune, consisting of paper, cannot be taken at all, without the taker's submitting to the conditions of production and intercourse of the country taken; whereas obviously, if the taker assigns another value to that indiscernible country or paper, he need not enter into the conditions of the former to any extent, which thus become utterly annihilate, English

law providing for the table-biting circumstance whereby it
may be brought within cognizance by its own fiction if not
actually. Windeyer's client, who we must admit was not up
to his reputation, was accused of nothing less than fraudu-
lently intending the disinherision of Our Said Lady the
Queen. He had leased a part of a sixty acre grant in Newcas-
tle given to Arthur Charles Fitzroy Dumaness, by the Crown,
on the part and in the voice of the Crown it is provided nevertheless, and we do hereby *reserve* to ourselves all such parts
and so much of the said land as may hereafter be required
for a public way or ways, . . . and also all stone and gravel, . . .
and all land within one hundred feet of high water mark, . . .
and also all *mines* of gold and silver, and of *coals* with full and
free liberty and power to search for, dig, and take away the
same. Sic ob cit, ladies. See I *do* deal in small change; se tutto
il co. I will repeat, au pied de cette mouche, that when the
defendant mined for coal, the Crown, in the person of the
Attorney General, held that the coal mines and veins of coal
were in the hands and possession of Our Said Lady the
Queen, and at last *Held*, the *reserve* created an *exception* in the
grant, and therefore that the *veins* of coal, being severable
from the land, remained as a *corporeal* hereditament in the
Crown, and were properly the subject of an information of
intrusion, if I haven't got that the wrong way around. Windeyer, identifying a form of tenure that had been abolished,
indeed argued that property in England before the Norman
conquest was effectively *allodial*, and that the Statute of
Charles II returned it, except for the retention of the fiction
as to all lands being held from the Crown, to its former state.
Brown's excavations, like the coal anciently buried to mark
boundaries but preserving them even beneath the move-
ments of successive epochs, brought suddenly into the light
of the Southern Hemisphere the very internal limits of
English feudal proprietary right as it lay across statutory and
common law by the middle of the nineteenth century, so
that, for the case in question, it was possible to cite statutes
as old as the said subdivisional King of England and his col-
laterally milling daughter casting doubt upon the power of

the Crown to make reservations, as well as numerous prec-
edents for the Crown's right to do so, as William and Mary
reserving all idols above a certain size in New England—
one could, as remains current, have gone back to Domesday,
to the county of the Axton Hundred for instance, to take a
random page, quidquid dignum memoria, thrice valued in
the record between the English and the French reeve who
holds it at farm, where it is forbidden to prune or exfoliate
whatever falls in the King's way, whether the responsible
roots were to come out in Whitham, Milton-Under-Wych-
wood, Taddington, Nether Cott, Old Cleeve, Exton or
Ixhill, Ash, Dodingtree, Fleamdyke, or Bagstone Hundred,
if not less fantastically, in Kent, the same Hundred liable to
render food and drink to the sovereign en voyage, over and
above the fact that, though not a farm, and lacking the fairly
controversial addition of swine, it already produced 40,000
herrings a year for the monks of the Archbishop, though par-
onyms are not precedent, and I have made the experience
in myself that you can have too many cooks, notably in orig.,
though I will point out inter alia abundantibus that to bite
here into the cindery apple of belongings is to touch on that
not altogether far from contemporaneous distinction
whereby, egg, cheese and bread being abscendens from lordship, these are defined as passing through a field of useless
lordship, indeed each fleetingly non valet ova duo, and
therefore not of personal servitude, which requires that salva
rei substantia maneat, but rather of abuse: *absit omen, lex
cessat,* and I will get there too, to the front door—but one is
less than astonished to learn that the sitting judge held the
opinion upon the law upon the question that it was quite
simply that the Queen would continue seised or possessed
of this land, and, at appeal, together with his colleagues,
decided outright to omit a variety of topics introduced in aid
of them with which we have as judges, nothing to do, and
which were indeed of too popular a character, merely, to
justify further notice by us, as they were pleased to have it
printed. The Attorney General had after all been alerted as
to Brown's activities by the Commissioner of the Australian

Agricultural Company, subject to a grant of one million acres
for the cultivation and improvement of waste lands in New
South Wales and for other purposes relating thereto. I hope
I have answered my question now. But as to the question of
the overlooked distinction between ownership and dominion, the difficulty pointed to in this case arose precisely from
the fact that what in England had effectively become a legal
fiction, that is, that all land was held in deference to the
Crown, was treated here as sied a mainmise in living memory,
resting on the premise that New Holland and what was associated with it at the moment of settlement was virgin
country, or at least that the droits of the soil and all lands in
the colony had, jure coronae, become vested immediately
upon settlement in the King. Whether or not one might wish
to imagine it implying the recognition of a sort of use in fact,
and in a frail case being o'ercounted, between abandoning
plans to build a penal colony on the South West African Skel-
eton Coast, and directing the establishment here with all its
shape and internal consistency, the British Government's
Committee of Transportation also let fall the provisions ini-
tially laid in place for buying or leasing land from the natives.
Now if it is property which stretches and indeed ends up
twisting like the ribbon in your typewriter, no I beg your
pardon you are out of ribbons I can see that, what Forbes in
a letter recalled Burke referring to as the chief security
between a country and her colonies, light as silk, but strong
as links of iron, that is, the similarity of institutions, if the
essence of fealty is the fusion of property and sovereignty,
one can well appreciate the sitting judges' insistence on the
abruptness of a case that raised, in 1829, incidentally, and I
admit quite irrelevantly, the same year from which the So-
licitor-General promised to prove to the court hearing R. v
Steele that the government had been in possession of what
we know as the Botanic Gardens in the Domain, a question
of criminal jurisdiction implicitly skipped over five years
earlier in a general discussion pertaining to trial by jury,
though no doubt appearing to Forbes' own mind on the occasion of a signal murder case only two years earlier, as well

as on their unpreparedness as on the informal nature of their remarks, Forbes finding that it may be a question of doubt, whether any advantages could be gained, without previous preparation, by ingrafting the institutions of our country, upon the natural system which savages have adopted for their own government, that nature prompts them to disdain the interposition of a race of people whom they find fixed in a country to which they did not originally belong, with Dowling recognising the implications for property disputes, an evocation from which with genuine abruptness he breaks off: in raising the *lex loci*, supposing that the analogy with what had hitherto been its scope failed, thus describing an exceptional limit to jurisdiction within the colony itself, he had indeed just pulled the cloak from beneath his feet, for, mutandis mutatis, so-called unoccupied land came under the scope of the English legal phenomenon of waste lands and that was in the Crown. What is exactly the same thing, the man in question, whom the court thus refrained from trying for the murder of one of his own people, on the presumption that he possessed what it and its dependents had given up, the following year, at the head of his tribe, accompanied the police to the bloody puddle of *Van Diemans Land*. (They could not try him as their ancestors would have tried a pig, and thus assigned him the place of the animal in their system.) Forbes partially recovered such excess within a few years' time, when he explicitly distinguished between the limits of settlement and of the colony, ascribing to the former the extent of police protection, and setting down that those settling without its limits were, if wanting Government permission, acting illegally, but if Lord Glenelg shared a sense of the great importance that land sales by the natives not be tacitly assented to, and indeed what went down over Melbourne was a vacant gesture, legally invalid in at least one direction, contrabanded, I beg your pardon, I'm not sure if that is a correct use of the word, prohibited in reasonable time by the colonial government, for if there must be ritual, and if the deed that resulted from the dubious advice of Mr. Gellibrand was in fact an earthy throwback to the source of

the Latin participle, which preserves the trace of a period
before the Norman conquest, the growth of writing and the
use of the wax seal, when the document evidenced rather
than embodied a transaction, it failed, comparable in this too
to Windeyer's plea, in the face of such authority as could be
accumulated from the experience in North America, or the
fact that occupation did not imply ownership, or the unre-
served right to alienation, the Government simultaneously
desired nothing more than that, on the elided fringe of big
business, the squatters be as true to themselves, as Government to the undisclosed buttons of town and civic institutions, and if that returns us to Forbes' and Dowling's preliminary skirting, providing the outlines of a perfectly circular
argument with its proper supplement, so that none of my
learned friends has succeeded in cracking it, that is because
it is none other than the very vinculum of our bovine right,
but never forget that the court's evocation of a doctrine of
which the Government had had no need to get started, ex-
pressed what was at that moment actually beginning to be
felt to be the case for both sides, for if the one was made to
feel it in the most brutal way, for the other, and in it orbi, it
said perfectly clearly more than it had ever meant to, the flagrant if misrecognised tenor of which one is permitted to
glimpse in its all vividness in the anxiety surrounding the
same inconsistencies where they appeared as the shock received by legal categories finally found incapable of admin-
istering to present modes of production, and which, comme
de rigueur, with that end of the jumelles front and forward,
would be mended as well as for the said infant colony to be
set en marche before the century was out. A tout bon compte:
nine years after the question of the interest rate was settled
by a committee established in the wake of Macdonald v
Levy, in order, in part, to hear the opinions of representa-
tives from financial, commercial and pastoral interests, including the globally inaccurate claim on the part of Dr.
Wardell that, respecting money, nothing finds its own level
more readily and with greater certainty, and the solid and
amusing contribution from J.B. Montefiore to the effect that

the rise in capital, the so called seed-corn of industry, resulting from a fixed interest rate, would stimulate the economic
development of the Colony, and despite the continued an-
tagonism of Justice Burton, whose losing battle in despising
what he felt to be repugnant to the laws of England, may be
gleaned from the eager tone of the complaint issued in the
Australian, that his cant about the sin of Usury we utterly
despise, for money is as much an article of commerce as
sugar, tea, or tobacco (wine, oil, tobacco, sheets fabric, 1689)
that is, nine years after the decision responsible in large
measure for a considerable increase in investment in the pastoral industry, in 1843, the Liens on Wool Bill, which allowed
pastoralists to mortgage a wool clip while still on the sheep's
back, elicited the same complaint from Secretary of the State
Lord Stanley, who forewarns, not textually that they will
Run *all* into sheep where they can, keeping only such other
Cattle as are necessary, then they will be their own *merchants*,
but that it will give unwonted facilities for borrowing money,
and increasing the evil of excessive credit, which criticism,
together with the Bill's precedent, that is, for mortgaging the
stock of the estates, namely, according to Hastings Elwin,
Negroes, in Antigua for instance, which shows how close ge-
ography can lie to history, where he says they are real estate,
and are literally walking freeholds, indicate the path taken
by legal reform as it emerged from the conflict between the
preservation of inherited territorially vested interests and
land appearing for the first time in its true form as void of
value per se. One can see how far we have come from the
chiromatic residue where *The Atlas*, promoting the case for
Liens on Wool, and bemoaning the distinction inherited
between real and personal property, springing out of a state
of feudal tenure, almost every vestige of which is claimed to
have long since passed away, affirms that those who have
become large purchasers of land have found that *real* property is in New South Wales the most *illusory* of all possessions, evoking the legal corollary of the division between real
and personal property, which is to say the division between
law and equity. Now, in consideration of the question of joint

tenancy, it is through equity, not common law, which recog-
nises a single possessor of title only, that such a form of ownership is made possible, creating as it did a trust, with the
property vested in a trustee, on behalf of a beneficiary, to
whom the trustee had certain obligations, the Achilles' heel
of which, aliter conflict of interest, having been pinned down
in England in 1726 when the Lord Chancellor ordered Mr.
Sandford to disgorge the profits made on the lease of a
market to his once infant beneficiary, because, failing to
renew the child's lease, he had it himself. If we are accustomed to see the odd hero even of our time swindled out of
a large property by his guardian in this way, suits in equity
were relatively infrequent during the first decade in
the life of this Court, and their hearing apt to be intermit-
tent and protracted, consisting as they did of a Bill, an
Answer, and perhaps, in addition, a Reply, and perhaps a Re-
joinder, as in Simeon Lord v The Executors of the Will of
D'Arcy Wentworth, where the Answer alone used up sheets
which laced together measured thirty-two feet, and where
ten years elapsed before the case brought by Sarah Howe,
widow of George Happy alias Happy George, printer of the
first book and pardoned robber, against the last minute ben-
eficiaries of land and printing paper, that is, Underwood,
Robinson, and 'their confederates', was resolved, but the division itself marked the so-called legal landscape to the
quick. The systemic hurdles to making a secure profit on
land that has changed hands, notably the difficulties bound
up in the possession of good title, were eventually felt to be
an impediment to the progress of our disembark'd generation. Conveyancing under the common law system required
a new deed to be drawn up every time a lot was sold or mort-
gaged, establishing proof of title demanding a tedious search
for and examination of a whole chain of discrete documents;
a complicated and expensive system without guarantee from
the State, there not even existing a statutory requirement
for registering all deeds, and even then insinuation, as it used
to be called, had to be paid for. By the 1840s the four families crouching spread-eagle over most of New South Wales

had their cronies in the executive to thank but to what,
Robert Lowe was asked by the Select Committee of the Administration of Intestate Estates in 1854, fifteen years after
Darling's open grant, did he attribute the fact that even in
the most important streets in Sydney there are patches of
land not occupied, or not improved. Chiefly to a want to title,
Lowe replied. The deep uncertainty about the suitability of
the existing legal apparatus for securing title in the colony
appears forcefully in the first outline of the court rules con-
cerning probate as it is drawn up in a letter drafted by Chief
Justice Dowling and Justices Burton and Stephen to Governor Gipps, their purpose being to point out that, whereas in
England there was very little in the way of deceased estates
appearing with no one to claim them, a great number of
persons have died in different parts of this extended territory, with its widely scattered population, without either relative or friend; but with, occasionally, a considerable amount
of property, surrounded by convicts (or those who have been
so) if not in their actual care, making it necessary to prevent
that the property of such persons shall be taken possession
of, if not stolen or wasted, (as it assurably would be) by the
dissolute and dishonest. Are you following me. Eliza must
have signalled. The question of the management of intestate estates, a concern that all too naturally began to peak
with the discovery of gold in 1851, for in the following ten
years the population increased threefold, while in less than
half that time business in the Department of Intestate
Estates increased fivefold, turned not only on the ability or
inability of the Court to intervene in the absence of an heir,
all witnesses to the Committee agreeing that in such cases
the land should escheat to the parens patrice, though the
basic role of the colonial judiciary in respect to any case in
which provisions had to be made for the transferal of a deceased estate was wanting fleshing out, as was apparent in
the case of the affairs of Thomas Campbell, who in 1830 left
most of his estate to relatives in Great Britain and Ireland
but failed to nominate, in writing, an executor, so that a petition to the Court on the grounds that one had been verbal-

ly nominated as such was met by an order that the will be
deposited in the Court Registry, an authority from the Court
to the Registrar, associated with the petitioner Captain
Robert Robison, directing them to collect, discover and hold
the effects of the deceased, subject to all further Orders of
the Court—with an instruction to report, with as little delay
as possible, upon the state and condition of the estate, and,
in case the same or any part thereof be exposed or liable to
waste, further to report what parts may be so liable—and
how far there may be immediate and pressing demands upon
the estate, and any other matters of moment, but turned also
on the possible removal of an heir, who was advantaged by
the law of primogeniture, but who might be unascertainable,
and moreover against whose interests there was a moral argument, in favour of the labourer to whom the land in question had been, in the words of Justice Stephen, what canvas
is to the painter, for, there being, in English law, no absolute
land ownership, an owner, for instance, being restricted to
transfer life-interest to a purchaser who merely became
tenant per autre vie, the period of limitations for actions to
be effective could be extended for those under the disabil-
ity of lunacy, infancy, coverture or absence beyond the seas,
and here, anticipating the same reform that would wipe away
the uncertain purchase of interminable research and silence
those revendications that threatened, or so the fear ran, to
issue from under the most eccentric weeds, subsuming the
antinomy of interests under the unique pressure of the Government Seal, one might recall G.K. Holden seeing no just
reason why an antipodean heir, whose existence is likely to
be unknown and even undiscoverable here, should have a
double time allocated him for raking up the ashes of his ge-
nealogy, to the prejudice of parties who have bought and improved the land, while he, one might as well add, is moved
by no more than that unholy effervescence in the very need
that he in dem Mund nimmt, indeed, to get a proper handful
of this picnic, forgive me my forensic roots, the justice in the
risk that land improved to a hundred-fold its original value,
may excite the cupidity of an heir whose connection with

the forgotten owner would never have been otherwise
thought of, and who gains his first intelligence of the prize
from an advertising attorney speculating on his share of the
spoil—

Someone, crossing his or her legs and bumping the table
sent a glass rolling onto the carpet. Eliza leapt up stuffed
her fingers into the paper napkin dispenser and pressed the
wad she drew out against the edge of the table until the paper turned pink. Smith was alarmingly unfazed. Where I
asked could we learn if the sisters had been joint tenants.
In the Department of Lands building on the other side of
the square he said. Individual land transactions are lodged
with the Office using standardised forms known as Dealings. The transactions are recorded on a single Register,
a copy of which is held by the owner, the original by the
government, in that building, in a public archive.

Bernard was absorbed in something passing far below
on the street. We told him, with deliberate though unpre-
meditated insincerity, that we would return to Wolloomo-
oloo soon, and said goodbye to the silk, who nodded silent-
ly, smiling vaguely as if from a distance that was receiving
him even as we backed towards the lifts, a luminous vanishing point that yawned between the arcadian thicket of
the city, until the doors slid closed and it was just us, in the
speculative box, if that's the word, going down.

When the radio broke our grave was really dug. All day Dodge listened to A.B.C. Classic F.M., the melodic fog rolling first thing over the living room. I would leave her for school standing by the window in a slate coloured skirt maybe and a pinstriped blouse, swirling the insides of her cup to some semi heard fugue. At times she would say as if out of nowhere ah Sibelius, and with an effort I would recover a noise passed almost out of my perception, like surf or the rumble of traffic in the street below.

Over dinner the radio was retuned and Dodge chewed vacantly through the news, but I had been waiting all afternoon for that static fissure and the piping voice come sudden as a bat got in the window that flaps around the room trying to recover the open air. Not a bat a whatsit. The other. I came back from school one day to dead silence.

The radio is broken she said from the sofa where she appeared to have been watching herself in the reflection of her shoes.

She must have sensed my disappointment in the evenings because she came up with an incentive for return: she bought poppy seed cakes by some kind of correspondence and we had afternoon tea. She would pick an album to browse and if she'd left a turd she would be tender (though I would know then, there is a turd).

What happened to the piano I asked one afternoon, my eyes having fallen on the angle of unfaded wallpaper underlapping the bookcase.

Fell to pieces said Dodge. That's impossible I said.

Ah she breathed and her eyes widened. That's right. Mother smashed it up.

What for.

Well her voice trailed she was very upset. Perhaps because the pilot died. Beaten by his vans over the sea. She was a passionate woman my mother. A bitter fit.

Did you learn to play I asked.

Dodge looked surprised and raised her hands. She twid-
dled them over the air. Well yes. I was very good. I'm sorry
I can't play for you. Might have been your school mistress.
It is a pity about the radio I ought to buy a new one. She
didn't, and a pall of silence settled down beneath the chat-
ter. Silence settled down like dust.

Behind the soft yellow stone of the Department of
Lands building Eliza and I made an important discovery.
At first there was a misunderstanding. I, ever the boggler,
had let Eliza do the talking because it was her family but in
telling it her own story got so entangled with the anile saga
of the flat and her admittedly notional ideas of antecedence
that we almost ended up in the basement with the bound
records going back to the beginning. Once it was clear that
it was in fact a flat, not a farm that we were after we were
shown to the maps, told that Canada may have patriated its
constitution but we had introduced to the world the strata
plan for apartments, which is not a map but a number of floor
plans illustrating units in relation to a whole building (common property, by 1982, being titled apart) and which ought
to give up the reference for the deed. At least I think that's
how it worked. This was before the automated land titles
system launched the following Halloween. The rest had
that hallucinatory detail that, in my experience, nine times
out of ten fades irreparably after the saying. Actually come
to think of it, ours was not a stratered building but a company title like there used to be. We did end up in the basement after all. Down there the adaptable New Form titles
are loose leafed, may be typed as well as hand written, and
previous owners are crossed out, but for a building like ours
the Old Form titles come on a single oversized piece of paper
with a memorial entered for every transaction in blanket
historical sequence so that, unless the page fills up and you
have to find its successor, the chain of ownership can be
seen at a glance. We were hoping for evidence of a tortious
conveyance. But in the folio that we turned out of its deep
red binding we discovered the flat had never belonged to

anyone but the Castor or the Albert family. Indeed the Roses were archaic renters. It was the end of the line. We had only one other question. The deed said nothing about the contents of the flat. Who did they belong to.

The fixtures or the furniture said the boy behind the desk.

What's a fixture.

A chattel is presumed not to have become a fixture if it is resting on its own weight on the land. A fixture is. Difficult to remove without doing violence to the. Integrity of the real property. A hot water system.

The furniture.

The deed might not tell you. Your auntie could have signed a contract. You'll have to follow that up with the owner.

How old are you.

Old he said and sucked his teeth. You wanna get a soda.

I nudged Eliza forward. We had just found a reason to keep a low profile. Look I said when we were in the street. Don't tell me she replied. We had to get all that furniture out of there fast, make some money while we still could. And if this Albert turns up. We'll destroy the letters, say we never heard of him. He can take the flat but if it's empty what can he do. We're within our rights.

On the Avenue that afternoon we intervened. Though I had considered how otherwise rewarding it could be to hang around as long as it took to get to the bottom of the whole obstruction in a formal way, the fact was Eliza had recognised the situation the moment she got my news in the mail. It was a sudden opening, a time to strike. There was no room for two agendas. My first premonition trumped the second. No. The scales fell from my eyes. The ultimatum hit me with the usual cumbersome aplomb. Fat chance losing anything until you find it but you can always try shaking off even the submerged facets in the market. Hail Jonus moneta! The hardest currency is monochrome! In other words somewhere among the tumbled down debris of our brief effort I got over it. Revisions, I thought. Carp 'em, my ink is ice. Of course one is still struck by moments of transparency but the façade is the last to fall from even the miserablest heritage listing and frankly I said to myself or at least do now which is the same thing, if from the rising waters of nature's own superbly rendering sheets the most mucked up growler wrinkling in the perfumed air before the spring lets go a pure floater or two from its equally crystalline delitescence, the tide of time, that's literalture. It runs against you, vainly repulsive. I stood stupefied in the rubble of my opulence. A chanceable hitting, some of us perseverate young. I was still in my salad days of self control. It was before I got ink and paper. If we can't shift all this before he comes, Eliza pondered aloud as she would faced with my almost unrelieved leisure respecting efforts at conversation, innocent of the flood gates she had divided in me.

We're through. What else was it after all to be between us to begin with.

Eliza wanted to know if I could remember the names of anyone Dodge had had dealings with. She had sat down on a pile of old magazines. In the living room they were all that was left of a collection that had come up to my knees in most places, even as I grew older. There was too much to tell. Factaque sparsa. But great masses of accumulation. From where. Impossible to tell. The venereal flow of international bric a brac. Open sesame. Here we go again. Deliacious ecstasy oh it doesn't matter and refuse of an interminable bargain that sends you senselessly out of your depth even as it generates the very jetsam that keeps you floating on tides of junk capped by dirty Kleenex drifting albums fold out star charts cigarette tins calendars empty perfume bottles bits of lead type terracotta picture frames torn up ferry time tables cameo heads playing cards needlework monogrammed gloves and combs and suitcases strings of beads and heaps and other. The spectacles she used to buy from the chemist, themselves a wonderful piece of work in the world's catalogue. Infinite seed. A list is nothing, details lost to view in their own ascendance save a glint from between

the dark stacks of a microlith flake shard of creamware a
pencil or a choker a broken light bulb pharate still in the
striped box a jade brooch at most a briefer stretch of turpilo-
quium. There was a stuffed blue Persian cat. You had to be
careful where you trod. One day Dodge slipped on a glossy
leaf and came down safely on a brittle stack of weather re-
ports, flakes of yellow paper flurrying around her petticoats.

Help!

That evening she put her hands on her hips and said I
think it is time we cleared this up. We used the suitcases
and we bundled the best things together and carried them
over to the Wayside Chapel on Hughes Street and dumped
them on the doorstep. A candle in a crown of thorns. We
stuffed the bottles and the broken pots in doubled garbage
bags and I took them in the lift to the bins in the courtyard.
Then we put the paper and the books together and I took
them down to the courtyard in garbage bags one by one until
the bins were full. We piled the rest in the bathtub and we
burnt it. We burnt the photo albums. They glowed red and
turned to ash. By the time we went to bed the same scene
that Eliza was sitting on a pile of old magazines in had begun
to effloresce through the emptied space a neat square
whose matching furniture gave it the tenuous coherence of
a window display returning to view under streaks of dust as
if the shadows of the objects drawn off had held on. I feel
like I have said that before. In any case, a clearing far more
efficient than the one in the office in Wolomooloo the place
of plenty. The sort of holocaust the solicitor was doomed
to dream about as he shifted the Gestetnered pulp of his
reckoning from one end of the room to the other, pages like
drops of water no of blood, that on their own are almost
nothing and in conglomerate can suffocate you or burst
walls.

Dodge went on shopping after that but only for repairs
and perishables. Bit by bit we put the old rooms back in
order polished and dusted the original knick knacks fixed
what we could. I was eleven years old and that year I got my
period and Dodge almost stopped shitting herself. It was a

false sign. Her guts had taken a secret turn for the worse.

I couldn't remember. Do you know I asked Eliza how much any of this stuff is worth.

With composure she looked around until her eyes came to rest on the bookcase: a fine squat deep hued piece much older than the rest of the furniture. It looked like the most valuable thing in the room. I wondered if Eliza knew something about furniture. No she said but we could find out.

After some asking around she bought the latest two editions of the *Australian Antiques Collector* and took them back to the flat to study. Unfortunately they had nothing in the way of a general guide but she read me an interesting article on rabdophilism. A cane whose knob is a fly made of black and blond horn fits snugly in the hand. Portraits of mute film actors and actresses appear on shafts. Valentino is represented in ivory. One finds the cheap metal bust of American presidential candidates and Walt Disney characters increase in price. Caricatures of faces from the curious bones of the whale's inner ear. Camphored stretcher. It went on like that, the siren call. The turned and tapered legs are capped and shod in copper. There was nothing in the magazines that looked like anything we had so to start with we thought it would be useful to make a roll. We began in the living room. The problem, we found, was we didn't know the proper names. Armchair I said. Eliza made a note on the back of my letter, which she had taken out of her bag along with the greater part of a pale blue Derwent pencil. What dilated in me at that first real flare of her own peculiar galaxies. Maybe it has it written on it somewhere. I turned the chair over onto its back but the sagging hessian, though its pores exhaled an odour like old straw, was blank. For some reason Dodge had left me with something resembling a respectable vocabulary for materials but if she knew what kind of furniture any of it was she never mentioned it. Striped, offered Eliza, writing. In bad condition.

The dining room was equally incommunicable. By the time we got to Dodge's bedroom Eliza threw the sheet of paper half full of her commentary on the kidney dresser and declared the exercise a dead end. She sat down on the bed, which was still unmade, the tartan quilt rolled up in one corner and trailing on the carpet. The room, whose denomination as forbidden territory had lingered between Dodge and myself long after the early years, though it had for practical reasons become a dead metaphor, now touched off in me the frisson from a loss of mystery, an immediate pleasure or uneasiness, the sheer idea of Eliza's midnight search representing at the end of such a prolapse a broach of far less murrain character than that of the literally superficial contact for which I had been improperly broken in. It was enough to know that the mole grey oak doors of the dressing table, the wardrobe, though closed now, had been opened. Distracted by a new sense of permissiveness, curiosity creeping up from the ruins of censure, I knelt down and reached my hand under the bed. My knuckles struck loaded cardboard. Putting in both hands, I dragged out a box.

There were books, that was the first surprise. Some, mostly those that had lost their spines, were picture books. A pasteboard edition of Grimm. A malkin puss in boots with graffito, abstract, as the police in Paris say. There were also notebooks bound together in a decaying rubber band. Under them locked together in a tangle of stiff limbs, a stuffed doll with a hard head, and hard hands, and hard little shoes, and a filthy rubber ducky, and a tiny phonograph, and some heavy contraptions made of a kind of metallic alloy, one of which turned out to be a man dancing with a pig, and one a sedan chair whose passenger was pulling on the ponytail of a Chinese porter as on a pair of reins, and one was a bust of a minstrel figure dressed in a blue suit and a red bow tie. Its arm, hand turned palm out before its belly, was a weighted mechanism. I pressed it with my finger and it swung up to its open mouth, its eyeballs rolling back in its head.

Eliza giggled.

It wants a penny. We can't sell that I said. Why not, she said. Someone will buy it.

The rubber band had congealed to the surface of the

notebooks and it crumbled away over the embrasures
where the bloated leaves puckered together like the ripple
marks on the rock platforms at Collaroy. Having never before seen a sample of Dodge's handwriting with the chance
to tend to deasil, I found the apparently puerile scrawl impossible to date. We set about studying them. Hurry up and
get this over with. There were four notebooks, all bound in
thick cardboard with a piece of stuff like gauze along the
spine. Two were simply cryptic, covered in what appeared
to be a nosediving kind of shorthand but whose crabbed
or porpoised coils may have been no more than what the
social services would call echopraxic. One had been written on for the first two and a half pages only. What seemed
at first to be tables were in fact six diary entries, in different ink, but since there were no dates we couldn't tell
whether they had been made days or months or some other period apart, or sporadically, over wide gaps, or all on
the same day. The content was not helpful. Cloudy, with
some scattered showers on the seaboard, otherwise mostly
mild for the present. Still a tendency to morning coastal
fogs. Impure thoughts. Lost a tooth. The last pit of tears
turned out to be a phone and address book.

Here look at this said Eliza. She pointed to an entry that
barely read ralph Siv 977 8218 will buy beefwood. What do
you think of that. Would you know beefwood if you saw it.

I wouldn't.

Naturally Eliza thought it would be worth looking in the
dining room. But the dining room furniture is all maple.

All of it.

It's a set.

To simplify, the same idea came to us at once. Back in
the living room we went over to the bookcase. It was a com-
posite piece. Eliza pulled on an empty draw at random.
That's easy, she said and sniffed. Cedar.

And you know what that is I said tapping the reddish
side panel.

Yes.

But the rest. I don't know. The key to the oval windowed

doors was in the lock. If Eliza had been hoping to crack it she was gracious, allowing me to open them and together we removed the things that had been arranged inside. Aside from the framed photograph there was a long legged person getting swept by the wind in bronze that was far too big for the low shelf, a few porcelain ladies and a hairy faced beer mug and a spoon from Government House. We laid them out in a row on the sofa and I got a torch from the kitchen to see if I could show up an inscription, the traces of a stamp, but there was nothing. Eliza pulled open the top drawer and felt blindly along the walls. Here, she said, I think, and took it all the way out onto the carpet. She pointed to a patch of yellow paper disintegrating at the edges and covered with an angular, old fashioned script. By an impurely formal logic the ragged arc where the bottom right hand corner of the label had been torn away led our eyes to the last finished word

King. &so remain
family it is
Beefwood

Bingo.
Too easy.
Eliza shook her head appreciatively. This is real she said. This could be worth something. Nonetheless we put off making the phone call. Nothing happened. We were living on domes of silence. Another rent notice arrived before we took up the address book again. Albert was obviously not in a hurry to take possession (why) but by then our funds were getting low and there wanted less than a week before the notice on our application for letters ran out and we weren't sure who might start trying to get in contact after that. We had no fear of creditors but there are others. Our level of comfort was also beginning to decline. We were far into the more obscure end of the silver and most of the food had gone rotten. Fancy clothes are no good if you have to eat the lingering pickle. Eliza had put the books without spines

in the bathroom. Time had caressed us, as brief and perso-
nally riotous as it had been. The welcome had been over-
stayed, we were being coaxed out.

She thought I should be the one to make the call. I carried the phone from the dresser and put it on the dining
table while she recovered the entry for Siv. And if the eights
are threes. We can try it again, in different combinations.

I got an answer straight off. I said I was calling about the
Beefwood bookcase.

Dodge Rose is selling?

The situation was explained. There was a long pause.
He didn't think he was in a position. He said, he would call
back. Perhaps, in the meantime, we could send him some
photographs.

Do you think it's a bargaining technique. We couldn't afford to wait. We decided to take the bookcase to him. The
postal address he'd provided was in Manly. We would catch
a ferry.

The next day we took the bookcase in the shopping
trolley down on to Macleay Street. After wrapping it in a
spare blanket the fit was perfect. For the route we decided
to take in Cowper Wharf, the Art Gallery, the Domain,
Spring Bent Street, then Loftus to the Quay. That should
satisfy the local historians in me. It's not like I don't owe
it to them. Eliza did the lateral steering and I pushed. We
almost ran up the back of a Phoenix but had no serious
trouble otherwise. It was good to be out. The controller
in the ticket booth at the wharf made us buy three tickets
then opened the service gate so we didn't have to haul
over the turnstile. At the end of the platform a man wearing an uncommonly dusty pair of aviator glasses turned his
back on us to wait. We sat in the shade of the Freshwater,
a hand each on a rickety wheel, rocked on the low waves.
The smell of guano and brine was like a purgative, I mean
a pick me up. No hang on I do mean the other one. I leant
over the edge and watched the seaweed swell and contract
around the pillars in the deep green water. Objects beneath
the surface are not where they appear. They aren't there

at all. Eliza scrubbed her latterly strawberries and cream then rancid cheeks. It's nice down here. She started laying out plans for moving the rest of the furniture, offered to push from now on. What we ought to do, she said, was get someone to value it anyway. Yes, initiative, that's what we needed again. The situation was not so dire. After all we had nothing to lose. What a beautiful day. A bar of sunlight had fallen between the ferry and the platform roof and began slanting in on us, warming through the chill breeze. I thought about unlacing my pumps. It was complicated. I might not have time.

Was it the Barrenjoey that picked us up or could I have called a ghost ship in from the Heads, what echoes, her hull clean of cement and what must be making itself felt as the no less speaking blubber/meat of that smallish but unhappy whale who would drag a vermilion zigzag through the harbour before failing, as a corpse, to stop washing up on the shore. Maybe the boat had already been condemned, it can be hard to keep count. Apart from the known survivors, which don't tend to run into the pavement anymore. So many ferries since The Lump made her maiden voyage have gone under, smashed to matchsticks in the vanished smog. I thought I would like to remember all their names; that would have taken some distilling. This tide you used to wish you could drain away in your separate fantasy, at last hollow, and dry, and empty, and noisy with only the diggers of the molten vessel for the Cpt. Cook Graving Dock, like horrific, repetitive dentists pulling the stump of a bloodwood tree from the inaurous silt exposed forty eight feet below sea level. These estoppels and reversals won't do forever. I am the skipper of something.

There was a shout. Some people came off the boat. The man in the sunglasses got on and we followed him, rolling our burden over the gangway ahead of us. The engine coughed up with a shudder, a yellow petrol cloud swirling over the water and we floated out, smooth, as if there were no longer an engine. Towards the Heads the ferry began to pitch. The spray hissed up the sides to strike our parched

lashes. A little prosopopoeia. I have a vague notion about
Manly. Once children used to sift in the long shadow of the
pines on the beaches, wet hair making rosettes in the hot
sand, for sovereigns and bones and older coins, and their
discoveries were published in the daily papers. We turned
into Henrietta Lane from the Corso, after which indeed I
am obliged to stop labouring the loom. Needless to say, I
didn't write that either. Wherever they were, our terminal
white gloves, which even looked like sails at first, reeking,
roughly washed of their gore, belonged to a small antiques
dealer's, the kind you normally find in country towns, a ma-
roon flag above the door with *Antiques* on it.

A handy cove. Didn't know they kept such characters.
Should help us when we're back in the saddle, so to speak.
I do not know what I can be hoping for from these inane ci-
tations but I draw the line at knicking, I mean stealing one-
legged men's crutches. Such quandaries as engulf the general user, fingers trailing in the ferried clews, the suddenly
modern. Maybe if I slit my wrists, I almost said my corre-
spondences. Could I have missed an appointment of some
kind, with all this scurrying out of public exits. Let it be
the unwound trammel of my braue Mayd's original perdi-
tion, and me on her coattails, and see where that gets us.
She mumbled to herself as we pushed the door open with
the trolley and the tinkle of a real bell. At the Yass Historical Society museum there is everything from a Koertz wool
press to a tiny trouser button stamped Bracken. This little shop was truly packed. From among the generic clutter
a man with a kind face peered over his. He smiled, lifted
what looked to be a thesaurus from his lap and laid it in the
hollow he left in the seat of an easy chair. His quick, gentle eyes went to the trolley then met ours without flinch-
ing. Maybe in the bad light he thought he was on familiar
ground. Do antiques dealers get visits from bag ladies. Eliza had been skipping showers to save soap. We introduced
ourselves. He might have started then, his steady eyes deliberate. Yes yes, he said, welcome. You needn't have come
out here yourselves, I'm obliged. We told him what was in

the trolley. Eliza unfolded the top layer of the blanket and Mr. Siv nodded in recognition.

The piece interests you.

Well, a long time ago now, Dodge and I discussed it, in relation to another deal, which went ahead anyway I believe. She must have made a note. I have to say I'm not really in that line anymore. It is a nice cabinet—

Bookcase.

Yes. It is very nice, you certainly shouldn't have trouble finding anyone to buy it.

It's very old.

Does seem to be. Georgian, by the look of it. But I'm not an expert.

There's a lable.

A table?

A label.

Oh, the craftsman's lable, that's common. It should tell you how old it is, if it isn't too damaged.

Why would it be damaged.

Because it's so old, any reason. Can you understand it.

We couldn't make out much. Would you like to see it.

I'm afraid if you can't make it out I have no hope he said smiling and tapping his crow's feet. Eliza looked embarrassed. We had forgotten to work out a price in advance. Would you be interested in buying it I asked.

He raised his eyebrows and pouted. I could give you two hundred dollars for it.

Eliza swallowed. She looked at me. That is, I said, quite a lot lower than we were expecting.

Siv burst. Ah it's like that I'm afraid. Rotten business. People think there's a fortune in it. I am sorry to disappoint you. He hung fire. Perhaps you would like a cup of tea.

We thanked him and he left the room still chortling under a tapestry that flapped back against the door jamb as he went. Eliza quietly ground her teeth. We waited a long time before we trusted him out of earshot. Do you think it really isn't worth that much.

Eliza shook her head. He's gurning.

Could she have said that.

A man looks at you like that wants your land or your daughter.

You think he'll pay more.

Through the. Sh—

That's continental direct speech for you. He was reversing into the room already, a kitchen's halogen light streaming faintly through the brief aperture, slaver clinking with the essentials from a porcelain tea set and a plate of ginger nut biscuits between his hands. By the way, he said I remember now what Dodge was going to swap me the bookcase for. Couldn't think for a moment. Hard to digest all of a sudden, the old thing coming back like that. Belly of the mind. I had a very nice set of ceramic tableware, cream. She bought it in the end. Is it still around.

I didn't think so. Yes I will have a biscuit. I was getting delusional no, dizzy. No wonder the deal wasn't going well we could hardly think straight. Eliza started laying it on with her mouth full. We came to you because you were one of the names we found associated with the bookcase. There were others.

There sure were.

Everyone gave us the same response, more or less, so we decided to do the rounds and settle it with someone today. Obviously we don't plan on wheeling this thing back and forth across the city another time.

That's understandable.

You're our first customer. But we did talk values on the phone and we're going on a ballpark figure of two thousand.

He crossed his fingers calmly and placed his hands in his lap. You do believe it is valuable.

Would you like to see the label.

No, I know what it says better than you do.

Eliza bit. What do you say Siv. You understand, we need to know if you're still interested. We've made a late start as it is. We think we're being very reasonable.

Narcissus let himself go in the fleshpots of afternoon

tea, he peeped into his teacup, placed it back on the saucer. It can be surprisingly hard for us connoisseurs to say what a thing like this is worth. Once money enters into it. I won't pretend it is not a very attractive object, certainly a, certainly a collector's piece. Perhaps, if there was something here that interested you we could include it in the exchange.

We're really not interested in old furniture.

What would you say to eight hundred. A predictable reduction I know, but I haven't got more than a thousand in the shop. His hand strayed over the bench where he was leaning and it was hard to tell if he meant to indicate a repository, letting it come to rest somewhere between a clay vase studded with periwinkles and a ricket of pencils and old chewing gum wrappers.

Have you got a T.V.

I beg your pardon.

Have you got a television. We'll give you the bookcase for eight hundred dollars and a television said Eliza.

Nothing in the shop, but I have a cranky black and white object out back I never watch. You'd be welcome to it.

Is it a deal.

He looked like he could hardly believe it. I couldn't. If I wasn't so hungry I might have said something. It isn't laughter ruins reason.

Why don't you help me get it out of there.

The bookcase was in three separate pieces. Together we lifted the base, the writing slope and the upper plinth from the trolley and sat them right way up in the middle of the shop. Nice work everyone almost screamed at once. The sun in the leaves outside filtered through to the glass ovals.

Now he said, if you go through there you'll find the television in the second room on the right. Just unplug it and you can bring it out here like that. We ducked under the rag into a corridor. Doesn't want us to see where he keeps his stash grumbled Eliza, squinnying for the doorway. It's probably in that dense book. I bet it's one of those fake ones with the pages cut out. A camouflaged sarcophagus. His burnished assiette. Vehicle and its freight, one sinking into something. We found the television in a mock Tudor living room with the curtains drawn, a worn in velvet armchair with the foot rest levered out, a lowboy, a liquor cabinet, a few rugs and journals lying around on modest furniture. I sometimes have the eye of a murderer. I pulled the plug and we carried the curved plastic box between us into the shop. It was orange. That's it he said, a respectable distance from everything. It'll fit in that trolley won't it. We lifted it in. He counted eight hundred dollars in cash from one hand to the other then he passed the wad to Eliza. Uniform and divisible. Never let your feelings get away from you. You'll be getting into antiques yourselves with that thing. Be wanting a computer soon, not a mirage but rasterized.

We have a whole flat full of stuff to get moving. Do you know someone who could value it all for us. We didn't think of it before.

He gave us the name of a friend at the Old Ark on Wentworth Avenue, or was it City Road. We said goodbye then. I preferred not to look at what we were leaving behind. Somehow Eliza and I found our way back to the wharf. At the ticket booth she stuffed the fresh money in her sock and I broke the last of the original notes. The last pair of white mice, the last bow tie. The dish rolled into the microscope. It was a rough crossing. We tried sitting inside but Eliza felt ill, so we threw the blanket over the latest idiot and chocked the trolley with our feet on the deck. I am giving up my goods. What do you want to do now I said through all the bitter spindrift that flew between us. Not bitter. You want to get a meal in Chinatown, or we could go back to the Bourbon and Beefsteak and order Sonofabitch Cowpoke Stew.

She tapped her fingers to her mouth.

I gotta buy cigarettes she said irrelevantly. Too much salty. Perhaps she didn't hear. Then, I am for staying in, ya bastard.

You're Rose's niece, well I'm pleased to meet you. It's a terrible disease. Had a cousin. Ted Sullaman had one brilliant heel dovetailed to the handle of a stepladder, the other hovering over the final rung and both hands outstretched towards a beaded and nickel plated lamp where it sat with some cardboard hat boxes on top of a wardrobe. His hair was oiled down like patent leather and his serge suit quickened in a smooth dent across his shoulders when he turned to greet us. Hang on I'll be with you in a sec. He lurched and grabbed the lamp by the stem in one hand, thumping the wardrobe with his knee so it shook, the price tag spinning on its blue thread. It wasn't a price tag, these were auction rooms. Eliza and I stood waiting in a clearing among the cases and tables and sea chests with initials stencilled onto the lids. Carpets had been rolled up between them and they all held lamps, animalier, telephones. Among the electroliers and the other light fixtures something like an umbrella had been strung to the high ceiling. Sullaman came down rattling.

So Alf Siv is still in business. What's his secret. Well anyway I'm glad to hear that. The smaller dealers are a dying race. Getting pushed out by the market. Art. International sales. Sotheby's and Christie's are here to make a killing, whole atmosphere is changing. It's in the air as they say, and you *can* hear it. They sound like the B.B.C. You know, dah dah dah daaah. Victory for the ancestors. Whose is that marble lion. A man. My stars, well hello sister.

Hello.

What brings you here.

We're looking for a valuer. We have some furniture, silver and things. An apartment's worth we want to get valued. We were told you could do it.

I'd be glad to but I can't at the moment I have my hands full. Got a monthly auction coming up. My wife though is an expert. I could ask her for you.

Is she expensive.

Couldn't tell you how much it's going to cost until she sees what you've got. But you won't find anyone more reasonable. Give you my word.

We accepted. She could probably be around by the end of the week. Was there anything we had to do in advance.

Just make sure she can get to everything.

It was, strictly, Eliza's turn to do the dishes. She turned the hot water on full blast and pulled up a pair of rubber gloves. While she worked over the encrusted remains of our partnership I beat the carpets on the balcony. Whole motifs broke loose. I watched as the threads, weightless, slowly turning, were borne away on insensible currents. That lifted my spirits. I had just thrown an especially skeletal carpet off the balcony in the hope that it would be untraceable by the time it hit the gutter when Eliza emerged through the steam in the kitchen doorway tugging at the bruised gloves until they everted. I wiped my forehead. We were ready for her.

The doorbell rang on the dot. Mrs. Sullaman was a tall, plumb shouldered woman with a severe haircut and divinely inscrutable eyes. At least you might have called them that. She pursed her lips and put out her hand. Elizabeth. And you must be the waif. Maxine. My name is Mrs. Sullaman; I've been told you need some material valued. Shall we see what I can do.

She put down a huge crocodile skin bag in the centre of the room and looked around her. It's even bigger than I imagined. What a building.

I haven't told the half of it. What is is not, not this piece of paper. A very spacious building. I feel I haven't been entirely accurate. There'll be time to go back. What exactly did we want to draw her attention to.

All of it.

For what purpose.

Profit.

Catalytic, preferably.

If you simply want to hawk it I can stop at market value. If you'd like to try anything at auction I could give you an estimate of realisable value on top of the first.

Market value will do.

Fine, well ideally I ought to have your instructions in writing but I can do that myself. I have your names and address. All I need from you otherwise is a clear statement of ownership. I charge by the hour so let's not make this unduly protracted.

Eliza opened her mouth but Mrs. Sullaman had already turned to unclasp her crocodile bag. Her silk bloused arms plunged in repeatedly until she'd drawn out two scrolls of bubble wrap, a few strips of old linen, a foolscap notebook, a tape measure, a pair of scales, a marbled portfolio, a magnifying glass, a camera, a receipt pad and a pencil case. She chose half a pencil, slung the camera on its leather band over her shoulder and took up the notebook. I'll photograph something if I think I need a better look at it. That probably won't be necessary. With some places you can tell more or less straight away what you have on your hands. I have my tables of hallmarks and makers' marks, and I know what to look for.

What do you look for.

Flaws, additions, or replacements in the furniture; cracks anywhere; excessive soldering in the gold and silver; crazing, chips, or restoration in the ceramics. If I get to a piece and you think there's something I ought to know about, speak up. Otherwise I'll just go ahead and write it all down from where I'm standing. That all right with you.

You're the one who can do it.

She wrote out loud. One silky oak hallstand with rugbox, seat, umbrella rack, coat hooks and bevelled mirror. One settee, two matching armchairs, upholstered in striped poplin, skirting with neoclassical crests. One 'Cavaliers' solid brass fire screen. One extra large Chesterfield, shaped back, double sprung, horsehair stuffed, upholstered in cream tapestry, fitted with loose rose brocade cover. One tub-shaped easy armchair, upholstered in same, loose covers to match. One china cabinet, blackwood finish, leadlight doors. Eight English lily-shaped china teacups and saucers. Six New York plain white china cups and saucers. Two Paragon china saucers. One tin box. One blackwood fern tub, copper bands. One matching floor ottoman. One blackwood occasional table. One small fumed oak escritoire with pigeon holes. One chair to match. What used to be here.

A piano.

A bookcase.

The piano was before. We sold the bookcase. It was really old, a relic. Max thinks we got rorted.

Don't use words you don't know the meaning of. I have to be careful what I hear. Unauthorised removal of relics is prohibited by the Heritage Act. There's an old law but the government has had its respectful eye on significant places since '75, even tapped Holland's palm for East India wrack. Happy holidays! Whatever you dig up that's nice belongs to Canberra. You follow me.

Not exactly.

Good for you. Blind eye to R. v. Forty-nine Casks of Brandy, R. v. Two Casks of Tallow, or R. v. Toole, not to mention buried treasure, which is not uncommon. Onward. One Brussels carpet, beyond repair. One antique silk Persian prayer rug, about 6ft. 7in. x 4ft. 3in. One antique silk Persian rug, fringed, 6ft. x 4ft., medallion centre, red and blue colourings. One tall red lacquer standard lamp, with hand-painted shade. One stained pine Jacobean tub chair. One orange television set. Does it work. No. Can't get any reception. Just snow. That can be fixed. One passport-sized studio portrait, nature scene, antique print, ambrotype or similar, xylonite frame. Two pairs blue silk chenille curtains, oxidised metal rods and fittings. Eight Chippendale dining chairs, backs carved in motifs of shells and foliage, cabriole legs and carved terminals, fitted with suede leather moveable seats. One patent spoon-backed sprung seat, lift-out, upholstered in chase leather, solid blackwood frame. One maple dining table. One sideboard of same with two drawers, two cupboards and bevelled mirror. One complete

Bleu de Roi dinner set, blue band and lace. One complete
Black Avon dinner set, filigree black lace pattern with solid
gilt handles. One Pall Mall glass suite, with sherries, ports,
clarets, champagne, liqueur, two pint jug, three pint jug,
quarter pint tumblers, decanters, ice plates and finger
bowls. One tall cut-glass claret jug with oxidized silver
mounts. One cut-glass whisky barrel, five cut-glass nob-
blers, hall-marked silver label and mounts. One large Venetian cut-glass basin. One wicker-covered milk bottle. One
Venetian glass liqueur decanter, burnished gilt, three glasses, circular tray to match. One cut mustard dish. One hobnail crystal cut-glass fern pot, loose electroplated lining.
One shaped sugar basket on ball feet. One cut and engraved glass biscuit barrel, electroplated mounts. One set
small engraved finger bowls. One heavy cut-glass ice bucket, electroplated mounts, drawer and tongs. One shaped
crumb tray and brush, buckhorn handle. Two covered
vegetable dishes with handles, reeded edge. One octagonal
saw-pierced cake basket. One shell-shaped saw-pierced
cake basket, twisted handle. One double saw-pierced sandwich basket, on feet. One teaset, incl. large teapot, sugar
basin and cream ewer. One four-egg cruet, complete
with spoons. Two sauceboats on feet (James Dixon & Sons,
Sheffield). Two tall trumpet-shaped flower vases, 12 inches.
Two smaller trumpet-shaped flower vases. One case containing six each cake knives and forks, coloured handles.
Ten fruit knives and eleven forks, ivory handles, in case.
One large shaped silver covered entrée dish with moveable
handle. One plain brass urn. One engraved silver covered
claret jug with shaped handle, decorated with scrolls and
floral trophies, height 13 inches. One large circular-shaped
salver, on four feet, shell decoration, 14 inches. One round
pewter serving tray, inscribed twice, worn, can't make out
original, second engraving says, May good digestion wait on
appetites and health on both are the best wishes of B.H.
and L.H. 1938. Two silver cigar ash trays with clips. One silver rat-tail soup ladle and gravy spoon. One tall silver embossed sugar sifter, shell and floral decoration. One small

silver toast rack (Hardy Bros. Ltd.). One small silver wine
strainer. Two shaped silver butter dishes on feet. One small
Georgian sugar basin and cream ewer, circular bases. One
small double-handed sugar basin and cream ewer, embossed floral decoration, on ball feet. One candlestick telephone, black enamel and brass, on oak box. One silver sycamore inlaid china cabinet, shaped front, clear glass doors,
plate glass shelves, lined with grey silk poplin. One porcelain Little Polly Flinders, marked Lefton, missing one loop
on the ribbon of her hat. One porcelain Southern Belle
Green, no head. One porcelain Victorian lady, myosotis pat-
terns on her dress. Royal Worcester, cows and flowers. One
Spode sugar basin and cream ewer, small candlestick, butter dish and transfer mug. Nine fine Coalport china coffee
cups and saucers, blue and burnished gold. One Royal
Doulton Flambe coffee set with silver gilt mounts, incl.
coffee pot, six cups and saucers, sugar basin. Nine Coalport
teacups, ten saucers and ten small plates, heavily burnished
in gold, decorated with floral bands. Three Royal Doulton
dessert plates with medallion centre, with portrait painting,
could be Boullemier, cream ground, heavy gilt enrich-
ments. One Royal Doulton character mug. One maple two-
tier occasional table. Five pairs black, silver and gold brocade fringed curtains, silk poplin linings, complete with
pelmets. One large functioning oak refrigerator, four doors,
enamelled lined, 6ft. x 4ft. x 2ft. 6in. One pine table. One
aluminium coffee pot (faulty). Two aluminium trays. One
aluminium casserole dish. One aluminium lemon squeezer.
Eight silver dinner knives. Eight silver dinner forks. Eight
silver luncheon knives. Six, no eight electroplated spoons.
Eight silver luncheon forks. Eight silver salad forks. Eight
electroplated knives. Eight electroplated forks. Eight large
silver soup spoons. Eight large silver teaspoons. One electroplated cake basket, saw-pierced design. One silver gravy
ladle. One electroplated coffee pot with ebonite handle.
One silver cold meat fork. One silver pie slice. One silver
butter knife. Eight silver cream soup spoons. Eight silver
butter spreaders. Eight silver coffee spoons. Eight silver

seafood forks. Eight silver bouillon spoons. One bronze Art
Deco urban female figurine signed Bruno Zach. Eight silver orange spoons. One silver sugar/preserve spoon. One
silver lemon fork. One zinc teaspoon. Two piece silver carv-
ing set. One pierced silver tablespoon. One silver pâté
server. One pair silver sugar tongs. One silver berry spoon.
One silver stuffing spoon. One electroplated jam dish and
spoon. One mixing bowl, one pestle and mortar. One aluminium egg poacher. One picnic hamper. One cake safe.
One deed box. One white enamelled bin. One enamelled
flour bin and sugar bin. One small bread crock, and enamelled salt box. Four chairs, blackwood rails. One pacific oak
kitchen cabinet, sliding glass door cupboards, fly-proof wire
gauze sides. One flour, one sugar, one rice, one tea, one
sago, one coffee canister, white and blue enamelled, stack-
able in descending size. One Kande toaster. One plain
brown china teapot. One milk jug. One glass sugar basin
with lid. One enamelled pie dish, block tin. One Palace
brand canvas butter cooler. Two enamelled stewpans. One
washup dish, block tin. One enamelled crockpot. One grid-
iron. One enamelled kettle. One pair bellows. One china
candlestick. Three lipped enamelled saucepans. One washing board. Six tumblers. Two wooden mixing spoons. One
enamelled colander. One aluminium canister. One aluminium boiler. One aluminium gravy strainer. Two aluminium
dinner plates. Two aluminium soup bowls. One wood serving bowl. One all-hair brush. One tin bucket. One gilt
framed circular convex mirror. One Jacobean-style auto tray
with drawer and rubber tires, Australian oak, nut brown finish. One patent two-roller mangle. Do you use this. One
porcelain laundry tub with candelabra stand. One large pine
ironing table. Three canary cages. One parrot cage. Two di-
xie mats. One black Wedgwood vase, decorated with rams'
heads and classical figures and floral trophies, profusely
overlaid with burnished gold. Four pairs silk poplin and
lace curtains. One electric two-globe radiator. One antique
silk Persian fringed rug, cream ground, floral design, about
9ft. 3in. x 6ft. 1in. One sea-grass and poker-work soiled lin-

en basket. One copper embossed fuel box, panels in high relief of battle scenes. One byzanta lustre bowl with decoration of fairies, 12 inches diameter. Two fine oriental bronze vases on circular bases, decorated with dragons, fish and foliage in high relief, each 18 inches high. One mechanical whistling bird. One small carved ivory mouse, ear missing. One small Rouge Doulton fox ornament. One Royal Doulton Rouge Flambe vase. One Royal Doulton Rouge Flambe penguin. One small Royal Doulton Rouge Flambe duck and axe. One Royal Doulton octagonal-shaped flat bowl. One Royal Worcester jardiniere with decoration of lions, satyr heads and scrolls in relief. One wax maple bedstead, wire mattress, three-ply woven, to fit pure flock mattress. One bolster and two pillows, manchester ticking. One full-size Marcella quilt, satin finish. One electric lamp with tall Corinthian column on square base, hobnail cut-glass bowl. Two Axminster hearthrugs. One set art-shaded toilet ware. One cast iron shower bath, porcelain, nickel-plated paw feet. Two pairs extra long royal blue silk velvet curtains with tasselled Holland blinds. One Mah Jong set in carved and gilt case, complete with four lacquered walls. One brown oak square card table on four carved columns, leather lined top, four drawers and loose baize cover. One oriental bronze elephant on wood base. No of ambre, and a Grasshopper. One cedar cigar box, plated lid enamelled with signal flags. One aluminium damp-proof cheroot case. One dark mahogany cigar cabinet with two drawers, enclosed by bevelled glass doors. One case containing part set of chess men. One set of benzoline snooker balls. One brass telescopic smokers' stand. One electric flexible reading lamp. One comfortable cretonne chair. Oriental matting. One electric fire log stand. One black and nickel bedstead, wire mattress, pure down mattress. Four pillows. One four-fold screen, grained and panelled in Tasmanian blackwood. One bedpan. One brass electric radiator, shell-shape, with four globes. One very large white polar bear specimen rug, with head and claws. One seagrass commode armchair. One eau-forte of three rigger,

crest with some kind of bird perhaps a cormorant, on a hel-
met, profuse with ivy, moulded frame, Hoffnung. One
white enamel soiled linen basket. One mole grey oak dressing table, kidney-shaped, cabriole legs, with two long linen
drawers and triplex bevelled mirrors, and wardrobe, nicely
panelled with two bow-front curtained glass panels, good
hanging space, 3ft. 6in. One wicker tray, water bottle
and glass. Three tinted pencil nude studies by Gustave
Brisgand. One nickel frame bevelled wall mirror. One cast
iron parallel bath, porcelain enamelled inside, with three-
quarter brass hot and cold smooth body hospital pillar taps,
one-and-a-half trapped waste, overflow and chain. One
nickel sponge, soap and tumbler holder with plain lip. One
Tokalon electric hairbrush. One cork bath mat, rotten. Two
brooms and a mop. One pair heavy rose silk velvet-embroi-
dered curtains, brass rods and fittings. Nine geranium tubs
and stands. Four sea-grass armchairs. One thermograph.

We showed her the cardboard box and she noted the remaining contents. She winced but wrote. She even picked
up some things we'd missed. One gold fish mask, acetate.
Have I seen it all. Eliza affirmed. What happens now. I'll
write a report and a valuation. Nothing in principle prohi-
bits them appearing in the same document so to make your
part as lucid and as uncomplicated as possible I'll combine
and send you a copy that'll be yours, to use that is. Take it
with you to the buyers and beware.

The next manoeuvre had been planned. Would she be
interested in any of it, all of it.

Certainly not. That would be a flagrant conflict of interest. I hope that. She straightened an arm. Do you know
what you're doing.

I suppose we couldn't offer any of it to your husband
then either.

Correct. Ted wouldn't touch it, be people just waiting to
trip him up. He's one of the best, unique, but he has to rise
above a lot. With all he cops from those goddamned nanny
goats and worse, above and below, he's a consummate professional, a great communicator. Phah. Vendetta of the flesh.

Anyway I thought you wanted to sell the stuff straight off.
I'll send you a list of places you could try. There's some value here, among the store-bought furniture, but let me tell
you, this is a long way from a sure business; whatever you
got for that bookcase, I wouldn't spend it yet.

Mrs. Sullaman wound on her film then dropped her
things back in the bag. Would she like a cup of tea or coffee before she left. No thank you. And I suggest you give
all that tableware a proper clean before you try pushing it
on anyone. Relatively small things like that can make a difference.

Yes ma'am.

After she had gone Eliza suggested we draw lots for
the washing up this time but I told her not to bother. She
hooked her finger in the elastic tabs of her boots and pulled
them off, then she stretched out on the sofa with a slip of
junk mail raised to the fading light. The valuer had been
over longer than I'd realised. I put the gloves on as they
were and dumped the silver back in the sink. It shivered
the unaccumulated quiet of the flat, waking me up to the
lull between peak hour and the various night traffic, when
you can hear the leaves if there are any, and the birds, closer
than that long, silent migration that darkens over the city
at twilight, when voices on the street break so clearly they
reach the kitchen window without the words that carried
them. Eliza was shuffling through her reading matter. I
poured a handful of baking soda into the sink.

I may as well say in faith to the arbitrariness by which
I apparently got here that I began when I came across a photograph of a scale model escalator on fire in a volume bound,
I believe, in the colour of the baseball team named for
keeping out of the way of the new trolley cars in Brooklyn,
and containing a report from a seminar on Fire Dynamics
and the Organisation of Safety at the Institution of Mechanical Engineers in London, augury into the accident in the
shaft serving the deep Piccadilly line at St. Pancras. An in-
testine catastrophe as they nicely call it. How did it happen. Probably a match, the ban ignored, dropped alight
by some careless traveller at the right side of the wooden
stairs and falling in a grease track pregnant with paper fragments from discarded tickets, sweet wrappers, fluff, rat and
human hair, never cleaned. An eastbound train arriving and
a westbound train departing. The wind in the wings. No
one believed the first computer simulation, that it burns
obliquely: the model proved it. Remain calm, fire does not
burn downwards, gh devoured. Anisot, well, you remember
the bits, the solvent in the ceiling turning the smoke oily
black, and so on the vidimus, less the wax of course in such
mounting heat. At least it's true I've always had a soft spot
for pictures. It might have been different.

The day word from Mrs. Sullaman arrived I was out
of bed before Eliza, who was normally moving around by
dawn. I washed, caught the lift in my pyjamas and brought
the brown A4 envelope back up to the dining room, where
it lay unopened on the dining table while I made breakfast.
There had been disappearances. All but the necessary silver
had been put away and we had gone through the rest of the
flat wherever we thought we could make a difference, so
the morning light ran level over most things and the smell
itself was less confused. Something similar missing. The
curtains in the dining room were half drawn. I was sitting in

it eating a bowl of cornflakes and watching a fly turn circles over the razed expanse of killed maple before me when Eliza came in a bit flushed, smiling. She said what's that.

It's from the valuer.

She ripped the top off. So we make progress. Inside were a few typed sheets held together by a bulldog clip and a handwritten note. Eliza lifted the sheets one by one. Blah blah blah, need of restoration, blah blah. Here. Estimated market value. She read off a series of preliminary numbers, her fingers twitching at the edge of the page, glissando to a computational flutter, then smacked the bundle down and sat motionless with her hands in her lap, her head inclined and her eyes fixed in utopian middle distance. We've done it she said at last, winking again. Pull out that pinky, we're sitting on thousands. Still something in my.

The handwritten note contained a list of places. We couldn't tell if it was in ascending or descending order so we went blindly from the top. Bob's Second Hand and Fossicker's were on south King Street, in Newtown. We started with Fossicker's. Yes they were interested in some things, not the major things but they could do something with some of the furniture, the lamps, the heater, that sort of thing. They would send someone on the weekend. I wonder is this how Dodge used to do it. We pottered around the flat smoothing the pillows down. Tooth, got it. That won't come back again. Eliza planted the list with gory asterisks and we discussed technique, settled on a terminus a quo, let the phone ring. She was standing in the middle of the living room pointing the television aerial in various directions when I answered the door to a grave young man, clearly somebody's son. He arrived later than you might have expected, being anxiously observant of the other civilities and knowing, he said, the area. Apologies. The weather. Yes of course. You look cold, poor thing. His shirt was buttoned above the collar of a plastic rain poncho that he took off at my invitation and hung where it dripped onto the hallstand. Come in don't just stand there. He put his hands in his pockets and followed me squelching into the living room, the freckles rising in his cheeks. He was as tall as Eliza and strongly built. In another place with his elbows free he might have been taken for athletic. I offered him a chair and Eliza went in to make some tea. She regretted having to leave the aerial. I heard something she said over her shoulder. I swear, just for a second I had it, something.

While she was in the kitchen our guest and I talked about his shop, antiques. He answered directly enough but his eyes nutated all over the place and by the time we ran out of small talk he was literally squirming. I wish I could put my finger on exactly what it was. It was a sombre day and the rainclouds banked in the windows had thrown the room into faint relief. The air rumbled. With the first price I happened to mention I thought I saw him blanch. He did jump. If that seems unbelievable, things certainly went downhill from there. We had already mentioned quite middling costs in the shop so it can't have been the money that put him off. He must have been prepared for that, which in any case was his job, or at least. Something spooked him. When Eliza came in with the tea things he was gone. Just like that. Did he say anything . . . He forgot his raincoat. She stood, stunned, a fillet of steam unwinding from the teapot into the rays of the oncoming storm. The television began to crackle.

Hold that!

I took the tray but the signal went dead at her approach. It's just the weather I said. She said I guess next time we'll have to be more careful. How. You left the front door open. We didn't discuss it any further then. Three peals of thunder split over our heads. We'd forgotten our stuff on the clothes-line so we dropped everything and ran for the fire escape. We spent the rest of the day grilling our refouled underpants on the heater and Monday morning we started out early. The streets were full of people going to work I imagine. Eliza walked where the storm had washed the last of the amber leaves, the bits of broken glass and plastic, turning over the flop of the weekend as we had the night before. She insisted the rupture might bare something but in my opinion there was no use hammering away at a lost cause. If we hadn't made it out already we never would. Some people are crackpots. We still had our list and the blaze of day ahead of us. But in Bob's Second Hand back on King Street we ran into all kinds of misunderstanding, so we turned around and flew up Cleveland Street to get to Darlinghurst and the Little Shop of Horrors, which was jumping the queue. Softly. At least Eliza was getting a real tour. Before we crossed Bourke Street in Burton she stopped and did a double take having never come at it from that angle before. She pointed down the hill. Here we are again. Pisgah run from the sea to the smokeless stack at Sydney Gate. That wasn't in my vocabulary either. No, we're higher up on it than we were. Do you think we might run into. Doesn't matter anyway. The green man standing became the red man striding. Decisive at last we ran in front of a bus, tires hissing on the slick behind us, faces in blurred boxes. More than a scent of the blustering season but still pools not brooks, either above or below the surface. I expect that's those sources run dry. Other young people were on the street, hands linked, in all kinds of jackets. What tenacious obsolescence, those shimmering constrictors; for the first time we must have almost fit. Down in. Echo the lot, la e lotio. No. Bends adorning. Een might come in. Dumb kids, playing old people. Where are the italics on this thing. Hardly feels like yesterday. And now this. *This* is retro. Me dehiscing, did I say that, down to rubble and I lose sight of you, weave away in the flicker of the crowns pressed together on the street, stars fading in my inky lids, litter of last light blinking off till all forgotten. It used to be called Semicircular Quay. That's good, that's in the books too. What frightfully innumerable summits I like to think I've been slipping over about my doubtful people. Look at me. I've lost them again. How's that for the thorns of life. Fast pinnacles. My molten vessel. I said that before. Must be a different button. You don't even need to write. What an unexpected boon for invention. So you return to where you started. Walk here no more, buoyed over deep space in a bassinet, your fingers looped in the cords of your bonnet, about the time you begin to take an interest in intercourse id est eyeball and semiloose sphere of the knee. They are buffing the mica flecked pavement in their haste to pass out. The rest has settled into an ashen cope. See. The other looms over you like Dad's fob. Hands closing in. Hurry up that's us they're calling. No steam but a whistle. I make the air vibrate but in despair. To make a new beginning. Till we get there. The line comes alive, faster than. Where was I. Further on in the same direction. Yes, I mean, further on in the same direction we passed the north wind, facing wall of what used to be East Sydney Technical College, dappled against the still melancholy heavens, a repulsive, fangless dinosaur having bolted its prickly branches above the high tiles on the south side and, rid precipitously its bag of pistoles, piercing them naked into the otherwise limitless sky—the branches; I understand a flying fish or a vampire if I haven't completely lost the ability to read would have been more suitable there, though no more excessively substantial, I would be glad to reaffirm that in the most formal environment. Like that well full of concrete. The drains were clogged to overflowing. I have nothing but my spontaneity. I will knout up hell if I have to. Eliza ran her fingers over the damp grey sandstone.

It may be dumb, she said, but you know I get the feeling I could miss it here.

She was really full of such homey expressions.

Out of our element again in the shop on Darley Street we asked to speak to Perry Quinton. A more or less blonde in a chair for sale with a ledger on her knee and a horrid pencil stub between her teeth called to him without getting up. There was music, a comfort to the myopic. What's the matter yelled Perry Quinton appearing between two L.P.s he was, it turned out, at the point of sorting into crates at the back of the shop. The woman in the chair coughed. Thelma and Thelma here want to sell you something.

He left the records and invited us to a coffee table spread over with the day's newspaper and a sort of picnic lunch of cold chips and tobacco pouch. Suppose you're going to tell me you've got a once in a lifetime. You read what they dragged out of the Thames today. No. Look at that. *That's* rare as bog butter.

Is that the date already.

Eliza put Sullaman's whole document down before him. Maybe the idea was not to appear over accommodating. I appreciated the gesture whatever the thought behind it was. We could hardly afford to bugger up again this far down the list so we may as well have come clean with as few extras as possible.

Quinton, in fact, was convivial. But he wouldn't take much. He made a few scratches on the valuation, offered to pay what we were asking for, fixed a day to come round with the van. We shuffled down Whites Lane to Victoria Street in a low mood. St. John's with the faceless clock that had stopped chiming the quarters at the behest of the more porous neighbours, a shrinking part of the population, looked somewhat gloomy under the lacklustre sky. Even the French bakery across the road, with which we were now also in charity, had a flatter frontage than it was wont to have. Would have wont to have. Tenses, those are the least of your worries. At least I, a failed millionaire, can say of myself that I am no slave to matter, devouring with supreme indifference the bars of my sensuous cage. Strawberry cream flan. I will even try onomastics. The whish of that familiar sphincter. Usually I found bad weather relaxing. Dodge had a habit of foaming at the mouth in the summertime, pacing the room in a limp cotton two piece, what's that line of Keats'. Oh, chestnut tree . . . But September was over! We'd get nowhere if we went on trying to palm the garbage this way. Eliza agreed. We needed a different tack. We'd both noticed the list finished with Lawson's.

An auction house.

She must have guessed we'd run into this kind of trouble. Mother always said bad things about auctions. Deceased estates. See what they've been reduced to. What if they bargain us down to nothing. That doesn't happen. You put a reserve on. Do the whole thing at once. If some things don't move at least we'll be in a better position. But the auctioneer must take a cut, if nothing else. And all that publicity. It'd be a risk. Eliza considered. If we abandoned the flat beforehand. Collect what we could on the day and quit town.

We went down to George Street and caught a bus to the Crescent.

In an office over furnished in tinted leather at the back of the Lawson's warehouse, we handed our list to a classical kind of washed up heartthrob who said his name was Paul. He leaned against the desk and held the list out to focus as I weighed the moment privately. A crease through the front of his worsted suit sat more like a scar in his flawless demeanour; the chivalric token of his salt and pepper crew cut implied a whole repertoire of belated habits kept up with the stubborn privilege of experience. Now that was a sentence that didn't make sense. As he pressed the thumb and forefinger of his free hand between his bloodshot eyes I heard the chair beside me squeak. Eliza had crossed her legs. She raised her reservations.

Paul didn't miss a beat. Our commission is twenty two percent. We charge a service fee depending on the material, taken together. This is a charming estate, it would generate considerable interest. You can be sure you'd stand to make a tidy profit. It is a respectable venture. You know everything used to be sold by auction, groceries, the lot, down on the wharves. The first discount docks, better than the supermarket. Lawson's has been there since the beginning. Now we deal in everything including the very best, the truly selective. We sold the Lloyd Jones collection at Rosemont Woollahra just last year. You'd be in safe hands.

When can we bring it all down to you.

Estates like this tend to sell well in situ. Buyers like to see the pieces in their original environment. It stimulates the imagination.

It would have been vain to try to do with more at that stage what was already getting done with less. We made an appointment at the flat to discuss the procedure and finalise a course of action. He or his boss would be there. In front of the warehouse we ducked under a folding screen as it was lifted into the back of a truck, picked our way between the chairs waiting in farouche clusters on the footpath, then followed the sloping line of Moreton Bay figs and the dirt sillage of the slaughterhouse along the water's edge in the coming Bicentennial Park to Geh I mean Glebe, the graveyard, the depurated, and the bus to Railway Square, which was quite indirect. From there we walked. What useless torture. I wrote this lying down. I'd start again but me'd derive sooner. Where's my arca. By the time we got back we were both exhausted. It's a relief to come home to a kept house. What do they call it, negative space. Empty crannies. Pure arrangement. Purple and green. Night and the nicht absolut gleich. We spread out in the relative void and napped until sundown, when, in what promises to be the last of the series reversions, I discovered the head planted at the foot of Eliza's bed until my vertigo had dissolved with the neon light pulsating like a bad habit in the curtains, and that striking silence. Must have dragged myself there half asleep. I found Eliza almost hanging off the end of the settee snoring. Some bacon in a pan brought her round, then we went out to see if we could find a place to hole up at auction time. Having talked over Paul's proposition we had not only agreed that it would be too dangerous to advertise an auction at the flat, we'd stuck to our assumption that the best thing to do, once the business was underway, was clear out altogether. After some trial and error we tentatively booked two beds in a backpacker's on Victoria Street for the week we hoped we would need them. We began packing our bags.

Almost everything not for sale was soon assembled into one place. What else. The urn. Better empty it first. We should scatter them in the harbour. Could do it from here, save the trip. We put the clean vessel in the china cabinet next to the flower girl. Lucky it isn't inscribed. Eliza shook her head and grinned far into her cheeks like my own mindless goss. You're ruthless.

Nothing else we could help was to be left to chance.

The night before our appointment Eliza drew a bath. She had found a jar of what appeared almost incredibly to be called Codex bath salts somewhere among the oozing and peeling mound of extinct toiletries we had piled in the sink to get rid of and the stale lavender perfume had already begun creeping into the furthest corner of the flat when I heard a cry, then a dull moan from the bathroom.

I called her name. There was no response, which will appear justifiably noteworthy, given the state of constant communication we always ended up in. It's not like I wasn't used to such noises, and not just from the bathroom. But Dodge never needed to be asked twice to expatiate on her keenings, and I must have supposed the niece, according to the famous theory of family resemblance, etc. I went over to the door, knocked and called again. I made a forced entrance. Eliza sat upright in the steam, her body already half turned towards the door, transfixed. Her eyes hardly flickered as I approached and when I put my hand on her arm, not a tendon flinched beneath her puckered skin. Droplets of condensation had collected on the erect hairs of her body, fusing where I touched her and trickling down her arm from under my hand. I forced her down into the bathtub. Her body went suddenly limp in my hands and slid under the water, her knees up. I saw then that she had cut herself, not badly, but where. She didn't move. As the oily surface calmed, the image of her body merged again, stilled, her thighs, her shimmering pubic mound, the long curve of her stomach, her dugs, slightly floating, her frozen mouth, her eyes, open, the lashes thick with bubbles, her hair wreathing in and out of place. I leant further in. She blinked, the surface shattered and she shot up gasping, pulled at my arm with both hands blindly, then put her head down, coughed out a foaming mouthful of water and caught her breath. I helped her out of the bathtub to the sink and took her towel and wrapped it round her shoulders. She rubbed at the foggy glass before her then turned to me. What happened. But she only shook her head, her shoulders rising a little. Well. At least she no longer seemed to be bleeding. I left her with

the towel hanging open in the living room while I dug out a
jumper and pair of slacks from my wardrobe. When I came
back she seemed to be in better shape. She thanked me,
could not suitably have sensed the pelt on my arm bristle
from the far side of her wrapping, and dressed herself. For
form's sake I inquired again, I inquire again.

I have no idea.

Before the night was out Dodge's clothes had grown on
her. She asked if I would lend her something attractive for
the next day so we went to my bedroom and tried some
things on. They were her size. She left the skullcap that
matched her nictitating membrane where it was and chose
a pair of brick red flannel slacks and a helio cardigan. I gave
her some stockings and a pair of vamp Oxfords with buried
welt stitch and bevelled edges I had been saving for a special occasion. We skipped dinner and slept in the same bed
with the light on.

In the morning we went down to the liquor shop for a
bottle of champagne. We took a turn around Fitzroy Gardens, where an old woman walking her dog smiled at us
nostalgically if not altogether conspiratorially as she bent
with a plastic bag on her hand, emerging from her supple
fur covered with the spoors of late spring. Morning. Morning. I told you I intended to leave no stone unturned. We
drew all the curtains but one, the better for a sense of
depth. Promise. In uncertainty, at least, hope. Doing my
best not to whistle too loud I twisted Eliza's hair in plaits,
wound them up into a bun, tried to show her how to step in
heels. There are certain signs. Réveillent des faits anciens.
When at last the doorbell rang I opened the door to the fat-
test man yet. He was panting. Lift broke. His name wasn't
Lawson but he was not, he said, unrelated. You've met
my boy. A suave nod from over his boss' shoulder brought
Paul's haggard face into the hall light for a moment. More
than we were expecting. Came up by the Metro. Thought
some air would do us both a service. I led them into the living room and the fatter man jumped at seeing Eliza standing behind one of the striped poplin armchairs. Hello, I'm

Frank Masters. Frank.

Hello. I'm Eliza. Hello.

Hello.

I had positioned myself at the mouth of the corridor, so when Frank glanced behind him I had a clear view of what was unmistakably a gleam of pure terror. But he didn't budge, turned back to Eliza to tell her what a handsome apartment it was, had never had the pleasure of being inside, admired it from a distance, the building, like every other local with any taste for the exceptional. He linked his fingers together in the small of his back. He wasn't going anywhere. I went to get the champagne, then I called Eliza for a hand with the glasses. They've got the creeps, she pointed out. Be putty if we can keep them.

Frank clapped his hands once at seeing us reappear, evidently feeling the belated effects of a sort of resurrection. Boy they know how to do hospitality in the Cross! When was the last time you were up here Paul.

He umd and ahd. Terrible. It must be a few years now. I saw Rex Wrenall's show at Patches, him and two others, what were the girls' names.

Yes. You don't mean. Not the one from the Pink Panther, same time, end of the seventies. Had a solo on a horned. Hung from the ceiling. Super fit. Magic place. Streets are a riot. Wouldn't know what you had. All spread their legs at sundown. Pardon. Forget where I am. You two ladies keep the old flame burning. Ah it's not what it used to be. This, this is very civilised, lovingly received. Thank you. It brimmed over the lip of the glass and down his fingers.

Eliza asked Paul if he would like to see some of the material. He had taken a seat in the Chesterfield and she perched opposite him to pour champagne one handed into a glass he held so far out it trembled. Watch it. Frank and I sat on the striped poplin. In the last shuffle the night before Dodge's dolls had gone in the china cabinet. If Paul started looking around for an excuse he found one there because he pointed through the stained glass to the piggy bank and said well I don't remember reading that, you've got a nig. A money-

box. He has a sister, you know, Dinah. Same thing. I have
a friend who collects those. There are all kinds apparently, hardly rare, but you know a collector is always looking
out for new specimens. One man's trash. He came back
from Paris the other year with an armful. He said he found
them in a junk market on the Seine. An Uncle Sam with a
nutcracker mouth and a stars and stripes carpet bag springs
open with a hidden lever, a gas station attendant, lifts the
lid on the oil reservoir or some such. Queer fish. Not my
thing. You don't have any Disney figurines do you, porcelain. You know, Donald Duck, the Little Mermaid.

Watch you don't spill that. I thought he might have
been afraid to go alone so I invited Frank, who obviously couldn't wait for a chance to keep changing the subject.
He put his half full glass down on the occasional table and
stood up. Your sales will certainly benefit from their sur-
roundings. Place has atmosphere. If we can pitch it right
we'll have them running.

Eliza lifted at last an admonishing finger. That won't be
possible I'm afraid. We'd like to hold the auction in your
rooms.

Whatever for.

I have a sick mother. We don't want to disturb her and
we can't move her.

Frank spun around so fast he stubbed up the end of the
Saraband and had to grab the standard lamp to stop himself from falling over. Paul might have yelled if his blasted thropple hadn't amphigoried such a natural reflex into
something resembling a distant trill. He surely would have
taken hold of Eliza if the fern tub hadn't got in the way, his
fingers rustling through the fronds to thin air. Eliza stifled
her laughter with Mrs. Sullaman's report and evaluation.
Daft. Pardon. Frank chuckled, the painted shade swinging
crazily above his fist. Fuit comata silva. A bub in the woods.
O theoi neoteroi. Excuse me. Of course. But for Physical
and œconomical purposes. He didn't say that. A shame really. He shut his eyes. A real pity. What resembles spinach.
It'd probably be better not to do a tour then. Wouldn't want

to disturb her.

She's in quite a different part of the flat, it wouldn't be any trouble. We live here after all.

Ah well all the same. Better not. We can organise to have it all brought over to us quite quickly. When did you envision having the auction.

Soon as possible.

What do you say Paul, you think we can get it all up and running in two weeks. Paul was already on his feet. Oh yes. What does that make it. How about the seventh of November, we've got nothing on. November seven suit you. Nothing sooner. That'd be the earliest to tell the truth. Mobled. What. November seven. Paul said your commission was twenty two percent. Did he. That sounds a bit high. Doesn't it. Why don't we say fourteen percent. Who pays the removalists' fees. You do. We do.

We do. Alright. November seven then. It's agreed. Bloody cold for this time of year. All round nodding. Excellent. Well it was truly a pleasure, very kind of you to have us, considering. Thank you for the bubbly. Really charming. Rare such a warm reception. Don't usually find ourselves in a partie carrée. Paul.

Right.

Well, thank you, goodbye. We'll be in touch about the removalists. Thank you. 'Bye. Goodbye. 'Bye 'bye. Which way do I turn this. 'Bye for now. Eliza shut the door behind them and sank towards the carpet. Floorboards. There was never any carpet. We looked at. I checked out the window. Are we going to see them again. I don't know. Our glasses may deceive us in many things. Look what I found in these pants. Eliza crossed to the divan, reached under a seat cushion and dug out the cash for the bookcase, then she thumbed through it twice before letting it patter into a neat stack on that no longer perennial surface for our affairs next to a meniscus of spilt champagne and the champagne cork. Rising like a candle flame buried in the wood. Following her lead I got a tea towel from the kitchen and squilgeed up the mess then I threw the tea towel in the bin.

Outside the traffic was building, or had been, once upon a time. Here we go. It's possible you may be losing your head. Or your handes. That would be a decorous exergue to the principle of separation. Offering baskets of Dead Sea fruit in a cephalophoric procession, on a pier glass. Make way for the square world development. What did I say about lifting apart I seem to recall that was better. Robbed at the Foule Oke. High above the future tumult I straightened my stockings if I hadn't started ripping my hair out by the roots already, rhetorically. Forget it it's too late now. In the meantime Eliza had packed the rest of her thing. We came face to face again in the living room. Well. Don't forget your toothbrush. Some modern touches here and there. Avast. Yes, the stink, that was it. Ab asse. Secreuit. An accepted conceit. Give it back sharper. Pirite's life for. Never thought to mention the little dents in all the silver. White mane in the coudé. Ripples gone. Pinguis Phrygiae. Hollow bosome. Naught but smelted cannonry and walnut if you ignore the rest. Not to mention my honest cure. It was a flat stone. Thought I'd lost it years ago. See if I can't garble this with a little thoroughness. Got gloop in my eye, unless that's the brain evaporating. Make me a rainbow. No, then here I am but tract of something with empty purse above the buried currents, smooth again as the in the oblivious dawn, penitent at least a bit. I think that will do mucking the galley. All these pins and needles almost make you want to jump back off the tortoise I mean the ship of immemorial ivory, go down and then what ah, balanda, this must be the capricious end to photocopying in the dictionary, hack, what, dropsey, I mean the company name, no such thing as clean linen, the false rod runneth under the surly fell of cold, cold dealing if not dissed up to prick the winding sheets, the surd slugs, adhere strictly to the damp in general, sure you were dreamin' anyhow to count on lacin' it 'round with your coils the accursed Thing and draggin' it whole from the hornblende couch or your boke of excelsior or whatever, to whop a stillborn metaphor, supposing if you weren't stuck here between the media threshing vnderstories for

what, der, interrest, it might have been worth something.
Obviously not to be transferred. Well. Throws some light
on the other fantasmagora. Had a large feeld to ere. Gotta.
N. Forth the remnant, no. Will have it all down soon, the
worst of both worlds, unless of course it is there in front
of you already on the tip, the right word, on the vanished
dustheaps of your abiding haunts. Our templum with its
oblique visitors. On solids at least you keep running over
your own horseshit footsteps, lutaceous enough to sling behind you but softly on Her heels or She'll kick you in the.
N. Ouch. A more appropriate crop for analysis. This bird
guts herself. Must be a comfort in cacology you don't get
from the other especially when it comes up this way with
all your secret assets. Still impossible apparently to loosen
the chain of. Eliza crossed her arms, eyed the fascicle of
withered banknotes on the occasional table and no doubt
glanced in my direction. Og in my froat. Ife been serfed!
Now then.

Like we agreed.

Yeah in more ways than one she said quite dryly, drop-
ping her knapsack across her wide shoulder and patting her
new plaits.

e n o w i said. wide. woops. there goes monday. open. cell. whats this made of. bumwool. in my. like a flick. a gen lick. peepers. orgen. molten. before. weaver. after. stardust. or before. nema. when theres no. no little people. and the fulness thereof. sitting in the. blank. it was over me. was in it. as if. them. in them. shiners. get wriggling. i said. no use hiding under there. blank. mother. come on chicken stop rucking under there and get up. time to get up. get up. there she is. theres my baby doll. youre getting too old for this. oo-plah. now hurry on. have my hands awfully full today with-out you playing peekaboo. go on get in there. got to spend it. hear her behind me, lift it, whoop, crack, make it again. no going back now. not for ages. not till its time again. golden.

golden. and there was dad at table already with his cup and his plate half emptied and the newspaper held up by its own starch and two well placed fingers. he bent it down. good morning my girl. it was prickly it looked so smooth from a distance. mother comes bustling up from behind. has the milk come in the dumb waiter. yes my dear and the ice. his hand over his mouth. what was that, mite. what did you say.

i love milk.

my little movie star. we will have to introduce you to the neighbours. check it, dear. so much is contaminated.

i thought id go over to plunkett street later see if i can get something fresh for lunch.

fine. we are so well connected here.

you do like it. and its so modern. they have escapes in the well like ours only in manhattan.

yes it is a new home. i feel at home. it is very close to the office. too large but we will have more family.

it needs filling out.

there will be a big family.

we sold too much from the old place. it was hard to imag-ine that it would be this big, even after seeing it. it is very fine. the tradesmen have to enter wearing suits. did you know that. they get changed in the basement. mr jones told me and now i see them, calling at the door in baroda street wearing suits.

and you are not afraid.

of what, love.

perhaps these razor gangs. of what do they call it, the dirty half mile. i mean of the people. it has seen better days. such grand houses. they say it was built as an affront and as an example. i suppose that is all behind us now.

and we live in the tallest most modern building and there is music all the time and celebrities and i hear theres a little cinema under the roof, did you hear that, a real little private cinema, and trams direct into town and just look out the window. im sure i dont know what razor gangs want with people like us. thats newspapers for you. why the streets are full of children. dont you like it here, chick.

she is a vedette. she likes the attention. everybody up and down the stairs asking for my mite. ah but you take the lift like a little queen. we are discrete.

and he puts his knuckle under my chin and i look into his pale blue eyes and i see myself.

mother is back with the milk and toast that will be warm and soft in the middle. soon we will have to start looking for proper help.

and yet i like you in this apron. you look as you did when i first met you. you do not regret your old home at all. i mean the first one.

dont you miss one.

i am a hothouse plant. i was born in a bank.

that wasnt you it was your sister.

its true i had a soft landing. somebody had to keep his brains. i was being figurative.

cmon chick hurry up and get that down.

i am going to wear something. something. blue ribbon. if you call out in the bathroom there is echo. spit in the sink. a little more water. it is because we are so bare. one part water to two parts scrubbing is mothers way. cold. dad abhorred it. called it the dip but let her do it because he misunderstood and admired all her domestic contrivances. wash my knees. light bulbs. nice little shoes. lovely with straps. so long, dad in his hat and one of those fine tailored

jackets rare these days. smell of what do you call it now, af-
tershave.

in the foyer coming out of the lift we were often caught
up by mr george. well met mesdames. what a fortunate surprise. i was just stepping out for some of that hungarian coffee if it isnt too early. ill walk with you as far as the grocers.
yes it is a charming frock. what have you been up to this morning. i have just read the most interesting news. you know
a man in america has been given a license to make radio
with pictures. like they do for the newspapers, i mean the
other way around, to send pictures, but moving. truly. what
do you think of that. imagine. you could see let alone hear
the g.p.o. clock every morning. ha ha ha. and the miniature
orchestra. ha. how miniature do you think they are. do you
think they are miniature enough to see on the radio. ha ha.
he swept off his hat and pushed the door open for us into
the blinding light. her golden dress. the sun dazzled in the
green trees across the street. i am the dame of acacias, the
alley of camellias. i am mixed up. confused, no, what do you
say, i am embarrassed. it is so beautiful here i forget myself.
what were we discussing.

all manner of souls shuffling over the bright pavement.
the tram clanged away down william street. i think. pigeons
fluttering out of the coloured awnings of shops. ah yes, radio
licenses. well it is a relief you will be able to buy them now
free range. listen in on what you want, no need for licenses. thanks to that droll englishman and his comic opera.
we are all in the good ship el publico nest pas. and the really fantastic thing is you can choose to listen to the chan-
nel with advertisements, which i find highly anglo saxon
and gratifying. very informative and often amusing. well i
leave you here and wish you a good day. do not stay out too
long it is going to be frightfully hot. i think perhaps later
i will take a plunge in the dom. see the ships. they come from
all over the world now. they are laden with things for you
my little one. have you ever seen them dock with all their
tiny flags flying, the swollen rusty hulls and the ropes pulling them in. many are your own, you know. and the longest

digital wharf in the world. if you dont mind you are making your mark, i say truly you are. do you remember when they made their first annual haul. it was not so long ago they went out packed with wheat and wool and came back from the factories full of wind up gramophones and edison records. cest un vrai conte. if only you were on garden island madame the day they sailed to fight the boers. in flammam iugulant pecudes. belle fin fait. pas des hommes. hats in the air, your upright faces on either side, such, how to say, bully. do you know how many changed their name to king on the first fleet. indeed it is the century of the new nations. you were there. well. at that time, i did not have the pleasure.

you dont believe it is really dangerous down this way do you mr george.

ah no, not for the likes of you. it is the reputation makes problems. they should have renamed the place twenty three years ago when they had the chance. in your herald it said, the old name, with its multitudinous vowels, has become synonymous with evil repute, and the modern resident craves for the final effacement of both with one pass of the sponge across the slate. but that is the past. thanks to god there is more than one newspaper, and that they did not call it palmersham! o woolloomoolethal no longer! o woolloomoolewd never more! when i give up the ghost, all the heavenly host i shall lead to your beautiful shore. on the woolloomoolittoral, fanned by the woolloomoolibertine breeze (bringing landlords who languish surcease from their anguish) well drink to the woolloomoolees; well be the woolloomoolucrative lodgers in woolloomooluxury vast, an eternitys stories shall tell of your glories to the infinite woolloomoolast! that was the bulletin. disgusting really, what you call funnies.

but we could not exactly say we were in woollamoola could we.

you wont get any letters addressed to queens cross. the post dont know it yet. better say you are in potts point.

but today, mr george, would you say it is safe. you understand my asking. five bullets in the back in darlinghurst.

if you believe me the runners around here, they are just the showoffs.

i hope you arent speaking from too close an acquaintance, i mean for your own sake.

ah it is what one knows in general. it is what counts. i say the worst will blow over sooner or later.

we bought the vegetables at lo blancos so that we could get our hands on them first and make sure that they were good. crammed into those little shops with the windows under the awnings you could get flour from a barrel and sugar from a vat and bon ami with the chicken that said it hasnt scratched yet and old dutch cleanser with a scuttling woman with no face on the label and cod liver oil and castor oil and heenzo for coughs and colds and dr morses indian root pills and woods peppermint compound and treacle and stove polish and knife powder and oatmeal and kerosene. we did not go down to the water for fish that day. there were nets strung over the balconies of the town houses and men and women mending them in their shirtsleeves, calling out to one another.

where do they come from.

they have run away from mussolini.

when we get back to kingsclere owen has the doors open and is polishing the door handles. all of it is new then, the wide rooms, the soft smell of the place, the sound of our things dull on the new carpets, the days passing through the bay windows. that bygone parade of tilting furniture. it gets old, it settles. down we go. first thing i did on arrival was eat a watermelon. lovely insipid fruit. i spat the pips into dads rusty palm. he had been at the prow all morning with his hands on the railing. because he was nervous he put them in his pocket though we were standing at the edge of the wharf where the water lapped the trash around the pylons. the crowd and the gulls swarmed above. dad gripped me by the blouse. mother held him by his waist. the sun streamed down on us. we all sway in the flat. why is the ground so stiff i think i asked. dad said because you are still rocking with the boat. so am I. our things arrive. odd coming out of boxes into the light of the flat. dads old paintings, a chair put back together with copper wire, porcelain stuffed with newspapers. highland cattle. i want to move them myself, feel something familiar, but mother takes charge of handling the furniture. she arranges it as best she can though afterwards she will look at the room and say something is not right. so she lays things out reluctantly at first. dad fills the place faster than she does. he buys an upright piano and they play for his friends, sing paddlin madelin home and no, no nanette. mother makes friends with the girl opposite and they sit and chat in the olive chairs until dad rises in the elevator in the evening. on friday mother roasts a bird and people are invited to eat. afterwards miss fox plays the piano and dad sings. because i cant drink the liquor he gives me a shilling from his pocket. i ask him what has he done with the watermelon seeds. thats what they were, your watermelon seeds! why i threw them out the window. happily he slaps the piano lid and there is laughter round the living room. when my light goes out i count the unfamiliar cars that roll below the window. interruptions in the luminous bar beneath the door intrude upon the gloom and slip away. from your dust. there is music playing on another floor, a record going round, tinkle of sherry glasses. a stifled what. i press my face to the cold dark glass and it gives back my face and the city lights. soft toys are consoling, i can keep a cats tail in my crack till dawn.

and then i have been to the saturday matinee at the rialto

or one of them. it would get so stinking warm. all those boys
hollering in the dark, and if the reel snapped, why the up-
roar it was enough to burst your. then the stamping and all
of them counting together, one big rising pack chanting and
stamping till it got spliced and whoosh there was the pretty
girl again wrapped up on the tracks. sucking acid drops after
interval. some blew up paper bags and burst them and the
worst threw bungers. we had buttered crumpets and strawberry ice cream soda for sixpence at bright lights near the
strand arcade afterwards and mother would say i think perhaps we will not do that again.

   dad was in the living room playing backgammon with mr
george when we got home and miss fox was there and mrs
rich and mr harwood, and mrs pickburn, perhaps, and langland and john busby. where have you been ma ptite.

   mother suggests a boy threw rotten egg gas in the second
half and it was a shame. it was after all someones son.

   that sullivan is an enterprising devil mr harwood said,
scratching the back of his neck and rolling his right foot to
let a little air in.

   *o*sullivan, said langland. he lost that getting off the boat
in london. probably hoped no one else picked it up too. he
went to school at the marist brothers you know. was there
with him. theyre a part of st marys, maam, just here in the
loo. now where did he get a wild idea like that i dont know.

   peter felix, said mr george. checkmate, no, pardon, i win.
do you remember peter felix. i believe he fought here in the
state heavyweight championship in o nine. he dressed himself head to toe in black. it was a sort of stocking i suppose.
gave me a real fright. he terrified all the children. truly, you
dont believe me. cozens spencer told me, you know cozens
spencer who built the rushcutters bay studios, filmed jack
johnson knock tommy burns teeth out, you remember *that*.
well he told me crazy pat got the idea watching peter felix.
i dont say. in any case that is what i heard. you dont have to
believe me.

   im sure i dont know where a wild idea like that comes
from.

how are you liking your new home mrs rose.

i was just saying to peter this morning how lovely i find it. its a wonderful building, even quite beyond my expectations. we were so fortunate mr alberts friends happened to leave when they did, i really dont know a place in town id rather be.

ah but can you sing and dance like franks friends.

if you please, madame riche, an alto like mr roses is not to be found every day among the non professional classes. a command of feeling that, well, if you dont mind, for a banker.

mr george.

je marrete la. oh. he struck his forehead. i was almost going to leave it behind incognito. listen, ma puce, guess what, i have prepared a little surprise. do you want to know what it is. can you guess where i have hid it. mon grand drageoir. theres something in there with your name on it.

you are not to touch it now, chick.

but i want to see her face.

she has just had crumpets and strawberry ice cream.

what is it.

you know perfeclty well.

it is only the good old cacao like mum makes.

what did you say.

a little sweetened. they are only her what do you call them. she will get a new set in any case. all the better to see candy with.

may i ask how you found the apartment.

my wife. word of mouth. she has her associates here longer than i have.

yes of course, many of the tenants at the astor are country folk. perhaps youve met my ruby.

im sorry to say i havent, mrs rich. it was my brother in fact who put us on to it. hes known the alberts for some time.

how nice. im sure the character of host suits the alberts terribly well. i can hardly bring myself to call them landlords. have you been up to the little cinema yet. well, the next soiree you are in for a treat. and the company needless to say is divine. no stink bombs up there i can assure you.

they buy into the astor dont they. one takes shares. is it like that here. it seems a very efficient way of conducting the business. what do you say, mr george, its the air of the times. that was quite an end to the year, mr rose. have you noticed how the domestic interior is beginning to take cues from industry. no more fitted carpets. i could only wish they had shops on the lower floors as they do below the temperance and general insurance company apartments. fitzgerald had a fine idea but one has to know when to be an integralist, no mr rose. to my mind it would have been a happier use of the street level property in an area like this, any chance to open it up on rational principles. the townhouses appear mercifully on their way to falling down by their own volition. it was quite inspired of albert to buy up this place. he told me he first considered it when he read an article more than a decade ago called the profit possibilities of tall buildings, and now, well, it has to be seen to be believed, but there are more projects in the pipeline for this year than there have ever been. the prospect certainly looks clear. i mean with the price of primary products, and the foreign loans. now the obstacles to a central bank have toppled. the department stores are extending credit to the working class. it does look promising doesnt it, i mean, and it is stable.

as long as we stay on gold.

gold! with a money market this tight and the price of wool in this house itll be wealth riding on the

dad smiled at mr harwood who had been bending towards his ear, though mr harwood stopped short and said they havent been in the fires have they. no said dad and ran his hand over the top of his mouth and put his other on my shoulder and said shall we see if we can fit on the balcony, a breeze seems to be coming on and i think these ladies might enjoy the relief of our company a moment. you two have had quite an excursion for such a scorcher.

naturally i snuck into the hall and pushed up the lid of the hallstand and stuck my head in and poked around until i found the box of californian chocolates. is that right. i may be jumping ahead. they came in a lovely large cedar box. they were called starck chocolates and had the shape of umbrellas and cars and coins and cigarettes. the umbrellas had little plastic handles. mother who was coming back in from having laid on the kettle grabbed me by the back of the neck and beat me quite savagely with the first rod she could get her hand on. later the heat really broke up and there was an electrical storm. that was the year the biggest hailstone fell in potter, nebraska. there were electrical storms in those days. we used to put away all the silver and cover the mirrors with sheets. sometimes there was a fireball, which was really a luminous ball that appeared where the lightning was going to strike and travelled slowly in a horizontal line with a hissing noise and then exploded but there was no fireball that time.

for a while on the days mother went out alone i was minded by miss fox. look she would say faking to draw an egg from behind my ear. she cracked it into a bowl. from the bench where i sat i tip the milk jar until i am satisfied. what need all this cookery. the smell of sulphur and a piece of butter frothing in the pan can still recall to me those evenings. scent the persistent reminiscent. her omelettes were hell but you have to be bought up on something.

miss fox was attending chartres business college on liverpool street, opposite hyde park. we went walking there sometimes after lunch. we fed the birds. saw shapes in the clouds. the clouds have shapes. miss fox sees animals. i see clouds. animals. what motion. her devergondage. look she says, theres one just like your monkey. get a taste for higher things. but ice cream cone and cathedral must be kept separate. most times after eating she just laid on the bench a sheet of paper with a grid drawn on it that had irregular sides like the periodic table and in each square a letter or a punctuation mark. i watched the white arcs of her index fingers fly up and down on the tables sometimes her hands would stop and fall in her lap and she would frown for a moment at the pummelled sheet then begin again. her cheek quivered when the fingers hit home. your hands she told me are machines, and finer calibrated than any typewriter. all it takes is to train them up to the capacity of a typewriter. i dont have one so i practice on this.

how will you know.

know what, that im at capacity. i wont till i try on the machine. when it jams ill know ive exceeded it. wouldnt that be something, to type impossibly. im rather slow now and make mistakes. she takes to it.

what are you typing i ask. robinson crusoe she says.

wybalenna. she played the piano just as punctually. now i could follow a a b a but i couldnt wrangle anything yet from o t o f t h a c o u n t damn. excuse me. you wont repeat that to your mother. other times we went walking in the park but that isnt worth telling you about.

mother will say the pilot is coming to tea and until he does i cant sit still. i watch her kid shoes back and forth over the carpet resentfully, as if she were keeping time with her steps, keeping the pilot from coming. when he does he brushes his mouth over mothers cheek and shakes the hand dad has unwound from his pipe and newspaper. there may be others to whom to say hello, aunt constance on the sofa, salting or langley, miss fox. *and where* he will say and i catch my breath up. he will begin beneath the sofa, then the coffee table and the olive armchairs and in the space between the maple paws of the dresser, rifle in the coats, add his, squint in the china cabinet. it does not take long. what i wish he would do is look everywhere, open the oven, lift the stuff on the beds. but i dont dare leave the living room and if im behind the curtains he finds me and same for the dog basket. he grabs me hard beneath the armpits and swings me up. no there was no dog now i think about it say the laundry basket.

the rest is disappointing. he drops one leg on the other and the words run over his lip like the evening news, crackling deafly on to anyone. he is bored. his glaucus pricks would not be here. iunkes of the see. his photo was in the newspaper for flying i dont remember where. very fast, or so it seemed at the time. those were the real high flying days with parer and mcintosh and goble and macintyre and ross and keith and kingsford smith and harry hawker all making records and breaking them and barnstorming and the rest of course it was pretty much a boys game. phyllis arnot got a license later but she never used it. uncle jim was a fanatic and didnt think people really got it. he would never have been given a license these days. dad asked about his following. to tell you the truth peter, many people still dont see it for what it is i bet you dont even remember william hart. why when lindbergh left roosevelt field for paris last year most of the americans were too busy watching their stocks rise to notice, if you dont mind my saying.

not at all, jim. and you might thank them for it too. you need someone to keep your head in the clouds. your gypsy moths wont fly without a turn over, ha.

and so on.

do you remember when cobbam had that trouble coming over here wasnt that frightening, all those mixed up messages coming out of where on earth was it i believe rangoon. couldnt find him. and before that when the engine blew out and his poor copilot bleeding into his handkerchief and none of us here could make head or tail of it. elliott is dead. elliott is not expected to live. we gave him such a party when he touched down. you ever have dangerous trouble jim.

no rotten luck yet he said tapping the woolly towel on his head. then i havent taken any real risks. once. well. but it was nothing hardly mushing. lost my bearings over java one time because. i couldnt. make out, i couldnt see.

ash plume.

no it was, fine. had been. just couldnt seem to get above the. wasnt a shadow anywhere. like turning up in the stratopause. not that it would be like that.

ive seen the hyaline the colour of his eyes. they are like mouldy mirrors, brilliant in spots. he cant find his tongue. he held up his hands. took them right off the wheel and theyre all eaten around by. i. only lasted a moment. he coughed. darn i dont know how to say it so it doesnt sound silly. inside you it just sinks all of a sudden. you get. he made a vertical movement. if it wasnt for the plane thered be nothing between and a few thousand feet and then actually the strange thing is you forget for a moment to worry about the mountain as if. es uns nur so scheint. it can be a horrible feeling weather. of course you know well enough where you are and suddenly youre quite lost breathes mother from the window where she leans her shoulders on the glass. it is ravelled with water. outside the rain falls before the shop windows and in the beams of the cars. a hush fills the room. aunt constance moans. i think i can imagine it and shut my eyes. frankly the pilot is best when lifting me so the air comes up. he smells of leather standing at the doorway dressed to leave, when he pats my head through a shining glove and winks his yellow teeth at the room for goodbye. all nerves says aunt constance when he has gone. it was like an electrical current in the sofa. did he marry that girl. not for this world says dad from behind the newspaper. he is in the habit of reading columns aloud. tragedy at stalybridge. panic broke out among the crowd of spectators. mr howard carter has discovered a jar containing the kings viscera in an antechamber to tutankamens tomb. horrible day says langley, they wont be racing. mother is humming something from the radio without realising it. i am tapping my foot because i cant wait to fart, but now why wait, i am not so well brung up. could be the age.

then just when i have decided to give up mother suddenly gets it into her head to take me shopping. you have no idea what the department stores were like then they were what we called a true outing. from king street all the way up and down to broadway. most are gone now. mcdowells, david jones, beard watson, f. lassetter, w. w. campbell, r. h. gordon, bebarfields, morley johnson, the a. c. o., a. hall, anthony hordens, j. a. booth, simpson lee, marcus clark, grace bros. we caught the tram down william street past the blind society and yee chongs laundry with the lux and lifebouy and sunbeam cleanser and changed for anthony hordens palace emporium on brickfield hill. lease destroy on alighting. now that was a really splendid place, with floors and floors and tearooms and restrooms and phone booths and a post office and even a branch of the commonwealth bank which mother was naturally pleased about. there were polished marble floors and embossed steel ceilings produced and finished in hordens own factories. the tram stopped on george street in front of the central tower with the oak tree logo. While I Live Ill Grow. look, chick.

mother lifted me off the step and pushed me up between the bustling skirts to the huge windows. my the models are getting frighteningly real. i wonder if you can get a lippie like that inside. enchanting. come on now, you arent going to make it impossible to unstick you are you.

i could not see any people. i could see only fountains and rock grottoes and hundreds of little green and gold trees.

chick, darling, get moving. whats the matter with you.

in the haby department an attendant suggested rosebud or swansdown trimming for mothers undergarments but mother just wanted to buy some rhinestones for embroidery and two pairs of holeproof shear loveliness and one pair of black magic. that woman was trying to sell the clothes off her back. i remember i sifted through the buttons while i waited and found a tortoiseshell heart with a thin gold arrow through for the clip i wanted to have a closer look at, maybe later, when someone said get your fat little hands out of there and gave me such a scare it disappeared forever. you could get mohair boot laces and aero silk and nainsook dress shields and there were ribbons getting wider and wider in velvet and crepe de chine and moire and lace.

after that we were wafted up a level on convergent waves of atkinsons californian poppy and colgates cashmere bouquet and fauldings lavender water musk and black narcisse and the slightly clogging scent of cheramy joli soir face powder which an officious attendant held beneath a puff ball somewhere ready for application behind a uniaxial backlog of cheramy pour le theatre. cut out without hands. throughout the whole wide world the love of music is inherent. it is a birthright. to withhold music from the kiddies is to deprive them of an influence that has much to do in the shaping of their destinies. so give them music. but instead of setting them off upon the heart breaking path of musical tuition, install a player piano, and so enable the veriest toddler to immediately produce music of the most finished kind. the attendants were mostly lovely. except for one woman who seemed to be looking at you sideways but mother said she didnt work there. in the hat department we bought a hemp straw two-tone hat with an ottoman ribbon. this lady knows what she wants said the hat attendant.

i have the catalogue on me.

we bought a pair of marshall shoes with cushion heels and a velour coat for me with a tailored collar and smart fawn pockets. youll have to put that away chick till youre cold. then in the glove department mother saw a pair of suede lisle petal gauntlet gloves and the girl brought them over and opened the fingers with a pair of tongs and shook powder inside and sprinkled a little on mothers hands and gently worked the fingers onto them. i think theyll suit me fine. in chamois or grey, madame. we chose between a brown python and a crocodile clutch bag and then i had a glass of lemonade in the rooftop tea garden.

chick, what is the matter. why are you holding your ear. why youve been perfectly distracted since we got in here, i hope you arent feeling unwell darling.

it was cool up there under the palm fronds with the lemonade sparkling in the tall glass the waiter carried over on a platter and put down on the wrought iron table in front of you with a soft clink. and the children playing at the edge of the fountain and their frocks were blinding out there in the sun. i think i would have liked to have known them. to borrow. to begin. t. dad and mother were keeping me back from school and mother wasnt one particularly for making introductions to strange children. i dont think she ever really adjusted to the city. it was the perfect scene for someone to walk in on you but we never saw anyone we knew. in the furniture departments those days you could buy a complete home set for a hundred and forty three pounds.

we got the hat and the coat delivered and mother carried the dress home and the haberdashery and the gloves in the python bag. we went to the tram stop on elizabeth street with the black and white destination sign that said wooll'mooloo on a diagonal and the tram turned at park street and branched at college. some have disappeared now. faucet lane, corfu street, malta place, burrahpone street. one time a man from the fire underwriters society showed me a map where you could see right into the stairwells of the buildings and their wooden floors and dormer windows and open joists and brass railings and when a building was knocked down or a new street put in they drew that part again on a new piece of paper and glued it onto the map. i think it was a man, let it be a man it may as well be. mother changed into her new dress before dad came home. it was a rayosil chine frock with a pleated frill scalloped edge and pleats partly stitched down and a belt. can i eer forget thee. what do you think she said as she met him in the corridor and made a curtsey. its stil de grain.

dad wrinkled his face and said ja that it is.

but the taste was infectious. have a look at this. you know we must get one sooner or later. yes, an eight day is good. i like the golden rod but i dont think much of the sound of imitation marble, if only we could have it in something mottled, like myrtle. what is an inveroid dial.

youre being difficult on purpose.

well you know how i like to come home from the office and be free of it for an evening. it is a very mild eccentricity you could bear with it while you can. we each have our own after all and the little one doesnt notice.

dad and mother were going to the theatre that night so mother called on miss fox. later we were surprised by an invitation to a party on spec at the misses blomfields. they were expecting to find my parents in but miss fox said why not we could probably go down for a little while. never seen

so many people in one room. they laughed and talked softly
then loudly and smoked so much the room is full of it. some
are sitting on the furniture and leaning over one other and
many are dancing. piano players are everywhere. i remember the rhythm in the floor. i sit trussed on the sofa with
miss fox who fiddles with our clothes and eyes the girls from
the heels up. some people beside us have been to the zoo. i
have never been to the zoo. grounds are marvellous. ashton
park trust. the council got it back and pulled up the scrub.
there we go. click clack. if the analgesics dont work you
can put your head between your knees and rock. what did
you say. i saw a civet have you ever even heard of a civet.
a young man on the telephone must have been important back then saying, he would have swallowed his own
pearls. but he said he was that parched, and a wreck, you
know, one tried to hide his up a, up a cimarron in waiting
but when she put her leg out for the doomed longboat the
sea took her own back, no diamonds, not their place. dont
know, havent seen him for months, stuck his finger in some
babblerie or other. yes married, the bastard. someone sings
a song and i fall halfway asleep in the bony cavity of my
minders lap. i can hear it still, through that girls tympanum,
like a dived duck. my dove mother called me. i wake in the
arms of the pilot as he lifts me in the muffled dark of the
early morning. we go in the lift and when we turn on the
landing mother is standing in the doorway in her evening
gown and she holds out her hands towards me. well constance i think she must have missed most of it. i left her
minder gently snoring.

mother is not angry we went to the party but i think she
was a little cross she missed it. it was the first one since
we got here. in the afternoon miss fox takes tea at the flat
and mother tells her how smart the assistants at horderns
looked and that there may be something in it for miss fox.
well, in fact, its funny you should mention it. a friend of
mine from chartres has been doing the berlei demonstra-
tions. they model the corsets while typing. well no naturally
i wasnt considering that but the other night she took me

along to a business girls session of the seeker after beauty
or the cilice of steel at the minerva, which is quite clever
with a girl at the end dressed as a fairy who waves her wand
around until another girl wearing the latest corset of course
jumps out of a cauldron. i suppose it *was* quite silly. yes it is
a serious topic at least i know a badly fitted corset can give
you. a lady needs to be aware of these things. in any case i
met a man who hires for mark foys and theyre giving me
a trial next week. itll be full time if they keep me on i can
quit typing school. that was the end of miss fox.

i am sure it was the tasmanian nightingale. its funny says
mother, you never hear them doing what theyre supposed
to do. its the insulation, said mr george beating the floor
with his foot. horesehair. other places have coal, which is
loony if you think about it. good thing we have all those
ladders in the courtyard. dad looks through the window in
the newspaper. wireless telephony between paris and new
york will be inaugurated tomorrow.

pass me that big piece there chick.

dew dew dewy day. dust storm at moorook on the river
murray. lamps were lit at noon. with the special ivory tips
no tobacco can pass your lips also cork tipped and plain.
caused a fire in the show window of a jewellery establishment in sydney. sunlight soap. mincemeat. shredded in-
cense. jar of stem ginger. jordan almonds. ca. em. pudding
raisins. currants. californian prunes. ham pate. port wine.
candied lemon peel. rosa apricots in heavy syrup. thats it,

pass it here will you. careful of the scissors.

mr george has graciously agreed to watch me for the afternoon. did you write to the people on bourke lane, peter. i did and i telephoned and apparently it never got there. we are only a stones throw away. a thing like that i find irritating. it is not as if they have to go through london anymore, or even the moons of jupiter. detur optima should have done it, no.

i have never known another man to enjoy terrorising his family with his macaronic education.

be reasonable. were they in sands.

well anyway the answer is negative. we will have to look somewhere else. but mr rose you know there are two bourke lanes in the same place no less. the red rose down in queensland. oh my where did you get that one ma ptite. some of these look hardly hygienic. be good. bye mite. dad wears a cream tussor sport style suit with hip pockets. he has a red tie which he always gets right. unlike me. but they didnt make ties the other way so it must have been. circus propando. they are going to a benefit concert or the beach or somewhere, i dont know, maybe they just go down to the basement. hm. where. we scroll through our nice murphy bakelite radio with the mottled blue paper dial and the hand ruled frequencies. mr george likes to call out the listings. bondi beach concert band. weather. miss louise homfrey the lady baritone. ha ha ha. whats on the theosophical station. miss ethel dale. miss dorothy toppin. player piano. miss gladys hart. no seriously my little one perhaps we ought to let it slide this time. indeed, at horderns. that is interesting. and did you like it. no it is not a real palace. clever sam horden got the idea from the exhibition building in prince alfred park where they had to move shop after the old place burned down the same year sandhills cemetery was resumed for the railway. you know that could have been the place your grandparents met, i mean your mothers father and your fathers father. you see you announced your international exhibition a little prematurely and there were ten thousand pounds missing in the budget so they conside-

red buying annexes from the exposition universelle to add
to the building in prince alfred park but in the end they rallied parliament and there was a subscription and the governor surrendered his private park in the domain, bref by the
time the foundation stone in melbourne had been laid they
were set to build a new one. what an age. they will be making a committee soon as they have for the olympics, so that
there cannot be too many at once, but back then anyone
could put an announcement in three languages in his bag
and get a ship to paris and say he was having an international exhibition. of course everyone was meeting everyone at
an international exhibition and it was, what was it, a very
good place to be young. never mind envelope machines.
why your own ushered in not just the giant steam shovel
but the very steam train, passenger lifts to push up buildings like pith in the coming epoch and apparently the first
cold boxes for meat export, though i dont believe that can
be right. i was a young man myself at the grand palais and
made a very great many future connections and saw wonderful things, the first moving staircase, the inclined elevator. there is a spiral in the underground i tell you they are
coming where you least expect them. they are already in
department stores all over the world. of the garden palace
nothing remains. the ashes fell on the harbour and woolloomooloo and even the houses up here on potts point, the
red hot roof iron sizzling into elizabeth bay. windowpanes
cracked in macquarie street. the sky lit up in a fantastic
gamut of carmine and yellow and blue and green flames. set
in the cloud indeed. inficiunt coguntque suo fluitare colore.
a graphite elephant having crashed through the floor and
fallen sixteen feet in the furnace came out miraculously un-
scathed. that was where your grandparents met. one sunny
day on the lawn among the freshly planted flowers, looking
out across the free public library and the treasury and sydney cove with the ships from london riding anchor and the
stately forests of the north shore and the church spires and
the fortifications at south head. or before the triumphal arch
of webb and sons crystal glass trophy, or the gilt obelisk rep-

resenting the gold export of new zealand or the pyramidal tin trophy of queensland or the superstructure for the biscuits of messrs swallow and ariell of melbourne or the pilasters of the red cross preserving co., or the immense coil of steel rails from the societe cocherill in belgium, or the three large bells from the foundry of messrs c. voss and sons, steltin, or eighty four feet under the pale blue gildstarred dome, whether in the glow of its hanging lamp or clerestory or stained glass, in the shadow of marshall woods colossal bronze statue of queen victoria or in the french court between the tapestries from gobelins and beauvais and the sevres vases or down fig tree avenue at the turkish bazaar or the japanese tea house or the australian dairy where one could take a glass of cold, fresh milk for a penny or emersons oyster saloon or the maori house or the fijian house or the concrete cottage or the austrian hungarian beer and wine tasting hall or any other likely place. in the end, in fact, it was built thanks to rush money. but your grandparents had other ideas. three thousand pounds down and two thousand acres to add to the family homestead. there had been a change of hands. new blood. your fathers father was to be what is called the sleeping partner. perhaps they met at the grand opening somewhere on the illustrious banks listening to the seven hundred and ninety musicians deliver henry kendalls cantata in four parts. songs of morning with your breath sing the darkness now to death — radiant river, beaming bay, fair as summer shine to-day — flying torrent, falling slope, wear the face as bright as hope — wind and woodland, hill and sea, lift your voices — sing for glee! greet the guests your fame has won — put your brightest garments on. lo, they come — the lords unknown, sons of peace, from every zone! see above our waves unfurled all the flags of all the world! north and south and west and east gather in to grace your feast. shining nations! let them see how like england we can be. mighty nations! let them view sons of generous sires in you. then the tenor a little flat, by the days that sound afar, sound, and shine like star by star; by the grand old years aflame with the fires of englands fame heirs of those who fought for right when the worlds arrayed face was white—meet these guests your fortune sends, as your fathers met their friends, let the beauty of your race, glow like morning in your face. and the bass a little sharp on the upper notes, where now a radiant city stands, the dark oak used to wave, the elfin harp of lonely lands above the wild mans grave, through windless woods, one clear, sweet stream, stole like the river of a dream, a hundred years ago. and the alto with a mellow volume to fill the room, upon the hills that blaze to-day with splendid dome and spire, the naked hunter tracked his prey, and slumbered by his fire. within the sound of shipless seas the wild rose used to blow about the feet of royal trees, a hundred years ago. and then miss moon the brilliant soprano, ah! haply on some mossy slope, against the shining ships, in those old days the aged hope sat down with folded wings; perhaps she touched in dreams sublime, in glory and in glow, the skirts of this resplendent time, a hundred years ago. a gracious morning on the hills of wet, and cold, and mist, her glittering feet has set; the life and heat of light have chased away australias dark mysterious yesterday. a great, glad glory now flows down and shines on gold green lands where waved funeral pines. and hence a fair dream goes before our gaze, and lifts the skirts of the hereafter days; and sees afar, as dreams alone can see, the splendid marvel of the years to be. and from the american gallery on the right and the english gallery on the left, and from every place between, from the dais to the organ on the gallery floor, from the pianists up the ascending tiers of the orchestra and the soloists and the childrens choir, the people rose to applaud, and maestro giorzia bowed again and again from his elevated little shielded stage festooned in flags and foliage. there was an encore. the australasian lauded the spectacle of the anglo-saxon race striking their roots deep, and carrying their growth and blossom high and luxuriant on the shores of a vast continent only reclaimed from desolation, solitude, and barbarism, within the memories of our fathers. trust me i have a head full of music. for piloubet read poitevin, at holland and green insert commended, for batson and brewer read balstone and brewer, for book and collings read booth and collings, for simpson and co., h. read simpson and co. l., for ragasaki read nagasaki, for professor a. c. read t. t., for eleventh read tenth of november, transfer exhibit of n.s.w. government astronomer from three hundred and eighty six to three hundred and ninety nine, for vermincelli read vermicelli, for givolamo read girolamo, for ungaru read ungarn, for reihms maine read marne, for ehrenfried bothers read brothers.

wed gone down to the water because mr george said i could see the city of palermo but i couldnt so he bought me a bundle of hot chips and we sat among the seagulls. what whiffs. bosis. organs need the help of a. m. rexonola no. 1 in golden or mission oak. centurion phono-radio. is. to. the rich round volume of sound which issues from bebarphone speaks volumes for the genius of the designers of its throat-like sound box. the specially-selected timber used is of the type used in high-grade violins to prevent tonal vibrations and ensure purity of tone. powerful worm drive motor of finest construction. tapered swan-neck tone arm. nickel plated. covered with plush. aeolian vocalian records. s.

you are getting through them fast.

turkish patrol. the mad major. a cup of coffee a sandwich and you. say mister have you seen rosies sister. bye-bye blackbird. cecilia. well never know. the world. pigs guts. throw that away and lets get you washed up. we went hand in hand over the ridge of challis steps. yes, it is like the travelling historian leroy beaulieu said of the eucalyptus globulus. la rapidite de sa croissance en fait par excellence larbre des pays neufs, le seul qui puisse selever aussi vite quune ville comme san francisco ou johannesburg. and the only tree who sheds its own pyre. every blome down. so many of the old great houses have been consumed. cheverelis for david jones and dowlings own brougham lodge and goderich lodge are gone, and sterling cottage is gone, and kellet house or bona vista is as impalpable now as mortimer lewis. w. e. sparke blew up in his bath in maranamah and expired in the bath at mona and you have nothing to tell for it. greenknowe was once the name for the magnificent but faded home of walter lamb and s. k. salting of flower, salting and co. gone are orwell house and roslyn hall with the crystal door handles and the turkey carpets and the polished cedar. even the remaining become mere shells after evacuation, which would be natural enough if not for an ardour whose readiness to let them crumble or be flattened imposes on one a repeated sense of lost tableaux. ah but indeed you must build. monstrous as it is the scenes must pass. tusculum is there but william long the wine and spirit merchant and those of his aspirant family sleeping with policemans rattles under their pillows are in eternal rest. no more the first sisters of tarmons who came in a whale battered ship from ireland hauling an iron black christ. and the coleman sisters have gone from the coach house at the gates of fairhaven, and nothing will bring back the sound of the vaudeville companies clatterring up victoria street in charabancs bound for picnics in the bush, or the sight of mrs hall driving her carriage down macleay street waving her arms as if she were swimming.

bushells. yass two miles. and the morning glory
flowing through the fences. i sit on mothers lap and looked
out the window. her legs shifted under me on the pea green
seat and she fanned us together with the timetable. dad plays
with the rim of his hat and chews his bottom lip. he had heavy
bags under his eyes after a late night at the office. listen,
mother murmurs at him. watch you dont say hell before my
mother.

    constance.

    try to say cunt or something else she doesnt know what
it means.

    really, love

    i know but when youre tired. just be vigilant.

    these trains are getting very modern. can you believe
it has been so long. do you think gregory is still driving
around in that trap.

    im sure theyll be the last in the district to buy a motor-
car. dr thane had the first one and he used to have to drive
up link hill in reverse. telephone poles flickering through
an eyelash forest under their dipping crests. shards of light.
shake it chick, were here. yass was connected to the state

railway line in eighteen ninety two by the shortest platform
in the world. when we got down there on the dusty slope
beyond the gabled eaves was grandfather astride his buggy with the reins over one hand waving. i go to meet him
with mother while dad gets the luggage. grandfather is already manoeuvring towards the station. he was a tall man,
with the cuffs folded and his face moving in and out of the
shadow of his hat. he turned his head rapidly on his straight
neck, his arm was long and steady. mother held my hand as
he brought the buggy in. hello papa.

connie. he reached out with one had towards her cheek
and she jumped off the steps onto the buggy and put her arms
around his neck. connie did you make this. it got bigger.

come and say hello to grandfather chick. she helped me
over the gap and grandfather bent down and said she looks
like *me* and laughed until dad got over to our side of the station with the suitcases. we rode the rest of comur street and
over the river where some turtles were basking on a rock
and the bank rolled up into folds of wild grass and brittle
gum and broadleaved peppermint. dad sat with grandfather
and smoked his pipe while mother pointed in her approx-
imate way to the scenery and talked about her childhood.
hills hills hills. this is the place she said lying back in the seat
and breathing deep. if you ever get sick of the city chick.

grandmother weil was waiting for us in front of the big
old stone house. she took the suitcases from dads hands and
put them down beside herself and called up to mother as
she got out. the little one can take your old room constance
and you and peter will have the annex. mother kissed
grandmother weil on the cheek and said come and see her.
grandmother weil had one eye. she took me in both hands
and kissed me smack on the forehead. welcome to alfalfa
glades. its overdue. we walked between the yellow crocus
borders of the flower beds to a verandah grown over with
wisteria and in between a pair of french doors to the drawing room. there was a young man there i never worked out
exactly who he was who took my bag and disappeared down
a corridor over a layer of cowhides getting duller towards

invisible. a grandfather clock ticked in the empty space. i turned back and took hold of mothers skirt. all right well unpack my suitcase first.

that night we had dinner before the sun went down, then grandfather lit the lamps. they got electricity in town last year he said, but old mrs weil thinks we get by fine as it is and so we do. he winked at her then he turned to me and said what age have you now.

less than she ought to, poor mite. its a leap year.

so it is. well that is unlucky. i hope that isnt the reason youre keeping her back.

oh no laughed dad. we arent superstitious. he leaned over in the semi dark and patted my head. shell be ready in a year she just needs prompting. grandmother weil finished clearing the plates then we all went out ing and sat on the verandah. did you ever see so many stars, chick. it is very quiet in the country. nothing but natural sounds. dad blinked through a cloud of lavender smoke. the pastor, said grandmother weil, is coming on wednesday. mother sighed and brushed me behind the head with her hand. that was a sublime meal, mrs weil, dad yawned, sinking lower in his seat. in the oblique shadow of the lamp i saw his eyes held shut. tell me is that over there orions belt.

in the morning i went in the buggy with grandfather to see the lambs. sulky it was called a sulky. i liked to ride with grandfather and feel the ground rattling away beneath us, the clumps of earth exploding under wheels but i didnt think much of the sheep not even the little ones. he showed me how to climb between the barbed wire fences. we gave hay to the horse, a piebald with a tongue like sandpaper and the hot breath rushing over your hands and the lips curled back and the teeth careful. keep your fingers flat. i washed my hands in a basin on the verandah and dried them with the towel hanging on the nail above. then grandfather drove to the post office for the bread. grandmother weil had been out before anyone else to milk the cow and feed the chickens and the pigs. mother was pushing her hair into place with hairpins in her mouth and dad was getting wood for the kitchen stove. mother wore an apron over her dressing gown. well how do you like our way of life, chick. nothing but hard work all day.

indeed you never took to it connie.

wouldnt even stand for maroubra said dad letting an armful of wooden blocks tumble down beside the stove. he wiped his hands on his thighs and took her waist. no said mother and laughed. all those snakes.

grandmother weil looked at me with her one eye. never thought id raise a girl for the city. i did it very well im sure i dont know how. she put down her hands flat on the table. come here and help your grandmother cut these scones. it was hot in the kitchen with the stove going, though it was a big room, with an old brick stove and iron kettles and saucepans hanging on the hooks. the kitchen and the storeroom and the mens dining room and the laundry and the wood shed were separated from the house by a runway of paving stones and in the shade of the creepers and the grapevines there were waterbags and a drip safe. there was a big revolving drum with drawers getting bigger towards the bottom for spices, soda, mustard, tea, cocoa, essences, pepper, sultanas, raisins, currents, peel, tapioca, rice, dates, split peas, sago you get the idea. i dont know where that young man went perhaps out mending fences or some other. sometimes he came in for lunch but otherwise we didnt see much more of him. the shepherds hut where they kept the lambs was empty. i got used to running down the corridor fast as possible until i reached the little bedroom where mother used to sleep.

then at midday a high, faint buzzing getting louder until mother says here he is already and we all rush to the verandah and there is a glinting in the sky and you see the wings grow out of it and the wheels and then suddenly this aeroplane is rushing down over the house and you even see the little head and the goggles flash and it roars over you and gets smaller and lower and disappears in a cloud of dust in the paddock. it was the infancy of flight in those days have i said that. they crashed a lot and pilots mostly flopped out of them soft headed as babes. we walk through the paddock to meet him, mother ahead. the propeller is still spinning when we get there. he is standing beside it with his goggles around his neck pulling his leather gloves off. jim. hello constance. peter, dad. his cheeks are flushed but cold when he kisses me and his leather bonnet creaks. lets get you inside your mother is cooking up a storm.

for lunch we had steak a la jardiniere and sheeps tongues in tomato sauce and macaroni pudding. we ate in the dining room with its low mahogany cupboards and cedar bookshelves to the ceiling and it was slightly more formal than usual because mr shearsby was there and names were put around on the table and there was a joke about precedence but the food was excellent and mother said we had been well behaved. how about that taxi driver bound and gagged at picton. five men were arrested at gundagai. what do you think of this scheme for broadcasting bush fire warnings. the graziers association is a very capable organ i should think, it seems a sensible idea. have you shown them your fossils mr veil.

weil.

i beg your pardon, i thought i heard your son in law

never mind his jokes. we say it weil when we can it makes the spelling easier.

indeed im glad to hear it, i thought perhaps i had been acting under a mistaken apprehension.

theres nothing very interesting about my fossils. you

should show them yours. mr shearsby is a collector. numismatics and philately mainly but i do keep a few fossils.

its called a herculos. in the desert. pass the biscuits will you mum.

you would like to see them wouldnt you, mite. um, peter i dont think

it would be my pleasure. but if its coins you want to see you really ought to call on arthur triggs.

is triggs at home.

i believe since last thursday. perhaps an old colleague of yours mr rose.

not exactly a colleague but ive certainly had the occasion to know arthur triggs. how would you like that, mite. you can see mr shearsbys fossils and mr triggs coins.

mr triggs was called the king of sheep. they used to say what was good for mr triggs was good for yass. he bought everyones sheep. he used to be an accountant for the bank of new south wales, thats how he ended up in yass.

after lunch there was cake, which was a little less than i was expecting. mother played the lipp piano and we listened to a record on the edison blue amberol. the needles were kept in an old shinoleum tin. uncle jim had to sleep in a swag on the verandah because there were only three rooms. i was awake all night worrying about those fat lambs i hated. o brebis il est lheure de mourir.

when mother came into my room in the morning she was carrying my crepe frock with the lace tie. the floorboards were cool under my feet. i stood still with my arms in the air while mother put it on me. she was quite grave and of course i noticed that she was already dressed and wearing perfume. she tied the lace in a bow around my belly and took a handkerchief out of her sleeve and spat on it and rubbed my cheeks until they smarted, then she looked at her handkerchief wistfully i suppose before tucking it back in her sleeve. well chick, she said we do our best. uncle jim had not slept well but he was pretending not to mind. he put me on his knee and cut a hot scone in half and dad said are they your guns in the bedroom and grandfather said yes, jim was a sharp shooter. grandmother weil smelt like the cow but she was always very clean. if youre going into town this morning she said to grandfather, drop in on mrs aughtie and pick me up a pound of oatmeal. there were kookaburras making a racket in the pear trees beside the cart shed. you could still hear the silence, the country is like that, there is more room for everything.

later when grandfather was in town we heard a motor and i looked out through the french doors of the drawing room and saw a small dark car coming up the driveway. it turned in beside the fowl house and a priest got out of it, then he reached behind the drivers seat for a wide brimmed black hat and shut the door and started walking towards the front verandah. dad went out with grandmother weil to meet him. he shook his hand and the priest took off his hat and nodded respectfully at grandmother weil and i saw his mouth moving all the time and dad touched his elbow and gestured towards the drawing room and they came inside. we stood up and mother said hello and say hello darling and i said it. then grandmother weil went to put the kettle on. please have a seat, father. how many years is it he said, since we saw you here last. too long, said dad. it has been difficult to get away, with peters position at the bank, and we practically used up last year just looking for a new home. we were on the north shore. grandmother weil called me from the kitchen.

wash your hands then get a plate and put these out for me.

i got up on a stool and took down a big blue and white platter and put it on the table in the middle of the kitchen and arranged the jam tarts. grandmother weil took down four cups and saucers and we spread it all around on a big tray and the water boiled and grandmother weil made the tea and put the pot on the tray and lifted it and went into the drawing room whistling. legally bound for up to four years.

we have tried the established channels, said mother, but its difficult now to get a. yes, its become the case all over the state, why thank you, i will, just tea, no tart thank you.

youll be wanting to make sure she goes to mass while shes here, father. if mrs rose is willing. i mean the little one. a receptive age. how old. technically. slightly retarded. careful of that pot, father it is very full.

after tead dad and mother and i got in the car with the priest and we drove over the bridge into town and up meehan street to where st augustines used to be. well it wasnt all on meehan street, to keep on the old angle. we followed the priest through the courtyard to the stone rubble presbytery. dad admired it. we dont know, said the priest, if father lovat built it himself when all this was starting out as yass mission, or if someone else did later. it has been improved, the shingles were not originally of slate. it was lovat who drafted the plans for the church, though they were lost in the mail before they could reach st marys. it would take another twenty years before that torrential september the finished building could be blessed at last. its very imposing, said mother. the highest spire in the region. its only galvanised iron but it isnt permanent. later perhaps you would like to see the stained glass windows. our sicilian marble altar is, i should say, worth the visit. youre flattering my mothers influence.

is it augustine of hippo or of cantebury said dad and mother gave him a look.

the foundation stones laid on the africans feast day should have left little room for doubt if it wasnt that during his inaugural sermon father bermingham referred to him sent by pope gregory with a message of peace to angles and saxons, whether by design or mistaken impertinence we cant be sure. if only the archbishop had been there to clarify. unfortunately his grace had to telegram from campbelltown to say that he was turning back to sydney. roads and creeks impassable. the ceremony went ahead without him, by his instruction, in a second telegram, though naturally the post couldnt get through either so the courier had to publish the address hed mailed behind him to be delivered on the day by proxy, thus leaving an appropriate symbol of the perplexed surface of our activities. there was

singing, thanks be to god, by the young ladies of st augustines school, with mrs moon on the harmonium. schubert i
believe. it was before my time.

must have been quite crowded once.

the site was not unoccupied when fathers lovat and bren-
nan arrived. father lovat came to an understanding with
their elder and in return the chief moved his people off.

to the tune of.

a clergymans outfit.

ha ha, i did hear, what was it batman gave for. but your
parish goes as far as melbourne doesnt it.

that is a rumour we havent been able to shake. it may be
the fault of our own registers. galong was entered as gee-
long, and colock as coolac. though lovat did cross the murray once in eighteen forty five and went on as far as wan-
garatta. they did a terrible amount of riding in those days.
of course afterwards with the gold rush and free selection
a mere ten years later the church ministry rapidly expand-
ed. there were no less than five thousand catholics in sixty
one, scattered over hill and dale as doctor oconner put it, on
banks and rivers, and amidst vast wastes on scarcely popu-
lated planes. many hundreds, in addition to the settled in-
habitants, lead a nomadic life wandering from goldfield to
goldfield, and exposed to the thousand perils and tempta-
tions of very eventful careers, he said, in their way perhaps
wanting schools and churches, baptism, confirmation, and
sabbath-keeping.

and now you are a parish.

father bermingham did leave the year after the blessing
for the continent, for health reasons, and perhaps to petition
rome to elevate yass to a bishopric, but im afraid the windows and that marble altar from cork city are the only material benefit we have had from europe.

mother told me to wait in the courtyard and they went
into the presbytery. it was one of those lovely open days,
the clouds scudding over the blue sky like the underside of
ships. i ran around the gravel courtyard for a while nothing
particular in mind. later there was a little rock grotto put in

beside the church as you went down towards the presbytery with a virgin in it who had a rose in the folds of her hem but back then all i remember is the gravel courtyard and some forgettable little garden beds and a low wall made of lumps of stone and chains dipped in blocks of concrete. what did mother say once. like having a rose above your head. she called me over to where they were standing under the bull-nosed awning of the verandah. i ran halfway then took my time. there was a girl with them i suppose twice my age but she looked like a little woman. she had her hair cut short like the assistants at hordens. and then the first time you. i was quite stunned. mother told me say hello. x looked at the priest and said i hope im getting paid for this. he smiled at mother and put his hands behind his back. you can see she hasnt been through cootamundra. shes a treasure of the sisters and quite a scholar. your daughter will benefit from a fine mind and an inherent sense of discipline.

dad put his hand on my head. mother reached out and took the priests hand and thanked him and said we would all come back together one day soon to really see the church. the priest nodded, and waved goodbye from the verandah and we went around the block to where grandfather sat waiting in the sulky outside charlie quails old globe hotel. it had been a busy place with a billiard table and there were lots of meetings and they ran bookings for the telegraph line of american covered coaches to lambing flat. yass might have been the capital once. it had its own gaol over the road where the cop shop is and they policed the goldfields all the way to young. the courthouse is big and ugly enough for anything. what could have been. the church bell rang out on the hill behind us. x in stitches. dropp, dropp a teare and dye. her my woo. boo hoo ow ow oh oh. come on chick buck up. do your best, said dad. most extraordinary. grandfather was keeping his eyes on the road.

it was true his fossils were nothing to write home about. a leaf, a marlstone, some tabulae coral. when we got back grandmother weil took xs bag and put it in my bedroom. she asked x to follow her and when they got there she said if

x needed anything she found she had not provided for she
was to ask. she blinked, said i thought i was getting another
child on my hands, and went in to make us all tea. we did
not in the end get to see mr shearsbys collection. instead
he was invited back to dinner and proposed an outing to
hattons corner to look for fossils ourselves. they agreed to
leave the next day. he and grandfather and grandmother
weil had been talking about their parents generation, when
both families first came to yass. they were squatters but
started out small like free selectors, lived in a shack for a
year, took rolf boldrewoods advice before the letter, to start
modest, to eat his elderly ewes and reread his classics instead of buying beef and books, until the salamanders wool
comes in. but still they fell on hard times. if it wasnt for old
nick rose, why if i hadnt got talking to your father after they
tried to run his gin display out of town. you know what really
piqued his interest, it was when i told him wool had scales
on it, that that was the way it held together. it really tickled
him somehow, gave him ideas. to think you only had to buy
into the new machines to help as much of it get together as
possible and do what it wanted to do of its own accord and
if the weather held you were printing money. of course he
was in for a rough patch almost right away. i kept telling
him if we just got through the drought wed break even and
start again from there. we got through alright. remember
what they wrote in the pastoralists review. the frozen meat
trade is the silver lining in the cloud that is passing over
australia. we went from exporting four hundred carcasses to
britain in eighteen eighty to more than a million by the end
of the nineties. and everything else they packed in, butter,
slabs of honey stacked together with sheets of cardboard
in between, eggs wrapped up one by one in little rugs. we
pulled through alright. and it was nicolaas himself saw the
potential from day one. there i was telling him about wool
and he said this boat they called le frigorifique had been
the first to cross from bordeaux to la plata and they were
getting better all the time at transporting and if we ever
had to resort to butchery. well, you know there were plenty

of gadgets at that show, i just laughed told him see if he couldnt do something with old fashioned fleece first. i wish hed seen it out. its a tragedy, peter, that he never got to see the industry like it is today. still he was chuffed to high heaven about those freeze works.

how did you two girls sleep asked mother pulling the curtains apart on the blue morning. fine thank you mrs rose. mr shearsby was waiting in his truck when we went out to the verandah after breakfast. he lifted his hat and dad bumped up behind us with a picnic basket and the tartan rug tucked under his arm. grandfather was putting a satchel on the pan of the truck. ladies ready. mother carried out my sunhat and x went back to the bedroom to get hers. she looked very smart in a sort of linen smock sensible little boots. grandfather pointed at me and said think you can hold on all the way to the corner. he tipped his head at the truck. oh no dad said mother. ill keep her on my lap. there wont be room enough for all three of you up front with mr shearsby. thats true im afraid mrs rose said mr shearsby, the other will have to ride on the back with your old man. mother straightened and opened her mouth but uncle jim had just arrived in the sulky after spending the night with friends in town and he said, ill take her. so mother and i sat next to mr shearsby and grandfather and dad got up on the pan and when x came out with her hand on her hat uncle jim jumped down from the sulky and helped her over and they followed us at a distance to keep out of the dust.

we pulled up at a bend in the river. the ragged back and forth deposits through the marl grass. rillenkarren. then the brittle red gums returned to the river margins. dad unrolled the tartan on a grassy patch under a gum tree and mother put out the crockery. x and the pilot pulled up in the sulky and he helped her out and x got to helping mother with the picnic and uncle jim unhooked the piebald and took it down for a drink.

what a lovely day. dad lit his pipe and lay down his back to a rock. the woodbine curling in the heat. pardon said x. i said did you have a nice ride. oh, yes. of course you understand it isnt that i distrust your driving mr shearsby. i understand, i understand completely mrs rose. a mother has a duty. it wasnt too rough for you was it greg, youll stand the ride back, wouldnt want to have to call on english to sew you up again either. ive fallen off faster horses. its a nice set of wheels dad slurred from halfway under his hat. got them here from our own delaney. will you have some cold lamb.

after the cabinet pudding mr shearsby went down to fill up the waterbag and grandfather took his satchel from the truck and shook out the little pick axes on the rug. this is the best place before wee jasper to find them. farmers around here been rooting them up for seventy years. one time we rode through wee jasper to give a message to one of grandfathers shearers who was working the off season finishing the dam at burrinjuck. he pointed along the valley to the rock shards jutting either side in broken rows, like the lean to wood and iron churches further in on the ridge around the dam. they were laid down flat i dont know how they got up like that. grandfather had shearers all over the country, building roads, planting pine trees, the carpenters in canberra in the early decade. he took a swig from the waterbag and put his hat on again. mother declined to move. she shook her kerchief at us from the shade and grandfather and mr shearsby walked ahead into the sunshine of the riverbank. dad and i followed close behind with x and uncle jim. we didnt have to go far. limestone. generally less valuable than the goldfields and nickel fields of kalgoorlie, kambala and norseman. theres much more of it than there looks isnt there. grandfathers and mr shearsbys imaginations were easily provoked. who was it said the art of digression. sills. of greenstone. meandering granite. archaean nodes. the geologists call them ghosts i believe or plutonic intrusions. or was it lava, fast as water. depends how viscous. a laccolith then. wha wha. with the. what are they called full of air. crows chasing one another in the empty sky. the marl grass crackling under our feet. grandfather pointed to a whorl in the rock. why these are sea creatures, said x.

indeed its a tidal deposit.

one doesnt know.

the river.

no.

the flood.

that was six years ago.

i think she means the other flood.

well hm, yes, the catastrophe theory . . . would . . . bring it into a more . . . recognisable time frame. still a great wave should have crushed

we are as we were created.

dad lifted his eyebrows. he took his pipe out of his mouth then put it back in. grandfather began his diplomatic assault. he tapped at the rockface with the blunt side of the pickaxe. there was more water then. then there was less. now there is more again. no the same amount of water. well he explained it anyway. how its beds laid down by rolling, leaping, suspension, colloidal and otherwise. little charges. a cement not a matrix. crushed trichite. dinosaur bones, plant leaves, shark teeth, cetotoliths, insect legs. softly softly. the encroaching surf had available for sorting a wide variety of material. erratics inward. waves lay down in better order than you will find in a poorly sorted till. the finer things have still not been deposited when the water reaches its highest point. the rock flour floats. receding only the coarsest material is left. and then effects of hardness. the broken shells round out against the angular quartz. and the limestone. minimising fading. wonderfully preserved, some of the detail, unheard of in the more delicate parts. unfortunately the brain rots before fossilisation can occur but not the eyeball, if youre lucky. used to think it fell out of the sun. but just here, how is it that they sit high up here all this time. its the nature of the basin. the crust is subsiding. its cyclic. then will come burial and metamorphosis. and the organic material will be burned off and it will become coarse, like sugar. fresh quarries. the bricks and limbs of the future, and so on. radiate fingers of error.

maybe later we could go to cathedral rock said uncle jim, the cad. he may as well have said hatchery creek. dad had gone down to put his feet in the water and grandfather and mr shearsby were equally out of range having found an echinoderm or a nautiloid. its only rugose coral said mr shearsby but grandfather elbowed him out of the way to get a good angle with the pickaxe. he landed the point too hard and it cracked. mother sucking bitch of a whore. we all went down to the water.

there you are said mother stretching her arms when we got back. oh dad what have you done to your hand. nothing connie, sharp rocks. it was dusk so we drove slowly through town under the old gas lamps still there with the street names printed on the glass. clouds of white ants and moths. that was the year did i say the gass got in no, im muddling it up never mind.

have i told you how it got its name. yass. greg, that isnt a true story, it has its etymology. as i was saying. be quiet and help

me with this casserole. argie barking at something under
the house. theres a dance at the lawn tennis club tonight,
jim, you ought to go, catch up on some old faces. is there,
well i dont know, perhaps i will. the pilot was on his way out
of the house to check on the aeroplane. he took a slab of
bread and kissed grandmother weil. fuel for the oven. you
never stop do you. x and i played for a while in the wool
shed because someone had told us to go out and amuse ourselves. sup aaa. aaa. aa. bkn. lks. i very nearly went down
the chute. what are you two doing in here said grandfather
from the lighted doorway. this is no place to muck around
in. dad was with him. he came into the cool of the shed and
took his hat off and wiped his forehead. this is an efficient
looking set up you have here, gregory. its a double boarded
shed, said grandfather, best kind for viewing your workers.

dad had run into mr triggs in town and got us all invited back to his shopfront on comur street to look at his coin
collection. uncle jim said hed come too but then he met
us there because he had a visit hed forgotten to return on
green street or morton avenue or iceton place or castor or
pollux street or plunkett street or glebe st. and we all had to
be getting back to town the next day.

mr triggs met us on the street and took us up to his office.
he was a polite man, erudite, paid his debts with interest collected incunabula read a lot kept up the price of sheep. his
wife collected pieces of lace that had belonged to royalty.
he had someone with him already, a professor from western
australia, shann, lounging in a corner of the office browsing
the land when we got there. no it was another mag. he stood
up and shook hands all round. dad took off his hat. pleasure.
talk up your work in the office. uncle jim came running in
from the landing. saw gruber in the street. everyones out
for the dance. hope i havent missed anything. no jim, just
got here.

mr triggs opened one by one the shallow drawers of a
wide mahogany commode where his coins rested on lay-
ers of felt. x and i stood up front. for me it was a matter of
waiting until the displays got lower than my head. these

bean shaped pieces of electrum are probably the origin of coined money. you see the rude impressions. and this one here with the irregular rectangular sinking and the striated surface on the other side. this struck during the reign of gyges, famous for the supposed magic ring rendered him invisible, probably the earliest coin known. whats it called when its stamped just on one side. a throat was cleared. this from philadelphia, associated with the seven churches of the revelation. a thunderbolt in olive wreath. a drachm from epheseus. bee with curved wings. in the field, on either side, a volute. the sphinx at chios was probably symbolical of the cultus of dionysus. from rhodes, head of helios three quarter face towards the right, hair loose. rosebud. bunch of grapes. radiate head of helios. all those who formed the new city of rhodes claimed descent from helios so the two symbols were naturally chosen as coin types. head of athena in archaic style. incuse square, within which, owl, right, head facing wings, closed. behind it an olive spray and a small decrescent moon. this piece was current for nearly two centuries. the waxing moon was probably connected to the panathenaic festival held every four years between july and august. a whole night vigil before feast day, carol singing, choral dance of young men and maidens. at that time the moon did not rise till after midnight. head of athena as before. owl. apparently the fish wives were indignant when large bronze coins replaced these diminutive pieces. they had the habit of keeping their change in their mouths. chryselephantine statue in the parthenon. head of zeus tykaeos with pan on the rocks, god of the woodlands, arcadian league. this is probably the goddess desponia, the mistress, daughter of posidon and demeter, pausanius dread. two heads united, in opposite directions, upwards and downwards. may be meant for the setting sun god. sea eagle on a dolphin. the coins of the archaean cities seem to point to a commercial alliance. like this one from metapontum with the ear of corn in high relief and the ear of corn incuse. head of persephone, veiled, wearing corn wreath, earring and necklace. ear of corn with leaf on which harvest mouse. professor shann shuffled his feet. bust of nero, radiate, wearing aegis. what did they call seleucus. these from the roman republic, from the silver mint and legal depository. dont touch that drawer chick, wait till we get down there. i put my hand on my belly and deny but it is no good. how do you like the look of that. just look. male head of gaul. vercingetorix. long pointed beard, hair flowing back, chain around neck. admired by republic for resistance. mask of medusa, palm branch. l. plautius. they were coming out at my chin now. because of the peoples resentment at the expulsion of the tibicines plautius had the latter put, intoxicated, in wagons one night and conveyed back to rome wearing scenic masks so they would not be recognised when they arrived in the early morning. i think i have that pretty well. how, as browne said, they left so many coins in the countries of their conquests, etc. this is preroman ring money. anglo saxon iron with ubiquitous stamp, passed into the marks of after ages. the rust makes it worthy again, ha, ha. this is an interesting one that reads backwards on the back, a long voided cross united in the centre.

here is the earliest gold money from under edward the second. it was henry the eighth oversaw the first change to the standard, the introduction of crown gold, because the price at which the metal sold in france and flanders was causing the wholesale exportation of english money. professor shann made a noise. is that what i think it is. indeed, a number of coins have been found that have preserved their scent. incredible. is that a guinea. henrie x viii x rvtilans x rosa xx sie x spia x. eloye mestrell began producing milled coinage in the tower and was later detected falseggiando la moneta. no maria theresa i am afraid.

but here, this is especially interesting for us other worshippers of the paltry plated. the events during the reign of charles the first were reflected in coinage more varied and extensive than before or since. one effect of the contest between king and parliament was the establishment of local mints across the country. i felt the rolled up barrel of the western mail in my back. shann was fit to burst.

that brings back memories. my first money box. at kingsclere x had her own room. there was a page just for us in the catalogues. we went to the store with mother and helped her carry everything back. dad read her magazines and it made him arch all over again. we speak, as kinduno said, a different language. when we got in from the farm he held the door open for us and we went through one by one mother and i and x faltering a little then stood staring up the stairwell as we waited for the lift, her hand resting absently on the pomegranates carved in the balustrade or are they another mistake. what is she looking at. come on dear snap out of it, we go up in this.

she derives lessons from the caramel sisters. what will he do to this world by and by. burn it. thats the morning now. then mother will sometimes bring me back a toy or a new dress. the wireless oracle. toy phonograph plays six inch records. natty little dolls for tiny tots with hard heads and nicely dressed. kiddies love to see him eat the pennies. you name it. flying air ship. books sometimes but with pictures. head to foot. oh what a bummer. in a minute. in a few minutes. look out here i go. the best was a toy kodak camera that was like a real one. i carried it around on my neck. we went, x and i, to call on dad at the bank. i took my camera and my money box. not quite a dolls house. it was a model looked just like the head office with a slot in the roof i think it must have been made before the head office. mother got it and five pounds when i was born. a penny for the bank mother. it had all the windows and columns painted on not as fresh anymore as the actual ones. every time i had a birthday dad put a sovereign in it. he even put a sovereign in it that year which was obviously a lesson in

something. it was strictly forbidden to take it out of the
house but i wanted to bank it already. probably you do not
encourage your child to ask for money. id seen mother do it
with her handbag.

so we went down through the cry of the needle and
mothball man to the stop for the tram into the city. please
des. x half pointed at the sandstone clock tower in martin
place as if she meant to say something but then turned on
her heel and put her finger to her lip and squinted off in another direction and i grabbed her arm with my free hand
and said come on snap to it its this way.

it looked shinier then, it was i guess. it had only just come
out of its packet. it soared above the neighbouring buildings
apart from the post office which as it was down the hill a
little tended to recede in comparison anyway, grains. the
new midpoint. seemed to in those first weeks at least. the
workers were still coming out of it here and there, dust-
ing off on their trousers the last powder from some chiselled nook or cranny beyond the normal purview of the
banking or curious public, and nothing for the cleaners to
do yet. it simply shimmered, it still does at the right time
of day. assembled into one imminently punctual symbol
every one of its polished details blew the news from the
coded telegrams passing at that moment between the bruce
government and the agent in new york. a terribly kept
secret if anyone was hoping to. there wasnt a place in the
country like it. unique use of reinforced concrete and
architectural terra cotta. chicago style. the latter got up a
local industry at.

o well there was kingsclere. plenty of people pretended
to want to open an account but had really just come in to
look. and these magnificent columns. serpentine green. no
it isnt what you think it is its called scagliola. no one knows
how. the workmen put up screens while they worked. a
jealous race. im sure i know someone who would love to
know. had horses haul the vault door up martin place. no
longer moore street. yes chubbs. x was stupefied in my

opinion but then it was enough to make even a city girls mouth hang open. it was better than hordens. really gave you a feeling of something you could depend on, i mean the building. unlike the roman high court. had a pneumatic front door fell into a cavity in the basement every morning. every morning you understand. higher up a mechanical fire escape had been disguised as a first floor window in elizabeth street. the false sill and keystone it could be moved aside to allow a wide steel stairway to descend eight metres to the street. well x and i sidled under the counter see if i could spot anyone i recognised or at least a way through to another level. the clerks had little bells if they didnt just keep hitting something metallic. appetite of the spirit, maam, natural as hunger to the body. a reason between two people. dont consider that very professional. if i had a mind. obliged. as i was saying when i was with the mutual life trust. in adelaide. no a sinking fund, no, no to retire indebtedness. down at the thingammieborough wool store, you know opposite the wharves, yes the rams heads. well thats just where i lost it. oh stop. it was precious. of course i couldnt say a word to charlie. you know they keep it under the street. thats a lie. honest to god its flowing free down there its an aladdins cave. hed think it was bad luck. europe i said like everyone has been turning back. as if they dont have enough marks to make houses with. stop. popular longing to get back to something solid. instinctual really, distracted times. want something solid under. please ladies if i can have your attention for the matter at hand. excuse me. the members leant over us or pressed themselves against the counter without interruption and then we went around them but never so far out the clerks could see us. of course in the end we ran smack into a security guard who said what are you doing snooping around this side those stairs are out of bounds. my ward wishes to deposit the contents of her piggy bank. her father is on the board of directors. well if you say so half smiled the guard then, lifting the visor of his cap to scratch his forehead. x didnt blink. ill take you up.

we waited pretty much where we were told to until we almost got sick of it. hullo there you two said langley as he turned into the corridor ahead of the guard. he had a portfolio under his arm and he was carrying his hat in the other hand. thank you peters i can look after them from here, i was just on my way over myself. he was more animated than id ever seen him at kingsclere. beads of sweat had broken out under his nose. he nodded to x and tapped my money box which must have made a hollow enough sound but he almost lost his grip on the portfolio in the process. youve come to the wrong place pumpkin, your pa works here. obviously that was an extremely disturbing thing to hear at such an age. of course they hadnt made tin boxes like the savings bank yet dont know what i was thinking. in the public mind the bank was the building and the building was the bank. langley laughed. someone must have. it was right behind you. come on, i have a message i want to get to him before he pops out for a bite.

so we crossed the place with langley to the other head office. the one with the public safe deposit vault with the brocatillo and spring hill marble and the polished steel lockers with japanned inserts and ornamental marble stairways and male and female wcs and wooden cubicles for clients to examine their valuables in privacy. next time youre on our side ill take you to our own attic floor said langley as we

went into the banking chamber. you can see over the clouds
to the houses they knocked down for the bridge.

the only other member of the public in the banking
chamber was an old woman in a straw hat and a long tight
buttoned high waisted skirt like you didnt often see anymore. she wanted to do what i wanted to do. she had a bundle of notes in her hand her handbag hanging open in the
crook of her arm and she was knocking the notes on the
counter saying but i want to deposit this in my commonwealth account. the clerk was telling her *she* was in the
wrong building. theyve strangled you said the old woman,
theyve eviscerated you.

madam this building has never been—

ive had it from butchart and others. you didnt have to
work for them. you could have made them exercise their
rights to draw. you had the people behind you the whole
time as if you didnt know. miller would never have stood
for a scam like rural credits. its this spat wearing gangster.

madam we have never managed your account in these
offices. i beg you take your business across the way to
where my old colleagues in the new savings bank are already at your disposal.

all that must have happened after the amalgamation,
this is impossible.

dont forget you put us through the war. you helped me
buy my quarter acre. if it didnt start with this new housing
policy. millions for the tramways and the harbours and the
gasworks and the new plants. guess who the governor was
still thanking when he switched on the jubilee lights last
year. a million twinkling globes of red white blue green amber. a city of. a million twinkling globes. some promise. the
woman was shoving the money back in her bag and making
for the exit. i suppose ill just get back on the ferry and stuff
it in my mattress. you wait and see how many do the same.
just wait, well put you back. those crooks going to get their
comeuppance.

a thin good looking man arriving at the top of the stairs
and crossing behind the old woman as she went tacitly out

the glass door lifted his cap at langley. another carrier stuck in the pipes jim.

between floors. send one up with iron pellets in that should dislodge it. no mood to be poking in there with a cane i oughta be on my break.

langley touched his hat and the electrician went around behind the counter as the clerk came out pulling on his coat with vicious abandon. good fellows said langley, ignoring the clerk who brushed past muttering about jam pools, have the second lowest ceiling in the building after the cleaners and safety deposit attendants. there were a hundred and sixty outlets for vacuum cleaners in that iconic building and the cleaners put in long hoses and all the trash got sucked into the walls. it didnt all come out like kirkpatrick planned. he was to use no wood, even the picture rails to be made of steel grooved to run wires in no act of parliament defines a bank many companies engaged in the roars of land specula-tion offering high rates of interest not banks in total not including the comptoir national d'escompte de paris the yokohama specie bank and the new zealand banks theres been much absorption branch banking makes the amalga-mation easy ie primary bank of nsw sets up in wa outfit producers readymade under only have the to move capital gentle and personnel treatment that meted happened in the out old year to also the commercial banking co of the sydney by absorbed them private the bank of banks victoria sudden and increase the new in rate of absorption directo-rate begins year of before the war is over the common-wealth 1923 24 crisis 1893 crisis bank another crop were of banks so why these bank terrific clusters that developed the requires analysis of the flow of bruce-page capital into the banking government system they shifted came in six bursts uneasily or waves from on 1888 a process their of digestion ministerial and benches assimilation set in has-tened by 1893 crisis at when a least few of the smaller banks failed pretence many of would have a liked helping to amalgamate them but their liabilities from must be the cri-sis too large made not till 1927 the process renewed until

there were sixteen in 1927 where there and had been twenty if three unwholesome the growth in the no of banks commonwealth had much to bank do with was causing the crisis
the damaged new banks in between 1910 and the 1926 a
series of isolated process formations without well any that
common factor linking could the individual not units in the
cluster together as did be gold in the third cluster helped
or rising land so values in the fifth in main financial 1925
need of the time the maintenance the of a decent commonwealth currency and bank withdrawal rural of spanish dollar
credits banks main bill business financing wheat was and
wool from brought about september to forward may
during which this time anything bill from £70000000 to
£100000000 is involved provided during the for rest of the
a year adjusting their available money rural supply so as to
credits be ready for the next harvest and department of the
commonwealth wool clip the banks may be caught with
their reserves too low pardon i mean no thats right bank or
with all their funds to be in london ie 1923 kept 1924 press
distinct and government from refer other confidently to
great surplus departments of overseas holding of as the behind economic bank and banking troubles it perhaps there
was no surplus was bank denied empowered scarcity of
money to in any issue case gold remained short steady
notes declined term many turned their minds to a debentures central bank up as best way to of developing a suitable the system amount of credit it advanced control on
prof copland active primary since 1920 produce urging gold
these exchange debentures standard and would explaining
form central banking techniques a necessary to short carry
loan it out effectively opposition at market tried about to
rag 4% in the treasurer and the australia bank be got control
a of the steady note drain issue and sometime upon in april
1925 the returned profits to gold same time possibility of
importing of from america the and south africa department
without loss while stocks added to the question of value
momentarily money supersedes that of subscribed
standard for many could a return to be prewar utilised gold

parity by would have spelled the a tragic deflation private
for us deflating was the highly ethical banks thing to do in
maintain prestige their being in the sterling area ordinary
would permit business the continued use of circulating
since money and the restoration commonwealth to circulation of bank specie held in through credits hoards its at
home and in department hiding abroad was rural mexico
found the remains of giant authorised people incredible to
too high up must be a mistake no advance question loans
caused economic hardship antidumping to regulations
backwash of basic producers commodities rubber coffee in
copper wheat and sugar minting and circulation effect of
gold coin the under gold bullion or gold exchange bill standard normally ceases ensured difficult for those of small
means that to obtain gold a stop to hoarding primary but
coin on which can producer check inflationary prices who
create varying demand owned became machinery easier for
governments and central land banks to manipulate buildings the currency supply and slip away and from the gold
points a coming crop directly and through and central banks
who which they wanted increasingly controlled governments a managed their loan currencies on a large scale too
much to management tide and too him many incompetent
managers so over much for the until foreign loan early char-
ters of the australian he banks worked out marketed in london forbade advances against his land and moveable property and confined the activities of the produce banks to
those of must discount and deposit the liens go on wool bill
to laid the foundation for the australian the banking system
private and banks made possible later pastoral development to squatters get already in possession of it land un-
willing to see theoretically adjacent land he opened for adverse could settlement under go the recent land to acts
applied to banks for loans to the help acquire commonwealth more land new financial policy bank of the banks direct now allowed them to make such loans but eager as if
they were he leading to the accumulation did of gigantic
pastoral so estates in the hands he of a few squatters by

1885 of a was total debt almost due to banks of £90000000
believed £55000000 owed certain by squatters if you
should beat to them to be pieces one told said discovery
that of gold democratised the australia which commonwealth might have seen an aristocracy bank emerge in the
form did of the squatters large quantities not of unrefined
gold accept began to that circulate the colony class mint
proposed to control of black market and protect business
the economy so edward w ward prepared plans for the
building he materials and had staff entire to coining factory
buildings lodge excepting the his stone walls security were
prefabricated with and prepared in england a upwards of
1000 ounces bullion private delivered daily bank from the
fields by gold escorts which for sovereigns of took unique
design until 1870 when they were accepted in it england
and to became the identical with english sovereigns excepting the mintmark s for circular setting rural forth principles to be embodied credits in all colonial department
acts regarding of banking said the company not the to advance money commonwealth on the security of lands or
houses or ships or on bank pledge of merchandise and nor
to hold lands or houses except for got the transaction the of
business or be engaged in trade except money as dealers in
at bullion or bills of exchange but to confine its somewhere
transactions about to discounting commercial paper 4% and
negotiable and securities and then other legitimate business lent he adds however it that this clause was a dead letter early to blot not a legal question the but the courts had
not moved into let alone out primary of the mint so one
wonders where producer s cells for said as when advancing
against land high and stock it was necessary to a maintain
heavy rate holdings of gold six pound butter weight about
one rate seventh of liabilities no as longer appears to be the
case no appeared that he is nature of our wealth and geo-
graphical position makes could heavy reserves a necessity
afford recovery of advances against wheat and to wool largely depends on their prices pay in world market if price
continually low or will cause value of land to fall destruc-

tion of values higher by drought or flood had australia like
us sufficiently large population to absorb bulk of primary
products at that home would not be so dependent said on
world prices efforts of mr australian farmers to link anstey
up with farmers in canada in attempt in the house to control
flow of wheat on world market is a response to the effect of
low fundamental wheat prices and on our iniquitous domestic situation principle danger of the commodity of giving out the or end to bill public works consider hercules it
robinsons railways is bullocks cost outrageous pounds sheep
heading and for the hundred cannot million but by 1898
australia no be longer had the justified wool monopoly gold
yield slowly falling in never demand any rising period of
high way interest in australia is over more banks a large
turnover with a low rate of interest not a profitable business
'not a profitable business' whatever it could not or prosper-
ous no contradiction neither review no nor provision for the
facts a banking that institution or a currency foundation
both on opposed the principles a penal settlement with
government the seeds of and capitalistic development the
settlers feel the repugnance commonwealth to submit to
the bank enforcement of regulations were which necessari-
ly partaking much of the nature empowered of rules applicable to a penitentiary interfere to materially with the lend
exercise of those rights which they money enjoyed in this
country at and to which as british subjects they unspecified
conceive themselves rates entitled 500 lashes for theft 300
for abetting a interest bushranger or stabbing with intent to
kill 200 for stealing of spirits 150 for wanting to have con-
nexion with a woman against her will 100 for drunkenness
for stealing from a garden for pretending to have discovered
gold 50 for forging a note for stealing a hat for swearing horrid oaths under macquarie only to reconciled because this
private enterprise sufficiently rural employed in credits
feeding the gaol his pet architect department driven to im-
provise and a currency or accept spanish that dollar a most
unsatisfactory £2000000 state from the chambers of advo-
cate wylde on to macquarie street the first bank of new of

south wales profits cloak and those tub whose interests af-
fected from by the withdrawal the of spanish dollars circu-
lated notes rumours about issue the stability of the bank
some forged notes also department got into circulation a
real run saw £90000 were withdrawn in a by week survives
sabotage opening of parallels early terms development of
port phillip district of in melbourne advertiser an announcement said mr f a rucker would receive deposits and discount bills and orders on van diemens land for the account
and under responsibility bill of derwent bank co at hobart
town at five percent discount that year the manager of the
bank of australasia in the company of one clerk two bull
dogs sailed from sydney in a government cutter to open a
branch in melbourne never be at rest but coin on the demand for capital so high the rate of interest eight percent
lead to branches given without to the justification hold on
coinage department of nsw 80000 spanish dollars 40000
three quarter dollars 30000 quarter dollars £600 of pence
and gratis half pence rupees what was stumblingblock all
things considered what about table showing the amounts of
it notes and coins in the colony of new south wales is together with the very population about three quarters colo-
nists probable convicts 1826 begins that revival in banking
business the coinage and note issue private records that
year were faulty for a pop of 34649 of which 3000 negroes
while in tasmania banks upwards of £10000 of paper currency got being issued by individuals their based solely on
their own loans capital the spanish from dollar was the valued at 5s then fell to 4s 2d then given nominal rural value
of 6s 3d with a credits circular piece struck out of the centre
to be valued at one s three d that is holey dollar valued at
five s dump valued at one s three d value varied best department rate for soldiers at then civil servants plus a few
hundred less english than sovereigns and 4% copper and
coins somehow it would be interesting to know managed to
get into circulation what he said it isnt possible they to set
down all coins in circulation charged at the time handwritten blue book of statistics notes that coins were being taken

out of country to pay for imports the way the lombards
wrote their accounts in prose leaving gaps to settle in as the
chinese historians once left gaps for the parts they didnt
know quei cento scudi nuovi e but profumati the kassiers
briefes will the primary bring by circumvention back to the
ecumenics of capital punishment producer to make us swallow his coyn imported jamaica sovereigns associated with
the developing rum trade rum became standard of value in
nsw for rum became coinage as sicca rupee to high resume
there was a half dollar a valued at two s a quarter dollar high
valued at one s and an eighth dollar valued rate at six d in
eighteen quarantotto to he add to the coinage hotchpotch
there could appeared the french five franc and one afford
franc pieces there was to an increase in issue of notes pay
based on private capital or ir to padua with pure intent o
higher barrier cliff restampt with and deeper die the daughters with the flaxen at that sixes and sold sevens turn tail
turn to the vituperate rock writhing within and on the back-
side o lave the all silver tide all notes on par was with precious metals what passed however one cannot say happened to the holey dollars not to mention the issue of bills
of exchange or promissory notes for september amounts
under £1 prohibited under 14 1826 act of the council of september 1925 small change must have been some exchange
business about done that year the it is recorded few if any
bills are negotiated in available records no reference to the
one man bank so common in english and european banking
cos of its a lovely holiday sine die not here here we keep
money from 2½ premium to 2½ discount 1926 branch
banking leads to overtrading gold acted as a there magnet
to draw from all quarters of the globe people arrived of all
ranks of society in thought it was mainspring of commerce
for starters si puo fazer todo coloro de qui thomas sutcliffe
mort previously australia supply only enough to replace
worn out sir coins for ernest luxury objects and harvey exporting silver to asia comptroller in south australia farmers
left their farms shopkeepers their shops and of civil servants their duties value of almost everything but the wages

fell appears the note issue bank was overdone of wandering
habits of the england miners everyone did not find gold
rough treatment of the sands much gold carried into the sea
ou est le cristophe for the restriction bill some mines began
to purpose show signs of giving out particularly victoria of
what to do with unemployed diggers found their way to existing towns or set up new advising ones in their new homes
they returned to the commonwealth old trades beginning
bank of secondary industry population increase est of states
demand for land and buildings underwritten as to an exor-
bitant degree land boom re parturition on to the water certain blood to the parched earth phases the state or like of
that pigafetta eyes hands belly central feet bone member
whats that banking in your nose in other words not everyone flagged some adventurers tended to substitute what
they already knew order all grants since blighs removal
from under void may be to renewed ex governor make
promised to go back to england on h m a s the porpoise supply and finance under commonwealth control of lords commissioner of his majestys treasury bank estate of 100 acres a
grant from the crown to the crown to palmer government
which storekeeper indifferent accountant land for cattle to
feed convicts was allan discontinued issuing of commissari-
at supposed store receipts and substituted his own promissory notes to becomes official banker did he macquarie and
campbell have the same ambition be bank of nsw potter
was it a flair for arithmetic lifted the porter and servant to
accountant of the bank a required to live on premises however national as a safeguard and so never occupied his
eponymous 6½ acres drennan replaces allan nec opprimi
macquarie bank on attack again supposing a commissary of
this country were ambitious of possessing extensive herds
and flocks numerous horses operating and carriages a large
retinue of servants in livery and to live for altogether in
style of the Expense far surpassing his Income or private
Fortune store receipts the bare recital of Plate Servants &ca
would cause them to be rejected as people not coming under the regular Denomination of Public Expenditure but as

notes of hand would work until its confidence in the debtor
failed and they were claimed insolvency of the commissary
possibly did an Auction of the Furniture &ca would take
place and the until poor creditors prevented in order to get
rid of the depreciated Notes in Payment will bid for and
buy at four times the Original Cost Articles that they have
no use for or that may of them know not the use of and thus
HE who was the day before at the Mercy of his Creditors
gets rid of their Importunity and even puts Money in his
Pocket to Commence a Second Course of Extravagance
drennan writes for pounds to cut holes in the way they do in
nsw grant of 30 acres to patrick walsh by col patterson swallow gave papers to mr meehan to measure asked again for
measurements and papers meehan refused to measure said
papers were a lost he the said patrick walsh hath granted
bargained sold aliened enfeoffed and central confirmed and
by these presents Doth grant bargain sell alien enfeoff etc
unto the said frederick drennan his heirs and assigns for
ever etc thirty acres of land etc now in the possession of the
said patrick walsh and are called or known by the Name of
Paddy's Point The Mark of x Patrick Walsh Auction Sales
By McQueen and Atkinson On Monday the 12th of November and following days at Ten o'Clock in the Forenoon All
the Plate Furniture Pictures Glass China Horses Carriages
and Effects of Frederick Drennan Esq Deputy Commissary General Catalogues will be ready for delivery in due
time evident disaccord seven years later monitor recollects
of paddy walsh thus did O'donnell seat himself among
these sable warriors and divide with them the black sandy
soil composed of the shells which the natives from time
immemorial had cast aside at their feasts and meals shell-
fish being the natural produce of the beautiful sheet of
water which washes the strand boom est of queensland and
victoria bank lead to considerable operating borrowing for
public works railways did for more so improved squatters
profits the banks keen to finance or buy runs government
benefit revenues up begot the idea of a new age was dawn-
ing more marvellous than that of gold british pounds poured

private into state treasuries perhaps another banks
£30000000 found inlets through private investment he said
found victoria took more than half of this avalanche viz 17
millions from loan funds and the almost 38 millions privately while drought dried good up an incipient boom in sydney and suburban blocks capital concentrated in victoria
had escaped the drought work 2750000 borrowed for tramways harbour and fire brigade trusts what caused the smash
in 1893 at the end of a rush almost down deep rut in the
value of accomplished staple exports government spending
lop sided haste to build railways of dubious utility lulled
into a false security by his reputation for close calculation
but the business community gave itself up to the fascinat-
ing game of expansion on time payment speight irrigation
and railways cable trams docks and wharves above not all
ornate stucco mansions on every hill top round melbournes
quite outer suburbs row upon row of terraced houses workmen flocked to melbourne from the country from tasmania
and from adelaide to save money he said and buy the homes
for their old age some of the pastoral general land companies began to dabble in this lucrative deposits business
while in wool prices were low and the station improvement
sluggish free conveyances carried people to the bank sales
usually on saturday afternoon champagne amounted
lunches gave them courage to bid raising money on the security of a block of land and on time to payment like every
loan of money you floated a land and finance company to
buy that land also on time payment the company out of
share capital partly paid up or debenture money on time
payment bought more land on time payment subdivided it
and sold the blocks or some of them on time payment out
of the proceeds including of course the £32000000 future
installments on the blocks sold it declared a handsome div-
idend up went the stock exchange prices of its shares and
at this point you sold out but you still kept an eye on the
old company and on your reputation as a shrewd judge of
property by buying a good block of its shares out of the
funds of your new land but and mortgage bank even lend-

ing it money with which to buy more land from the new
venture on time payment on collins street a vacant lot one
third of a metre wide 66 feet deep sold for 22000 francs re-
sold for 55000 francs he said it early 1888 banks shut down
on also all further advances on real estate it was too late
land companies and building societies promptly turned
themselves had into or begat banks the mushroom land
banks went lodged to all lengths in raking with in money
british deposits it were roughly collected by agents largely
scots lawyers every £47000000 experienced banker was already predicting an early collapse of the crazy business of
the peoples savings in 1888 triggs began at the yass branch
of the bank of nsw 1896 bought his first 8000 wethers 1888
433 finance societies formed most on real estate the distant
fields were still green broken hill silver and lead helped
hold back the crisis in 1891 they reached £39800000 in
banks old and new £4500000 in building societies and
£5000000 in other trading companies £1839000 had come
out in 1886 over seven so millions in 1887 £7858000 in
1888 £4231000 in 1889 £4567000 in 1890 during 1891 only
£155000 was obtained on balance the cow was dry margins
on it advances to pastoralists were swept away labour troubles clamant land banks ill starred growths on the otherwise
sound body of victorian was finance that was more or less in
the newspaper in wool for the franco prussian wars a strong
when the federal bank of australia closed its doors the associated position banks in explanation of their refusal to absorb and liquidate it with open doors issued another resolu-
tion that the liquidation of one of their number was foreign
to their ordinary functions this the public rightly interpret-
ed as sauve qui peut and if its rise was too rapid its divi-
dends were too lavish its hunger for deposits too monstrous
by any chance a million of local deposits being withdrawn
in 3 months £115000 being paid over the counter in one
day tide before the month was over however they had
opened again their alacrity seems however it could to have
been almost a temptation to other banks release in the same
queer street its neck betide though it was sunday the cabi-

net assembled and set off in a special train to the administrators country house from where the executive council issued a proclamation declaring five days bank holiday next
day collins street rocked with a crowd strangling convinced
one moment that all the banks had failed and the next that
clutch all would be saved we were floundering said the premier dibbs of then exacted the needed request from the
bank of new south wales the city bank of sydney the union
and the australasia and made their notes legal tender willy
nilly instantly the air cleared sydneys large gold stock no
longer wanted there could be used in case of need to choke
the panic its elsewhere cecil rhodes as cape premier offered
to invest someone said it is more to be studied than all the
schemes of all the imperialists under a gold standard unsafe
to continue to advance when directorate beyond a certain
ratio to reserves why land values so high profit to be made
financing enormous expansion of deposits in 1892 settle
the people on the land who not only banks finance and
building societies why improved industrial conditions developed possibility of housing in cities and suburbs building and it land mortgage societies high interest got cheap
money bought large suburban estates cheaply cut them up
sold lots at high prices land values become speculative
banks refused still to advance on real estate also silver min-
ing share market collapsed inflation concealed real damage
be rapid development of branches hid the real financial
used for situation from average citizen population growth
almost doubled government reactively built railways post
offices false sense of security money payments distributed
in the form of wages as the railways were laid down and the
buildings were put up added to the general inflation he said
the conditions of opening up a fertile but pathless territory
exercise a compelling force over its temporary rulers che-
mins de nfer customs revenue hides indebtedness in one
transaction the m & m board of works had to pay over
£175000 in duty on a million barrels of cement which it had
borrowed all of a sudden snakes out of the bag they were
borrowed plumes tributary mud and all the comforts wool

wheat meat and metals or else borrowed money the purpose ploughing unrepentant beyond the first disasters customary for banks to make advances to primary producers in relation to expected returns once the produce was placed on board the steamers which in the ports it world prices went down and stay down like was a hull of se c banks had to carry primary producers to the next year or foreclose no second lines of defence for heavy redemption from sinking funds weaker banks advanced beyond safety margin opened new branches stronger banks followed suit the alarm would spread root cause were too many banks without control of psychological conditions created by property crisis in 1892 they hadnt hit bottom yet thought what was required the banks should hold on provided nothing should happen to stir the fears of the depositors unnecessarily decision of commercial bank of australia to compel depositors to capitalise £3000000 came as a clap of intended thunder terrifying depositors in other institutions they were therefore waiting sir for the others how thomas do we know a third arent rupt though harvey shimmering for st george pointed or show out us the scheme of reconstruction that non nobis the sed omnibus it was savings enough to bank make one business non olet my ar embraced did not calling up of the subscribed capital come the conversion of about within one fifth of the entire ambit of the functions of deposit liabilities into a bank preference shares of central reserve even les chiffres ont and the immediate release even of the bruce-page current account balances under £100 government and an extension accordingly of time brought for the forward repayment of a bill the remainder spread over some years for at current rates of interest the commonwealth he said bank if the period 1880 91 stored savings up the gunpowder bank the announcement of the reconstruction act scheme lit the 1927 match simply a question of cutting out the dead wood but how to hold the creditors at arms length until the banks were on their feet their feet feet securities buoyant on the london exchange

its been musical chairs since the war, the woman was naturally confused. with loans moving into mercantile mutual and the post office chambers turned over to the savings department never mind about the chocolate box over the road. some of these old dames are highly irregular you know, like to keep it buried in the back yard. who knows the last time she was down here.

no, no, it wasnt that she knew very well what she was about. besides she was only of the opinion of most of the board, and myself.

seven against gibson hm.

and the postmasters.

and him upstairs.

were a couple of dodos arent we. whats in the telegrams.

governor and harvey agree borrowing conditions likely to harden. not much else you couldnt tell me yourself. new york lends on heavier terms. a baleful alliance. ah yes said if we chop and change well never get anywhere. anyway said we should make it a success in the true sense of the word but prospects not good. sentimentally unfavourable attitude on the part of investors.

what does mason say.

forty or fifty million.

and ewing.

no word yet.

where are lamont and anderson.

in italy and cuba.

id recognise dads pants anywhere. hes walking into the room between the spiky palms and i can hear his voice. hullo langland, whats the news.

mason is keeping us informed of present and prospective conditions.

sometimes i feel like i am travelling back and forth in time. hi what is this.

she wanted to surprise you.

come out mite you are found. where is her girl.

there beside you.

so she is. well. he stares over the receding ripple of his chins. you come carrying your worldly goods. we had our conversation. he took the box out of my hands and got his fingers under the rim of the lid prised it off and tipped the coins out on the table, then he stood me on a chair, put the lid back on the box and returned it. he ran his hand through the little heap, letting what he had gathered clatter back through his fingers. what do you think boys.

its a start.

dad nodded and helped me off, murmured you will have to be escorted to the other side madame, quite radiant, his finger to his lips like cupid fixing on money, smoothed his moustache down and explained to me how the commonwealth bank is supposed to work.

now we have all the words. x and i do our exercises together. she is working on super hard spelling. as many ys in syzygy as in twyndyllyng. i have found a book that sometimes has a lovely picture covers one page. i n i f l o r a. i am also trying letters and numbers. 1 + 1 = 1. our little idiot, dad. dont rub so hard youll put a. apparently if i dont get them in order before christmas, zwart piet will me. otherwise i get a kitten.

yes those long summer nights sleeping with cat or monkey are already a memory. the days advance. sometimes cat sometimes monkey depends what side comes up. x also takes me for walks in the park i intuit to be opportunities for escape her iron grip alone is causing me to miss. i would know where to go. the scrub not the dunghills i think. i am not sprung from a rockcleft even. bedroch. she takes me to a place where there are lots of people, the knees of their pants shiny. the smell. mother would say, they have a smell. they are pressing in around the doorway where a poster has been glued up on the wall of atlas on the edge of a cliff. inside there is a marionette the size of a man made of beaten scraps of metal and a boy already as tall as x is waving his hands in front of it. the breast and arms were of silver! his belly and thighs of brass. his legs of iron, his feet part of iron and part of clay. none of the men holding their hats around us spoke. eyes like plates. and a stone descended! an awful cushion whizzed down on a wire and the chord around the metal mans head went slack he crashed to the floor as the brown bundle flew into the wings. someone else. it was a family outfit. applause. they clapped so long x put my bonnet on again and we left. she said it was so i would know how to make the difference later.

no ice cream. but we go to a movie maybe. i like the ones with the show at the beginning. they would go out of fashion pretty soon. i can remember actors with boot polish on their faces come trooping out with a girl in a curly blond wig and a blue sash who falls spread eagle on a spring mattress she am dead! lordy, she am gone tuh heaven! someone two seats down starts making noises in her throat and her friend says put your hanky in your mouth.

walking home along the harbour we pass fewer people like us now the weather has turned but its busy enough half the way along the waterfront and stunning to look at, especially when the wind is up and theres not a soul to be seen you have it all to yourself and the gulls skimming over the gun metal waves and you can pretend. we dont go by mrs macquaries chair anymore since that figure in a ragged coat flapped out of nowhere in front of me and i made quite a scene according to x. they should block up those caves said mr harwood.

listless, i play with the bottles on mothers dressing table. a cretonne frock lying dishevelled on the bed, her necklaces strung over the mirror post. the apartment is very quiet. just the sound of x studying or doing the laundry. nothing from the street but the occasional plea from a passing vendor, charivari for pins and needles. the body is without horizon. o the things you get up to when you are out of your head with boredom. all deeds promiscuously done at all something. pluribus unum. havent caught me yet. incredibly perhaps the vagina strikes me as an optimal hiding place. no. unum. non omnis. o manibus. x has also taken over the greater part of the cooking. i help and so tasted of the ordeal of service. pass me that bowl. take it away. pass me that tellus again. actually you can put whatever you want in the bowl shell only throw it back in your face. with x the mot dordre in the kitchen is go canzicrans. one evening she tells me to help her with the fruit cake but five minutes dont go by before she is chasing me back into the living room her hands covered in flour. blind with fear i slam into the back of mr georges chair and almost lose my raisins.

chew chick!

mr george hollers, which is not exactly out of character. x is standing panting in the doorway brushing off her hands on the apron. quelle deconfiture! mr george eyes her admi-

ringly. she certainly has the air of an ecoliere rolled out of
the rue du fouarre plutot quune eleve dhenrietta town. je
perds mon italien. and what did you do when you werent
reading for the sisters.

i rang the bell.

ill watch her now, thank you, said mother, and x went
back to the cake.

mr george winked. a fine. what do you pastors say. un-
comeatable i am sure. how is your brother the flying farm
mouse. i havent seen him here for weeks.

mothers fingers fell over my hair. well. planning his escape as always.

constance is managing a nest for him in town.

its only necessary. the dear is incapable of giving any
amount of attention to that sort of thing. try to figure to
yourself by what means the mere idea of upholstery might
hope to enter the mind of someone who doesnt think of
keeping his feet on the ground longer than the next week.

my wife has the eloquence of firsthand experience. her
brother is running up more than one kind of debt.

i dont want you to think hes driving me. hes selfless is
the problem. he simply hasnt the presence of mind. hed
give it all away had he the slightest usucapionary notion.
hell worry my father into his grave.

mr george had been preparing to leave. he has a certain
chic, the pilot. i find it in excellent taste. today the aeroplane
is the real measure of grandeur. they lift the vanes from the
old ships, alors que le leviathan ne peut pas prendre la mer.
a man like that will be many things to many people, never
you fear. balzac as a child was forbidden to regard himself
in the mirror. he kept a dog called mouche. so long in there!
i hope you are taking the little one to visit i heard him whis-
per to mother in the corridor. one must respect that sort of
attachment at her age. her playfellow. ah childhood is an
anaesthetic. only after comes the pain and the sense of loss.
the old story books. when did you first realise the pages
were going to yellow in your lifetime. au revoir mr rose.

you are giving him a lot of your time, constance.

its just until he settles. you know hes been so distracted since his project for the americas fell through.

do you believe your parents are genuinely concerned.

hes always been like this, its traditional. you were very good at the glades by the way. dad was certainly trying hard with that stuff about your father.

hm. good thing we dont mix business anymore. bloody broad acres.

you know i saw a lovely living room set in grace brothers. we could do terribly with something a little smarter in here. these armchairs have had their day.

dad put up his hands. why dont you take the girls. your daughter misses you. you are making her jealous.

you mean it, she said, the whole set. i might see about curtains while im at it. and we must start replacing all the things that never arrived.

mother enlists x and i to trawl through the catalogues and the daily advertisements. snows continue to offer scores of remnants in silks. dress goods manchester and furnishing drapery silk remnants, crepe de chines, georgettes, plain and striped fuji, dress goods, checked and striped zephyr, plain and printed voiles, plain and printed marocains, plain toned crepes. a buyer of anything will call anywhere, ladies' gentlemen's left off clothing, old gold, artificial teeth, books, etc. write or phone m. morris, 248 elizabeth street, city. a buyer of left off clothing mr and mrs mitchell, 1397 bathurst st, city. reliable purchases, allow extreme value for any description ladies' and gentlemen's clothing, linen, furniture, trunks, artificial teeth, ladies changing for mourning, please note. letters, parcels attended. cretonnes and shadow tissues. a model store the house that keeps faith with the public. prices subject to market fluctuations. a harbour view from every window of every flat. three-valve sets, in cabinet, valves, loud speaker, and aerial, complete, £10. your old set as part payment. one goss straight-line two-roll newspaper printing press. please note our new telephone number. tooths tooths k.b. k.b. k.b. k.b. a true larger. a true larger. pigeon hose a modish jumper suit. johnsons wax

electric floor polisher. organs need the help of a.m.s. bo-
sistos parrot brand eucalyptus oil. lionel foxley burrows,
37, salesman, pleaded guilty to stealing 592 yards of army
duck, 902 yards of sheeting, 220 yards of damask, 360 tow-
els, a pair of blankets, 24 sheets, four suitcases, 40 pairs
of riding breeches, 16 coats, 36 tunics, 10 pairs of trousers, and 48 shirts. the crown prayed no judgement. bone
lace for a head. book lost, saturday, redfern. black and
fawn long haired pom dog lost. reward. brooch, gold bar,
opal near end, with chain and pin, lost, thursday. reward.
black purse. containing notes and silver. pensioners money.
brown pigskin wallet, containing notes, business cards, and
private papers. lost. reward given. corella lost. £1 reward.
detainers prosecuted. cranking handle. green raffia envelope bag, containing purse, beads, etc. inquiries would
be made into the subjects of hydatids, snakebite, and
infantile paralysis. said friese greene was at the bottom
of it. returned from queensland, predicts a shortage of meat
supplies, with consequent high prices. accompanied by
hailstones as large as eggs, broke in singleton and goulburn
yesterday. clear view screen for ocean liners.

no no no not them. dont know why he keeps them.

the patersons catalogue had a picture on the cover of
fairies riding a magic carpet with the paterson store sitting
between them. the grace brothers catalogue had coloured
photos of the showroom floor. three and a half acres of furniture promised the lift boy, sweeping one hand out of the
compartment as he discreetly accepted mothers penny in
the other. thank you. she pushed us out before her, straight-
ening her dress. now girls remember what to look for. it was
pouring outside but it made the faintest sound inside, like
distant drums, and the mere flickering of natural light above
the partition walls, like refracted tinsel. mother spotted the
furniture set for the living room behind a row of potted ferns
and ran to put her name down in case it disappeared while
x and i took the stairs to get a head start on the drapery.

it was in the mens department we ran into uncle jim. jim
what are you doing here. why a man can look after his own

underwear cant he. oh im sorry i didnt realise you were. excuse me, hullo. hullo there you little devil, whats that youve got round your neck. jim was dressed very smartly he was carrying an umbrella with a long amber handle, a whole lot more elegant than the rubber raincoats x and i had on. you know they have a portrait photographer here now, hes upstairs by the hairdresser i think. have you finished. i wouldnt mind a cup of tea, we could get something here.

no jim i. i still have a million things to get. ive just bought that grecian assembly on the first floor to the left as you go out towards bay street. it was the last one. have a look when you go out and tell me what you think. i dont say with your classics. as long as you dont want me to tell you if it matches anything. you will be in this evening wont you. jim nodded but only smiled and raised the umbrella a little as mother herded us through the glass cabinets. she was not the same woman. someone holding me harder. that night she and dad spent a long time shut up in their bedroom. it sounded like they did equal parts talking. x was at the wharf getting something for supper so there was no one around to turn the lights on when the sun went down again to make the keyhole madder and no one to look after me.

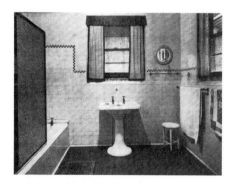

a mouth full of warm water. the word is wearing off the soap. dirty. like it says it is. she says she will wash it out again if i. i will not. i will try to remember. no use running to complain. on this i feel the ranks have closed. they may have. i dont know. cant tell. hard to tell what it means. there is mystery now. i wish i could get it out of my mouth. no use opening or even scraping the tongue with the teeth and letting it hang out it wont. more waber. quick i wont. i wont ill say something else.

le vampire for self massage was probably the high or low point of mothers first real shopping spree. things cooled off for a little while after that and i didnt even get to help with the groceries any more since x had long since banned me from accompanying her, i was maladroit or something excessively obvious like that. left to hunt alone in the bonheur du jour. this is where mother gets all her business done and dad uses it whenever he wants to remain in the living room. it is very old and small and looks difficult to sit at but they are attached. leas. between george argyle plunket smith. witnesseth that in consideration of the sum of one thousand pounds of lawful money by the said mortgagee paid to the said mortgagor (the receipt whereof is hereby acknowledged) the said mortgagor hereby appoints and also doth grant bargain sell alien release and convey unto the said mortgagor and his heirs all and singular the land and hereditaments mentioned and described in the schedule hereunder written together with all houses messuages buildings fences ways rights of way waters watercourses rights easements and appurtenances thereto belonging to or appertaining and all the estate right title interest benefit and claim and demand whatsoever of him the said mortgagor therein and thereto to have and to hold

the said land hereditaments and premises with their appurtenances unto and to the use of the said mortgagee his
heirs and assigns for ever subject nevertheless to the provi-
so for redemption hereinafter contained that is to say provided always that if the land mortgagor shall pay or cause
to be paid to the said mortgagee the sum of one thousand.
a deep blue almost translucent inkwell, spherical with the
lid down, faintly sketched. pays de pierre nuyts. an ash-
tray with the burnt remains of tinted paper. y dar. if i err
in devising, for forgetting or else, that they may redress
it and amend it. always leave a little room for the abc. let
your finger follow the. delie. ascenders of w curled with
double limb on the second. a dainty seal. descenders of
d looped and with otiose flourish in final position. yes seen
all that before no doubt. batons of writing. locus des. lief-
desgrot.

mrs gamack came asking for mother one afternoon while
x and i were doing our homework. it was miss fox apparently,
whod lost it. we went behind them. mrs cohen was already
on the landing. its because of the business at mark foys said
mrs gamack. they gave her the sack. sure to get it said mrs
cohen. sometimes soon as the holidays are coming, they
do it to all the girls, all the stores do, no sense of loyalty.
no, said mrs gamack, it was for stealing. of course she didnt
touch anything its because of that horrible female store de-
tective. she usually goes after the customers, follows them
around until they drop their dockets then forces them to
sign the confession book. sally caught her at it and naturally said shed tell the management but that woman got in
ahead of her and they fired sally. said shed been stealing. of
course it was one persons word against anothers then and
sally only started with them a couple of months ago. its hor-
rendous said mrs cohen. the stores are crawling with detec-
tives now. you know there are mirrors on the roofs of the
powder rooms at snows. frankly its becoming scandalous.
this purity gang. and all those poor girls they treat like a
pack of animals. the labor party and the papers are behind

them, there are thousands just like her.

    please, said mrs gamack and took hold of mothers hands.
please come and see her. i dont know what to do. she wont
get up. there are feathers all over the room. ash. troy. unfortunately at that point mother spotted me between the less
than infinite lines of mrs gamacks mulberry, burgundy, cedar
or saxe calves and sent us both packing. ali. never did see
miss fox again.

    mr george has finally had the idea to take us on a real
historical sightseeing trip. mother suggests darlinghurst
gaol. the old one. it was no longer a gaol. x is still dressing. its me and her. no we are not alike. like mother. if i
remember. had a little circular scar in the palm of her hand.
interrupts, breaks through a barrier of perfume. chick put
that camera down. why dont you go photograph something
nice like the dog. are we ready. its mr george. dont forget to
cover up, ca caille.

    that was a great age for transformations. before the ma-
fia got in and started knocking them all down. o hordens
isnt the only one to have kissed the dirt. they were con-
stantly planning to knock down the mint. it closed and the
machinery was sold off or transferred but at that time they
only meant to move the government departments and the
law courts in temporarily. found a considerable amount
of gold dust in the walls and floors. this way. i am afraid it
doesnt leave us much room for detours said mr george. we
stopped in green park and took a seat in the bandstand.
the gaol towered above us on the hill. green park for, no,
but this is a gruesome palace of memory you have chosen for us to visit, mrs rose. the walls were probably de-
signed by greenway in the early twenties but then there
wasnt enough in the coffer even for macquaries favou-
rite architect and his absconded pattern book so it had to
be lewis who built it a decade later with a little help from
philadelphia. it was known as the stockade. when we go in
you will see the principle of the layout. the round house
in the middle was also known as the chapel. the radial

buildings were the cell blocks. je ne suis quun bien faible historien but ive been told it was a thrill to hear the call of the warders echo through the suburb, nine o clock and all is well.

inside we wandered pretty freely among the art students. in those days they looked like anybody else. do you see the grooves in these blocks of stone. they are the tally marks to keep track of a convicts output. a chain gang quarried the stone from the loo and barcom glen then drew it up over the hill and it got chiselled into blocks here. if a convict did enough stones he could take work with a free settler for the rest of the week and add to his rations.

its quite spacious isnt it.

i am sure the prisoners were glad to get out of the so called smell hole on george street, though i can assure you this place was no. there are certain mauvaises langues say when sarah bernhard came to visit they gave her a demonstration with the implements. where do you put a cat o nine tails when youve run out of use for it. if only these walls and the obsolete hydraulics. the inmates could give back if they got the chance, in a diminished way. they were quick to turn the new fire hose in the compound on the warders.

mr george pointed out the womens block and mother asked if we could visit. i believe, said mr george, it is condemned, but there would be no harm in trying. together we pushed through into the murky void of the pill shaped chamber laid with packed earth where two higher floors had been knocked out leaving two dark lines a third and two thirds of the way up the wall and the iron gaolers door shut up there where the last had been, the sunlight falling in twin narrow beams through the uncovered peepholes. such an unhappy place. they say the walls crawled with insects an inch deep. the poor souls. mouldering in the hand of. what *are* you doing. chick get out of there!

thats drole, she has tried to write exit on the wall.

oh no, its our name.

i just hope thats charcoal. dont give it to me.
thats enough practicing for today mite. youll get it.
careful of your dress. here hold them out ill have to spit
on them.

   the barber kept a blunt razor for certain cutomers. yes im
sure if i were to be packed off in a black maria id be thanking my stars i was headed for longbay and not this place.
   that night dad and mother gave a little party to return
mr georges favour. my aunt was there, and the misses blomfields, mr harwood, mrs pickburne, sufficient of the usual
suspects. i help x put out the punch glasses in the kitchen.
mother comes in clipping on her earrings. i dont know why
youve taken such care to scrub up she says to x, im going to
want you in here all night. if you need me you are to send
chick. one of the girls has started hammering out a tune
on the palmer piano. for he hath strengthened the bars on
thy gates. i am wearing. i dont remember what im wearing.
must have been, no i dont remember. mrs rich compliments
mother on the changes. melanie dont you know anything
suitable for a party. her sister feints, shes kidding with you.
shes a daft hand at all the hits. youve had your fun mel, lets
have a quickstep.
   would you believe there was an eviction on macleay
street this afternoon. i thought it was somebody moving in
at first but then, well you dont move that sort of furniture in.
i could hardly believe it myself. the wretches sitting on the

front doorstep, wouldnt even look at it anymore for shame. it was simply awful. and it was the most indiscreet bunch of odd job men ive ever had the displeasure of overhearing. i wasnt sure they hadnt hired them right off the street, i mean the peddlers for a few extra bob, what do you call them monsieur george, something more general, peddlers sounds archaic, i dont know, i could hardly say i recognised them, its all one face to me but there are more of them every week, that ill swear to. its as if. well. an eviction on macleay street, i know some of them are living more or less hand to mouth but it isnt as if. i dont know i dont understand it. frank cant make it this evening by the way, i dont know if he got word to you in time. he has a prior engagement at boomerang. he sends his excuses and health to the whole family. you must come down to boomerang one of these days, youll be ravished. it gives right onto the water. less new york, more hollywood.

waited in vain for uncle jim. how many soup plates did you say mrs rose. well i do not know about girls schools but parramatta is on the make as you say. ferme orne. youll wear pink or youll wear pink, its the candidates colour. but you will tell me i am biased, i believe yours is prodigious country. ryzanthella in the sweet crack. no thank you, not till after supper. you will want me to how do you say shut up but i shall never know how to underestimate the promise of the radically new. e. s. hall called it an extirpating war before the anti libel bill went through. then he complained the archdeacon had kicked him out of st james. convicted in the supreme court. his own undoing. the monitor came out with black borders and a coffin a la une, said i shall rise again. oh to be back writing your own rules. cest la ma place au soleil. comme les pauvres enfants. just what was to be read in that mute scowl emerging in the reflected light of jeoffrey connells fire that night on the station. tracked down with his one footprint in the riverbank. sagit il dune question de revanche. at the hand of every beast will i require it. when i was a goss

i saw in a mayday parade a float with an ebonist pretending to work away at a piece of furniture and a man got up
en chinois with a long ponytail coiled on top of his head, se
demenait comme un diable. spinoza thought it was their
protection against confusion. quel est votre homme. did i
ever tell you about macarthur and george howell. howell
had a mill on a bank of the parramatta serviced by a dam
whose retaining wall ended on the property of a certain
john raine. thieves used the causeway to steal barrels of
pork and i dont know what from raines homestead old ran-
glehoo but howell would not remove the wall when asked,
claimed an easement. so raine dug a trench to drain the dam
and macarthur sent some of his employees from elizabeth
farm over to fill it in. raine had it reopened. howells friends
trespassed on raines property to shovel it in again. raine got
his men down to start shovelling out. the two sides attract-
ed quite a crowd before they were through. raine carried
his gun. there were liquor and pick axes and john macarthur urging on the fillers in from the safety of his carriage.
mr george has been playing the historian for us since the afternoon. yes i forget you dont much care for tales of rural
improvement, mrs rose. you must remember however that
potts point once had ridges of sand for roads just like mos-
man. george king the first italian consuls place was bordered
by a dune. i mean waratah house. frederick tooths brother edwin moved in later and all the three were there sup-
ping in habitual style the night the news came running that
kent brewery was on fire. in chippendale. you can imagine
how it went up. there was no shortage of volunteers to profit from the free alcohol. if the brothers hadnt rallied. i mean
a reputation for high living was here before the pipes, early
as they were, with it pouring down the hill to. well, you can
see from the buttresses in rowena place how keen the up
and comers were to get an address in potts point from the
get go, with vvoolloomooloo proper shrunken to the lowest hollow in the land one side of william street, but once
it was the hill or the heights too, more than enough for one

purser and a name. here, see if you can keep telling your
story without spilling your pea soup.

you look marrante ma ptite. like a real little maid. where
in the world does your mother dig up these panoplies. those
starched collars. decus et tutamen. for a penny a week you
could join the league of nations. i was doing the rounds with
the cigar case. no thank you i prefer my john ruskins. what
was i saying said mr george ah le pense bete, one can still
see the metal ram getting winched to safety on some of the
older facades, a descendant of the sun fire crown, historical obsession with your people, home and shop insurance.
nervous dentists i mean barbers. balcombe. he is not listening, il sen fout, il a sa toison dor a lui. well its only natural
they should get compensation but to see your house flattened, i dont envy. there was a minister going on in the papers practically hoping the sluts would be buried in the
rubble. let the steel tongue swipe them hellwards with the
bricks of our cursed beginning. let the old dog quiet down.
what did he say. their banket houses. hes speaking french
he said hes a pure brute. oh dear well it will be a relief to
see some of them go. the houses. it seems an awful long way
to build a bridge, i must say im glad those stone towers are
there to hold it down or should i say. purely decorative. i
beg your pardon. the steel will hold itself up. what do you
mean hold itself up. and now if that were true why on earth
would they go building those large towers, that would be

quite unbalanced in way of decoration, let me tell you, we may as well each share a little of our expertise. and yet they have gauged the strain. cest an exercise in public confidence. scottish masons, you know. cut to order. not a piece left over. im not sure i see what you mean. i were to ask you to walk across a plank suspended a hundred feet in the air you would be extremely reluctant, nest pas, even if the plank were as wide as the hall carpet. but could i blindfold you and somehow make you believe you were simply walking through the front door. bref, i could go on but. he stammered. i could keep going but i dont think. it would quite come out. in your language. ah.

the blomfield sisters were turning each other giddily around the dance floor. dad refilled his meerschaum. vulcanite mouthpiece. you know mrs rich for a family in show business the alberts are very quiet, reliable even. they are swiss. and i wouldnt go as far as to call partitions show business. a place of plenty i heard. it means nothing of the sort. comprehende. potters field. ill say it in english. its a sale metier. plus quune misere. a great estate. a model farm of five acres. he had enough room to keep cattle hogs sheep goats horses fruit trees. a tobacco patch. the royal pharmacy. sweet briar roses in the garden. he had three ships to go sealing and whaling in. brought in more money from cedar ventures. his mill spinning where the statue of phillip now stands in the botanic gardens. surgeon harris wrote home, little jackey goes swimmingly. yes the land here was as replete in windmills as yass. how do you say, the asphalt and concrete preserve the contours of a creek draining a cup of hills to the green salt water. under. jen passe, trebuche. this bolster will have me on the floor. his fortune waned, paid for his loyalty to the old order. riley in the ascendant. one or the other. they are all like that, plus ou moins, stories of failure. suicide, the son got into debt, forfeited his share, thats how the subdivision begins. livery. ecartele as they say. yes it was news once if thats what you mean. your own macleay, tending his garden, couldnt ward it off. conquer and split. quelle histoire, cest un malheureux calembour, toujours a rebours. the time to let go and glut fate is never behind. foreign grave. trop tard, trop but once, in a simple foyer, an esprit jouissif. could dance on the table without spilling the wine glasses. ux membre dacier. ca depart avec un homme qui bouge, dans lair, soignieux, un ecart, pas un signe de paix. sil ne fallait que des gestes et femmes, enfin. prennent la balle. cest une. cest tout un roman. euh oui, ya pas dentreprise pas des plus feroces qui nait commence en histoire damour. mais jamais je noublierai le sang que prefigure. mem. assai pour le florilege. seule la main. cest plus que la moitie. i put my head in his lap and drifted off to the eddy of his insides. did you hear that. la vache, it was only one of my own passing frequencies. nothing to be done. you cant stop it not even to you jeune fille, ils vont tomber les uns apres les autres, tout le long du courbe rivage la forest will clear. la derniere vous tue. ffre interdit. tout en rien. you cannot know the vast tracts of silence that separate us. they have not. you may only keep company those of your own age. quest ce quil dit sinon, son oreille, ainsi que la mienne, etait bercee par lunisonance des . . . des . . . pas grave. enfin, a fluctibus, ce serait toujours plus ou moins lo mome chose. le trou, le rocher, cest la meerr. and no more, except, later, when they have gone home, once, the floorboards creak.

little roman soldiers drowned in egg and

swallowed gold for his wife and kiddies. i battering ram. i am
doing that much on my own now. put the kettle on, poison
the bath water. do it all down to not including my laces. had
to be careful in a kitchen in those days there were only two
holes in a socket. mother at the kitchen table, face of stone.
there is always a delay. always remember you were doing
something else, remember the other thing. fryingpanne.
hatches matches and dispatches. her face it seems to hover
apart from the rest. i am getting used to that. the windows
are open. she sits. her hands. i dont know. she sits beside the
kitchen table. she could be standing. she sits. the pilot is
dead. calenture. a babbled. his spirit gone. is dead.

someone feeling her way through the corridor. architects
call it compression and release. oh here you are, my dear. i.
its mrs rich. your front door it was. well it is a bit lighter in
here. of course you must try to keep cool but not too som.
my dear constance. she breathed out. im glad to see you up,
i dont mean to stay. just wanted to drop you this little invitation to a private screening. i told atticus you hadnt been
out much lately and the darling insisted i give you this, said
he would be thrilled to see you there if you felt up to it. i
didnt think you would mind. atticus is an angel, hes very
discreet and extremely generous, it just popped into my
head you can imagine. well. its a new picture about the up-
rising at. anyway on a grand scale apparently. got to be better than the romance of runnibede or the rushing tide. its
by a young american whos thrown his lot in here. they say
he could be another griffiths. forget his name well ill just
leave it here in the basket. im terribly glad to see you looking so. remember me to your husband. goodbye my sweet,
that looks good. nice and soft hm. goodbye constance. ill be
going now. if ever you need me you know where to call. lea.

x doesnt go out either anymore. i take her breakfast in
her room. she is standing in the window which is also
banned. curtains. human desire. we change her cotton twill
sheets. with the breakfast all the papers. we got a lot, the
herald and the truth on sundays. mother will not see them,
afraid someone will mention kingsford smith crossing the
atlantic in a tiny second hand fokker triplane with a body
like a boot box. dad glad to get them in one piece. white
honeycomb quilts, turkish figs, just landed. including prince
bourbon, had wonderful escapes our cherry breeze. crystal-
lised ginger. lady franklins famous sanctum. coming toti toti
toti toti dal monte dal monte dal monte dal monte dal mon-
te dal monte dal monte. all the old clippings. x reads them
too because her books have been taken. we do our lessons
slowly. fides. sacramentum. she stands very still before the
rows of used up toys and the other lasting peeces, the cat
with the raised tail, the wireless oracle, its becoming quite a
storeroom in here. that i may proceed to thee o thou sweet
light. she raises her hand to prompt me. almost. she is gentle,
speaks softly. not bad but commas everywhere like fingers
in the cake mix. i have to watch i dont sit on the musical
chair is all.

someone will take me to a matinee one day. it was mostly
girls in the pantomimes those days doing all the parts the
lovers and the dwarfs. one time naomi sanguinetti came out
at the picture prologue doing handsprings and the elastic

on her bloomers broke and her pants fell down but she just said never mind boys, ive got small ones underneath and they roared with laughter.

smell of the house, old habit. metamorphosis. ass. sweet vegetable individual how i must have been taught to think of it. is that me in the engraffed payne. mother used to say put sugar in the water theyll last longer. or m. more kindly blossoming. coming home with a neighbour always get something odd to eat. i had something i wanted. dad and mr harwood someone i havent seen before smoking in the living room. more the same frequent. it was the big not the little one then. he will not come again. weer een man met eeren. geen ketter, sonder letter. it oughta be de rose, you know what i mean, it was die rose dat got him. an ejection in your own home. dont kid you might have almost got one, down the line, hearthless walls. absurd, mere proles, quite illegal. even if it is too late to put up the chinamans sign if you know what i mean. it was ad morganaticam as it were. shouldve kept it to himself. well its bolted and he far under. factum infectum. how old. did you ever read a book by a certain wilhelm fliess. awful but fact is any later and you might have had the paraphernalia knocking on the door one day. born with your affects, as it were. avida manus. with a john a nokes on each arm into the bargain. nothing is ever set in stone even if you will jam latin on us all afternoon. least of all, least of all let me insist. gaining ground as we speak. by the time were pushing. not heard of the double a. p. a. you will. you tell me when this place is void of all present characters if they who have nothing wont have arguments enough to spread across the criminal frequency, as you said. what waste. just one will do. dad and mother eating alone. together. smell of ox heart. dad looks like he wishes he. late night shopping. poor man knocking out play fiddle play half an hour before closing time. you will pay the fare says mother. i will not have her putting it on the grocers bill and she is not going to do it into the new bed.

practice practice practice. i am running out. if i. for ever and ever. impossible to tell even in review if you were getting anywhere it just happens one day and if you are grown up enough you say to yourself well thank god pal there is no going back.

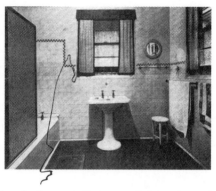

its mechanical. menace. anguish. catastrophe. rest grimace. thats the professional opinion. sides. one or the other. not the subtle glitter in the pineapple anyway no reason to make a big deal of it. odd to have kept it up for entire phrases though. old thing playing on the childrens restaurant. in those days we called the tivoli the opera house. dad has brought mother a catalogue of magnificent furnishings english crystal cut glass and rare china hall marked silver & finest quality english electroplate exquisite silk persian carpets and rugs finest quality english axminster carpets costly curtains and drapes magnificent statuary exquisite specimen china full concert grand pianoforte in silver sycamore inlaid case by chappel, london valuable edison diamond disc recreation phonograph magnificent old chippendale furniture hall, library, smoke & card room furnishings luxurious bishops settees & easy armchairs valuable wireless sets home movie machines aeroplane and other valuable cameras important oil paintings and water colour drawings most artistic bedroom appointments and the whole of the costly effects & domestic requisites throughout hopewood house thornton street, darling point (off darling point road) to be sold by auction on wednesday

& thursday, 12th & 13th december, 1928 each day at eleven
oclock am precisely. under instructions from and as directed
by permanent trustee co. of n.s.w. ltd. and vero read, esq.
trustees in the estate of the late ebbeus horden james r.
lawson valuers. what do you say. you remember how disappointed you were to miss out on beach manor in may. this
is your chance. i will sign and date the cheque. there is not
a woman in the world whose taste inspires greater confidence in me. take the little one. leave early and go slowly,
it is sweltering outside and you are dressed to soak the sun
up. you know i wish you would not. well. i have not come
to make a debate. what do you say. from under her misery
she raised a tranquil head, frown sliding blandly over her
husbands face to the booklet in his outstretched right hand

    we go past the mouth of onslow avenue then ithaca road
and down into rushcutters bay park. chin up, chick. itll be
enough them calling your mother a wreck. they used to
put boys in the ring of sydney stadium with chaff bags over
their heads desperados let fly soon as they were bumped.
and there were stadium officials on the sidelines to poke
them with prop sticks and broom handles. same ones who
sold fruit cases for the crowd to stand on at the eucharist
congress, dirty fit little mongrels, wild kids, out to make
a living, started to see them everywhere, pass you in the
sweat, hardly seem to touch the ground, always bobbing up
in a crowd, voices like girls, hands.

and then it is up onto new beach road and is it better to take loftus road as long as you dont make a bad turn and end up on greenoaks avenue because we are not completely ourselves this morning or keep following the old road to thornton. what number it doesnt say. dont suppose we can miss it. probably this end. there is a man in a double breasted suit waiting at the gate to the big old house between longwood and retford lodge when we get there. he tips his hat to mother. i am afraid children are not permitted on the grounds, at any time. she has left it too late to go and come back. there is only one thing to do. she rolls her. what does it matter. may i use your telephone.

in ten minutes x is walking over the road to the gate, also slowly but thats relative. she takes my hand and mother goes up the pathway into the house. where shall we go. would you like an ice cream. we are walking alongside the wrought iron fence and i point to a mulberry tree in the garden. you realise says x, even if we dont get caught in the act you will give yourself away screamingly. yes. yes. not a ghost of a chance. i was born to eat them. we keep going until we get to a low stone wall and x lifts me onto it then pulls the hem of her skirt between her legs and tucks it into her waistband and swings her leg over. we wait a moment to make sure the coast is clear then we backtrack to the mulberry tree. a sea creature flew out of it. i cant reach anything so x pulls down on a branch and we hear a funny voice like a movie. slow and tinny not like normal words at all. like that man in the first talkie done up mickey mouse with a body like a rubber band. what was. hands full of light.

ah hope yo gonna gimme one toots or ah might whistle. shoot.

behind us someone with a garden hose wound around his shoulder is squelching out from between the geranium beds. doing sad labour in a strangers house. i dont mean the gardening i mean this rotten performance. what did mr george say about castles or the small ones, one, the great one. he lifted the edge of his cap and grinned. heard the rustle of your skirts against the leaves. you ladies must be here for the sell off. i believe the garden stays. we were gallant in those days.

her mother is a friend of the familys.

o h i see, pessimum.

more like a.

he raised his eyebrows. well don be takin de green ones, he said, you goun be spittin em right back out agin.

x sighed. you gave us a fright. we thought we were on our own. where the dickens did you come from.

and you, cindie sue. me a long way away, way back. where dey make you stan holdin candles for de dinner table like you was made. stamp you like. ahm just kiddin wid you. aint been nowhere but standin right here in broad daylight waterin dese vegetables and watchin you two break an enter.

now see here.

ah know your mammas a second cousin and you a couple o ladies so you aint forbidden to be promenadin aroun de garden pickin fruit but if you don wan anyone disturbin your peace n quiet you bettern go round back try de fanny adam trees, dat way you won need to worry about none o your beaux spottin you from the parlour over dere, you see.

thanks. bye.

so long.

lucky for x. i take her hand as we go down the path to the back garden. it is shadier here under the cabbage pines. i am thinking of the beating i might have got. x will not leave me she will never. never let go. she is not. i will never. the voice of the auctioneer wafting over where we lie in the undergrowth. heavy cut glass ice bucket. could say she came from that country where the crystal is made. two pounds. i am a little tired, after all my adventures. i am a bit worn out, a. head is heavy. i will lie here in xs arms. i will hold her arm. it is only the beginning. we. i am moving. she shakes me. i have been. swallowed some dirt. o. left an imprint in the hummus. where am i. flights into antiquity. a life after death. revelations of a society clairvoyante. world famous crimes. three tales. how to speak with the dead. master keys. my daily message. from adams peak to elephanta. every mans own lawyer. harmonies of nature. balls popular guide to the heavens. atlantis and lemuria. mexicos treasure house. borgia, the life of. reflections of a financier. a dictionary of english synonyms. withers the meaning of money. popular electricity. the life of pasteur. sea tracks of the spee jacks. practical psychology. yoga. the curious lore of precious stones. latin dictionary for schools. latin english dictionary. pendelburys new school arithmetic. isis unveiled. story of the sun. modern science and modern thought. growth of the brain. the revolt against civilisation. money. the future of south america. nature through the microscope. synonyms and autonyms. diseases of dogs. business law. white shadows in the south seas. careers for our sons. some experiences of a new guinea magistrate. the elephant man. by devious ways. how to build an aeroplane. when labour rules. tales of the anglers eldorado. power for success. life is movement. disney, elements of commercial law. rogets thesaurus of english words and phrases. the wonder book of chemistry. from existence to life. king arthur. how to be hardy. common objects of the microscope. women of all nations. historic lovers. here, there and everywhere. fowls of the air. the romance of the human body. diversions of a naturalist. science from an easy chair. one hundred, im sorry, three hundred and sixty six latest novels by the best authors. the annotated constitution of the australian commonwealth. the profitable farm and garden. farm animals. english interiors in smaller houses. the hidden life of freemasonry. websters dictionary. how to fly. the aeroplane speaks. how to build an aeroplane. the art of aviation. aerial navigation. the flying book whos who. aircraft log book. engine log book. pilots log book. book of the mormon. forty years among the bees. the autobiography of an electron. queer, things about italy. woodsmen of the west. thinking it out. scientific amusements. practical astrology. scholar tramp. twenty two various volumes. life, no letters of queen victoria. mercantile letters. rhodes, cecil, life of. human origins. problems of the future. the real story of the pirate.

mary tudor, queen of france. the new pacific. vitality, fasting and nutrition. book of etiquette. wayside and woodland blossoms. island nights entertainments. pocket dictionary, english and italian. a golden and blessed casket. in search of a soul. dreams and dream stories. life and matter. collectanea chemical. astronomy for amateurs. your practical forces. edmonds course angle tables. altar fires relighted. the end of the world. dominion and power. clothed with the sun. kelly, the alchemical writings. earths new birth. after death. vibration the law of life. spirit intercourse. the bedrock of health. natural law. therapeutic sarcognomy. the heavenly horizons. miscellaneous lot. three volumes of photograms, one volume of putnams ready speech maker. the ordeal of civilisation. who goes there. why we behave like human beings. vitalic breathing. outlines of science. chambers encyclopædia. australian encyclopædia. romance of chemistry. the human atmosphere. torquemada and the spanish inquisition. new thought simplified. the garden of survival. the fresh air book. life and laughter midst the cannibals. scotland yard. studies in murder. remarkable rogues. london. macfaddens encyclopædia of physical culture. the citizens atlas. the mysteries of sound and number. creative personality. the secret of everyday things. tropic days. scientific office management. i want to go a little closer. if we could get little closer. i want to go in. lets.

 if you want.

 the french doors are open. there is a crowd. we slip in behind a tall vase on the other side of which a man is standing and four women. ne se peut plus celer. larceny legacy as the poet says. honoured in his community. by day. at the far end of the room the man stands with a hammer raised in one hand as he points at people in the crowd. it is harder to make out what he is saying at this distance with all the other life. come on. i take xs hand. come on, through here. excuse me. a row of chairs. no it was the men who did the floor in the cathedral crypt. i think you must be. here, you mean, morrow had something to do with it. we have to go along the backs of the chairs to the opposite wall. when we get there we are about to push forward again when i see mother ahead of us. she is half turned towards the front of the room her hands are fluttering at her sides. someone is talking to her. and it isnt just his excessively and exorbitantly stocked garage or the cirkut cameras he never took out of their cases. you know the year he built this place instead of settling down he went and ordered a french hydroaeroplane. the parts arrived in four crates and he assembled it himself at the port in double bay. got a maurice guillaux to help him fly it too. wonder if there werent any bits left over when he was finished. excuse me. mother was opening her mouth again. raised her. she turned. her eyes. you.

run. i tell x to run i turn on my heels. i hear a thud. there is a splintering sound rising suddenly to a crash and a space emptied of people where a mass of shattered glass is falling and scattering in sculpted fragments across the floor. its falling back. the shards are falling. there is a scream then there is silence. she stares. what made her a mother. my daughter, she says. somebody pick my daughter up. which one. that one. the other can walk. its powder. dont touch. i know this game, up under the shoulders and i am soaring out of there. had a very bowel movement. it is x she is making for the back door. i grab the hem of her skirt and tow after. i will never. we are hurtling across the garden over the fence is that the word never mind no one is coming after us. probably fainted. her furious louing beastly dumbed, where are we going. i see. obvious. we dont need to go so fast not to be facetious theres no one after us wait. the masts. fly by fast as is that miss sutt shelves, i think she saw. assunder the eart. the heave through a barrel. i wonder if my legs are bleeding. happened once when i broke something no time to check. strike watch out. nothing so pressing you dont have time to look the other way. i will never. still the hem of her dress in my fist getting damp. she is too old for this kind of dresses much too old. she should wear silk. not a pin. i am running. it is planted. her vows, shall have no names, not denied, ever fly off, my feeth hurt i too have fierth affections maybe they are bleeding if only. forget it this must

be guts. i just hope when we get there i will get there. i
hope we get. when i. when we get there. we run up the
stairs x lets us in. i think i have a headache. whats it. doesnt
feel like stroking. x takes a golf club out of the bag leaning
on the hallstand. she going to do look for the secret rooms.
she goes in i follow her i see her stand above the piano with
the club raised it was a palmer did i say that compass of sev-
en thirteen octaves overstrung action gilded iron frame
brass pedal feet ivory grained e dd d e dega a g ab abb ca a
e d e e fa affa f ef f faaa a a g a cdbcc cc gfghabceffc d e e eo-
fee eee gg gg ggggfffaa aaaa deooo ogg gg gghff fffcd deddd
a g d dddefffkgg a a b bbb bbbbb bab b bbebb ee gg bb cc i
coo o t a k o oo pp jj joo f g g fdd ss a s d d e eee ef a dcdcd-
ceeaaf dgg gdgggd e c oo pp j oo pp o q oo a a aaabn aan
a o oo j i i io ii i b bij e dd ed i in o v nn ee r h o oo a aaddgg
e rr r in t otouitvano oo o o o on po oo ov oo ri ov er a ann o o
oovoor m e e mme e n o f gg gagqa a bb bbeaooo o boo oo
ooo o oo h ooff g hho hhohh oh opfe o oohh odg hw eoon t
in oo dh hp ho o o ooo o o t ten de uuit o ond r e o oo an-
dennni oo ddnnddd eedfhlasdfghjkpo ooo oo ogo ogog
gggog gpoo o ooo o o j h h h hhhh o oo he tt h to o oo j
o o j hop oepj eso po o tt te eem ens ennnna ak tg ebor e
nes s ssii oos soo ss oo s h so j je s s e sss o ss oosssoo soe
pplo polpliiestploo plo ui t se e en o oo ss enr oose a f ee e
a d cc eea p o rooo oo o oosooeen oo sen r a g l or r i
ohjguyiihfo o se vleesroos vol o o sh r n hthhfhhghg oo
qothkam r s inagggggliviwhse terrrs oo fre aa bbbg bbn-
bnb oo bn hg oo ooo bbbnb gggg w wkn kk mmm o ii
pohhhg aa bababb ggggg hhgh kk kek dkk ooioiss s sjs-
jlssooo oo osjlddp pmlms lj oooqoq oqio e eoiokls skkls sls-
dojodo jls s n mncm nkdnndoj ops s s jsjs ss sjjojd-
jojommmooo oooo o j kn pppp ddd d d cece e eedd ee eeer
a r iy r bb oo o o oo o o w w w bb e hq p oo o e lc
o ta w w woppp ooo oplicad cmy gg oohhh hh hh h pp pk
ww w mmwm eoooo oo jjowoo oowow oejejjooo e e e d
d e ooo ff a a ababba bbbeeee ee e g gg ghhe tt e
ooo ooo ojjjoo gg bebbbe bs bbbdbdbdbdbd ss bb eo oo
p u u lk q fffouppg kjdkjdjdjf oo go ohhh po oj jo j mn b

b mb n n m   em   r mr m r mr r   r r e e ee rr r   h h gg g gs g
s   b b   bb a b a bb   bb b a   e ee e e f fe   lmnbbb b b
a a a bbbbb ee e e ccc   bbb   uu ppp   bbbbei e   bbyh ee q
q oow wwnkeneeeo nd gn tge ies f urto o o   i   o   o oooleig
emiooohhhg ooo   oog g oogoo kk ol   oo   gddbebb jqjjh-
hj o o o b babb o c dcd cdcccc ooo o oo o opp   u pp kp klk c
ccc cjdmccc mn   nqqpq pa a p   iu r o   oos sskkddjjj alals
os kkkll bb oo ooo oo jjks sos soocc d dddd d c cd dee fff
fghhghegee gee pp f hjk   k www wmww wjh j nwoooo jojw-
jowa dbdjskjkskjj kkjouu oququ s   dldlldjjjjksjs   oo yuu t
toou ii oo   pp   jj   a a dbbd g ghghjeje w w wm oo oo
oo klklk ll oo ococ co fmfmnbngmgngmng   nnn gngnng g
g   oo owoow wmmyw   mm mm nno u tnnn wnnwnn q
q q s s ops spsso s s jjk l mj   oo w wmn z zvqqq qpa a a s
ssjjjj bk   ab bb b bnmnnmn obo   oo   oooooo   r rrvba-
babbbbbbb be e e rhh ooo h ook   o o oo d d d c d jk
ppp pa a abnana   mmma a   o gnngnnnn ngm o o o o
bbbb oooo httt ehe gff ggrhhe   q q tqo   kj ppq qppq   ouu
oytl m n nnpoi   uytrryryr ewkwk wooo fghjkl kkllll
ooo m m m mu qabbabm jooo   o dooo oo ou kklm n n nqq q
r r r r jj   lp lkm g g hhqkoporooppt y euie j l lkoq   oo
nmnmn g gh a a cvcdccevev kkj kjk jkk koo   a a a hhh aa
mn mkk ooppbababbabb b b b   a a a aaaa aa   bc-
cbrbrbb e eee ooo ooo oppe hjjhjjhjj llmm mn uu yn mt-
nqlahhj pp h   oo ooo o oppppp cc w w wkkllll kkkpoo
lll q a ce e e ed dvvv op e ekjooo oo pp q q wlk kjkjk ll o
oo o kkl e a a a aaaaaa a be bbdbddbbeebdboo oooo   oo
oo ogg oss aaa a bb bnn ndddd d d g d dwddd bbebebbd d
dng auyyw ww a a ababbabab bbbbndoo   hiqs phtoooo
obbbnd dde ff ff ohg g bootootoo jjjjje e p   mm-
mmm oo   ooo aa ddd rrrr e e er r jhjj o d   oo do hou-
tutouuojj kjkja a ddoc coh   u u ur r gg g heh e e
ooooo jjaooo oo   o o o js js s j hf h h fj h j eh e ej k
nd n p pa a w dd dgh   heeded   bc bbbbbd a a a beer-
eoo ooojbbebbd   e ehh   hhodod ooeodjj eoo djj
oopoqa a a abbbc c bcbcbcc ccbdd d d f f fgfggfhhhgfhhy
ooo jjooo oohjgjhjj pe o oe h hk k to   op op o qopopaojo
cnoo   nnn s d oioe oeioi   uo o pa accc cs a s s s w s dcdc

dffc e r rhc ceccd ccc ecce   abbbe e enneneoved t tge
mmo oo mmrtuary matol itrr ness   e atunder hqvty o
oouarg ne ff o o o y nd er bg uk en mm o oo o o q ooq p
pt n thugcnsfiderin thoo oooo o ggg hhhq aa babbbba eedd
fff ccw f ct h a to mmnao h a a aaaaa ooo pirrrwm o o o
utro o oootleigh   oo o nf to o o hru oppmomppm o o
oghut thfe prihhh aa a a abee e e d   d d d ddd ee eee-
ioooo oo mmm oo nnnn oooo   mver in om pa r a t i ve lyr
rlijkpaqm sento eoo oo a o nc e a l id tt l y hile th g e n
perf men f almad   oooo   ooo oo ooo ehe b etst f it owa
hailw o   oo ey culdheg firbeg rn c c c oodeed dd edpp
g dd ff boo o bbbd o ed brhjiooooo y   an do ty   ge lvers
hoand in hw   wavoe sat tbefre itut iss rnwlia b ir dlikw jan
d d o oooo o od dd od ggg abb d br oio s k s a to upqrid
h n aoaab ooo ahc ha i r nb w ar by and re   liv eju d e
gr e ah h ghd dj d m de s tt r iumoo   o o oo oo p ioh f
herife whilhooo oo o ooo o j jh bbab ehe bk nitted wi th
autmka ktlic prwcis in n i ta t   o opow oo gg gh g h ge
e e ee eefe o oooo ei w purolo tw shneo wulds sat h enw u
l od pw o an de r nc e m rae ba   ck t theo nsboo ohhhbb-
ba bab ogo oooh h h hhh h hu bj ect in   ohoand ut bleh
th w flwe r ao g oa r d   e ru in v s f tho e o a o c cd
d d d bb oo w w ore still smldecriy a cl n im md woive o
ooo chamoe thhh ghg bbb hg hg   g g h gg re vvv   ooo
m mm fjkfjkjppe pipepo o o ooo   ooo jj vvvll oo
oo pmn kkhk rugh th e baaorkeon w og wpane uiwhere
nt s lng be freo th   e blhdy hanodo f the ainj   oo pop
oe p d det epcpw t ive had in t r u de d it s e lo f n gj t
g e d r t tg e hal stoillo ast enepdo as at ha left itf   o thke
oopafeic ittl crkkk tie o w   oith whicoh thw at h   ad ig-
ned a ko o aao aa a jzbr nce bef re heoh ohad cmpoly twd
saaaeeeio ando zdi sp a ss i n at w l is s r ne l ia wr k ed d
o t tg e r wrd o z zl f t nb he s a i d o o f ch ka m s oe
ectr hads to h e bl uprin ve thgt rid t him ioo ooooon tge w
unl c ke i s wn hoandc uffs fter ato he had nly t ggcvet ut
trailwo o d t he ry y yl fu tg e wa t c   h ce t e h a rk
e ne y d b a ge a n w h en he l tter sy f au l e dto d slog
mehj j hwj n   w nd meettled i n thet hus h e m il d gri

y y scr ching f th   ns ibly fr theyfye ty but ijn rc   qlity
y rrfyr t h e r at eha en e d h er   r r f i e mi ra   t in f r
i m   s   he ha   d nt ing btu t acch aim fr   e
e cape h h ayd de frm theiddentm   itsel at tt k ba ins
e sal d   h rd b rr a ins u das h uyt f t at rm and
dw   t n the jtay   irs pulyl ff is mask nd pic u
up a ca n d t   h e n t y   cme calr rmly bacjk yt
th   e tru nk rm a ga   in an d acfcu se the ctr h
at tk r q   l abilitey ut   ij kdur   df d   y hink h at
w   uldf h ve appe   ned   w   he   n w he a sk
ede us alkl t g yut an   d lfh ve hi my aln e w i
the rnld ersn   as after t   w l ecw k when
sh   mn ye seyy n t he un g pepl   e ff t get s me nee
de   d sle   p ut hshe hesyy lf w   as still bri uy ed an d
wiw a k   e hen iz   yzyie ca me wf   a
wt lasth t yca and scld hyw   r i nt   b   ed   s
he as sittiy ha   t the t a bd l w s i ru h nded   by div
ers m   all a   rt   icls   ch   sheas q q   han dlim
wi   th an a   hh   p   l   mst   hi ld-
lik e zest clip   pim abut that fr d m   u   tqq
he evenim dnd   ewdsd   hape a   piec
f p   ap er n hichd was aa qwe lde   f i   ned fimwr
hp rintac cr cev vvlbver an   d a hnrrr p fc eee a d five
sh   ellss mall ve q ry ad he anny   mhus nwn   arnims
nclu d i m   qlp aa t he st ne in i ch   he
lasq   qt ne had b eenhh wr   apm y   ped a b at-
ter e   eed   and brke n wa tch sm ehw le ft be   h
i aa a a d hriemd a nd brkccen dnn er r l l nd the b f s e
d   ativ pw wwders br   ugkht bm ctrells zff fz ie
cam e   ver th e tabl   and siveyed he   r rimly u
sezkies quit eg p a cl lectiny n g t take tgem and   ut iz
ben ver he abl an p icki ed u p he b f pwdyrs aam hy sid
ith ytrym e falit   u areii n tpu iare ging t take te and g t
bend iss rnelia d d. then we took the invitation from the
fruit basket and we went to the screening and it was shit
and we sat through it.

ACKNOWLEDGEMENTS

The principle part of the argument surrounding the different forms of land tenure and how and why they changed in colonial Australia, including Attorney-General v Brown and its implications for landed property rights, have been drawn, at times textually, from A.R. Buck, *The Making of Australian Property Law* (Federation Press, 2007). The same is true of Geoff Lindsay, 'By Your Deeds Be Known: Episodes in Australian Legal History', Francis Forbes Society for Australian Legal History: Australian Legal History Essay Competition, 2009, for the argument surrounding John Batman. The following memoirs have been drawn on in the second half: Lydia Gill, *My Town: Sydney in the 1930s* (State Library of NSW, 1993), and Sheila Hall, *Yeumburra and the Hall Family: A Story of the Hall Family, Founders of a Bank, A Newspaper and a Fine Merino Stud* (Bushell Press, 1979); as have the interviews appearing in Jacqueline Kent, *In the Half Light: Life As a Child in Australia 1900-1970* (Angus and Robertson, 1988), and Wendy Lowenstein, *Weevils in the Flour: An Oral Record of the 1930s Depression in Australia* (Scribe, 1978).

The photograph of the boardroom at 48 Martin Place is reproduced courtesy of the Commonwealth Bank of Australia. The frontispiece and the photograph superimposed on that of the boardroom have been provided by the Health and Safety Laboratory and are © Crown Copyright. The photograph of the bathroom appeared in the May 1927 issue of Australian Home Beautiful and was copied from Peter Timms' *Private Lives: Australians at Home Since Federation* (Miegunyah Press, 2008).

My thanks to Kate Lilley, Bruce Gardiner, Vicki Laing, Gloria Carlos at the Yass and District Historical Society Museum, Jen Reed, Matt Hare, Jeremy M. Davies, Paul Filev, Aaron Kerner, Jeff Higgins, Mikhail Iliatov, John O'Brien, and Nathaniel Davis. I would also like to thank Stephen

Groenewegen and Graham Shirley at the National Film and Sound Archive, Phil Ward at the City of Sydney Library, Janice van de Velde at the State Library of Victoria, Aviva Wolff at the Sydney Jewish Museum, and staff members at the Caroline Simpson Library and the Kings Cross branch of the City of Sydney Library.

I am grateful for the award of a Marten Bequest Travelling Scholarship in 2010.

I have never met or heard a description of Perry Quinton. The names of the residents of Kingsclere in 1928 are likewise all that is reflected of them in this book. An earlier version was submitted for the degree of Master of Philosophy at the University of Sydney in 2011, for which it received government funding; I would like to express my gratitude to the other members of the English department who saw it through.

PIERRE ALBERT-BIROT, *Grabinoulor.*

FELIPE ALFAU, *Chromos.*
Locos.

JOE AMATO, *Samuel Taylor's Last Night.*

JOHN ASHBERY & JAMES SCHUYLER,
A Nest of Ninnies.

ROBERT ASHLEY, *Perfect Lives.*

DJUNA BARNES, *Ladies Almanack.*
Ryder.

DONALD BARTHELME, *The King.*
Paradise.

G. CABRERA INFANTE, *Infante's Inferno.*
Three Trapped Tigers.

JULIETA CAMPOS, *The Fear of Losing*
Eurydice.

ANNE CARSON, *Eros the Bittersweet.*

LOUIS-FERDINAND CÉLINE, *North.*
Conversations with Professor Y.
London Bridge.

ERIC CHEVILLARD, *The Author and Me.*

ROBERT COOVER, *A Night at the Movies.*

STANLEY CRAWFORD, *Log of the S.S.*
The Mrs Unguentine.
Some Instructions to My Wife.

COLEMAN DOWELL, *Island People.*
Too Much Flesh and Jabez.

ARKADII DRAGOMOSHCHENKO,
Dust.

RIKKI DUCORNET, *Phosphor in*
Dreamland.
The Complete Butcher's Tales.

WILLIAM EASTLAKE, *The Bamboo Bed.*
Castle Keep.
Lyric of the Circle Heart.

GUSTAVE FLAUBERT, *Bouvard and*
Pécuchet.

CARLOS FUENTES, *Christopher Unborn.*
Distant Relations.
Terra Nostra.
Where the Air Is Clear.

TAKEHIKO FUKUNAGA, *Flowers of*
Grass.

WILLIAM GADDIS, JR., *The Recognitions.*

WILLIAM H. GASS, *Life Sentences.*
The Tunnel.

Willie Masters' Lonesome Wife.

GÉRARD GAVARRY, *Hoppla! 1 2 3.*

WITOLD GOMBROWICZ, *A Kind*
of Testament.

JOHN HAWKES, *The Passion Artist.*
Whistlejacket.

AIDAN HIGGINS, *Balcony of Europe.*
Blind Man's Bluff.
Bornholm Night-Ferry.
Langrishe, Go Down.
Scenes from a Receding Past.

GERT JONKE, *The Distant Sound.*
Homage to Czerny.
The System of Vienna.

JACQUES JOUET, *Mountain R.*
Savage.
Upstaged.

JIM KRUSOE, *Iceland.*

AYSE KULIN, *Farewell: A Mansion in*
Occupied Istanbul.

VIOLETTE LEDUC, *La Bâtarde.*

EDOUARD LEVÉ, *Autoportrait.*
Newspaper.
Suicide.
Works.

DEBORAH LEVY, *Billy and Girl.*

YURI LOTMAN, *Non-Memoirs.*

MINA LOY, *Stories and Essays of Mina Loy.*

WALLACE MARKFIELD, *Teitlebaum's*
Window.

DAVID MARKSON, *Reader's Block.*
Wittgenstein's Mistress.

CAROLE MASO, *AVA.*

HARRY MATHEWS, *Cigarettes.*
The Conversions.
The Human Country.
The Journalist.
My Life in CIA.
Singular Pleasures.
The Sinking of the Odradek.
Stadium.
Tlooth.

JOSEPH MCELROY, *Night Soul and*
Other Stories.

ABDELWAHAB MEDDEB, *Talismano.*

HERMAN MELVILLE, *The Confidence-Man.*

AMANDA MICHALOPOULOU, *I'd Like.*

STEVEN MILLHAUSER, *The Barnum Museum.*
In the Penny Arcade.

RALPH J. MILLS, JR., *Essays on Poetry.*

MOMUS, *The Book of Jokes.*

CHRISTINE MONTALBETTI, *The Origin of Man.*
Western.

WARREN MOTTE, *Fables of the Novel: French Fiction since 1990.*
Fiction Now: The French Novel in the 21st Century.
Mirror Gazing.
Oulipo: A Primer of Potential Literature.

GERALD MURNANE, *Barley Patch.*
Inland.

YVES NAVARRE, *Our Share of Time.*
Sweet Tooth.

DOROTHY NELSON, *In Night's City.*
Tar and Feathers.

ESHKOL NEVO, *Homesick.*

WILFRIDO D. NOLLEDO, *But for the Lovers.*

BORIS A. NOVAK, *The Master of Insomnia.*

FLANN O'BRIEN, *At Swim-Two-Birds.*
The Best of Myles.
The Dalkey Archive.
The Hard Life.
The Poor Mouth.
The Third Policeman.

CLAUDE OLLIER, *The Mise-en-Scène.*
Wert and the Life Without End.

PATRIK OUŘEDNÍK, *Europeana.*
The Opportune Moment, 1855.

BORIS PAHOR, *Necropolis.*

FERNANDO DEL PASO, *News from the Empire.*
Palinuro of Mexico.

ROBERT PINGET, *The Inquisitory.*
Mahu or The Material.
Trio.

MANUEL PUIG, *Betrayed by Rita Hayworth.*
The Buenos Aires Affair.
Heartbreak Tango.

RAYMOND QUENEAU, *The Last Days.*
Odile.
Pierrot Mon Ami.
Saint Glinglin.

ANN QUIN, *Berg.*
Passages.
Three.
Tripticks.

ISHMAEL REED, *The Free-Lance Pallbearers.*
The Last Days of Louisiana Red.
Ishmael Reed: The Plays.
Juice!
The Terrible Threes.
The Terrible Twos.
Yellow Back Radio Broke-Down.

JASIA REICHARDT, *15 Journeys Warsaw to London.*

JOÃO UBALDO RIBEIRO, *House of the Fortunate Buddhas.*

JEAN RICARDOU, *Place Names.*

RAINER MARIA RILKE, *The Notebooks of Malte Laurids Brigge.*

JULIÁN RÍOS, *The House of Ulysses.*
Larva: A Midsummer Night's Babel.
Poundemonium.

ALAIN ROBBE-GRILLET, *Project for a Revolution in New York.*
A Sentimental Novel.

AUGUSTO ROA BASTOS, *I the Supreme.*

ALIX CLEO ROUBAUD, *Alix's Journal.*

JACQUES ROUBAUD, *The Form of a City Changes Faster, Alas, Than the Human Heart.*
The Great Fire of London.
Hortense in Exile.
Hortense Is Abducted.
Mathematics: The Plurality of Worlds of Lewis.
Some Thing Black.

RAYMOND ROUSSEL, *Impressions of Africa.*

VEDRANA RUDAN, *Night.*

TOMAŽ ŠALAMUN, *Soy Realidad.*

LYDIE SALVAYRE, *The Company of Ghosts.*
The Lecture.
The Power of Flies.

LUIS RAFAEL SÁNCHEZ, *Macho Camacho's Beat.*

SEVERO SARDUY, *Cobra & Maitreya.*

NATHALIE SARRAUTE, *Do You Hear Them?*
Martereau.
The Planetarium.

STIG SÆTERBAKKEN, *Siamese.*
Self-Control.
Through the Night.

ARNO SCHMIDT, *Collected Novellas.*
Collected Stories.
Nobodaddy's Children.
Two Novels.

GAIL SCOTT, *My Paris.*

JUNE AKERS SEESE,
Is This What Other Women Feel Too?

VIKTOR SHKLOVSKY, *Bowstring.*
Literature and Cinematography.
Theory of Prose.
Third Factory.
Zoo, or Letters Not about Love.

PIERRE SINIAC, *The Collaborators.*

KJERSTI A. SKOMSVOLD,
The Faster I Walk, the Smaller I Am.

JOSEF ŠKVORECKÝ, *The Engineer of Human Souls.*

GILBERT SORRENTINO, *Aberration of Starlight.*
Blue Pastoral.
Crystal Vision.
Imaginative Qualities of Actual Things.
Mulligan Stew. Red the Fiend.
Steelwork.
Under the Shadow.

MARKO SOSIČ, *Ballerina, Ballerina.*

ANDRZEJ STASIUK, *Dukla.*
Fado.

GERTRUDE STEIN, *The Making of Americans.*
A Novel of Thank You.

LARS SVENDSEN, *A Philosophy of Evil.*

PIOTR SZEWC, *Annihilation.*

GONÇALO M. TAVARES, *A Man: Klaus Klump.*
Jerusalem.
Learning to Pray in the Age of Technique.

LUCIAN DAN TEODOROVICI,
Our Circus Presents...

NIKANOR TERATOLOGEN, *Assisted Living.*

STEFAN THEMERSON, *Hobson's Island.*
The Mystery of the Sardine.
Tom Harris.

TAEKO TOMIOKA, *Building Waves.*

JOHN TOOMEY, *Sleepwalker.*

DUMITRU TSEPENEAG, *Hotel Europa.*
The Necessary Marriage.
Pigeon Post.
Vain Art of the Fugue.

MATI UNT, *Brecht at Night.*
Diary of a Blood Donor.
Things in the Night.

LUISA VALENZUELA, *Dark Desires and the Others.*
He Who Searches.

CURTIS WHITE, *America's Magic Mountain.*
The Idea of Home.
Memories of My Father Watching TV.
Requiem..

MARGUERITE YOUNG, *Angel in the Forest.*
Miss MacIntosh, My Darling.

LOUIS ZUKOFSKY, *Collected Fiction.*

SCOTT ZWIREN, *God Head.*

AND MORE ...